Herself

By Leslie Carroll

HERSELF
SPIN DOCTOR
PLAY DATES
TEMPORARY INSANITY

Herself

Leslie Carroll

A

AVON

An Imprint of HarperCollinsPublishers

FIRST EDITION

Interior text designed by Diahann Sturge

Library of Congress Cataloging-in-Publication Data

Carroll, Leslie Sara.
  Herself / by Leslie Carroll.—1st ed.
    p. cm.
  ISBN: 978-0-06-085995-4
  ISBN-10: 0-06-085995-4
  1. Women speechwriters—Fiction. 2. Politicians—Fiction. 3. Political corruption—Fiction. 4. Manhattan (New York, N.Y.)—Fiction. 5. Political fiction.
  [1. Self-reliance—Fiction.] I. Title.

PS3603.A77458H47 2006
813'.6—dc22   2006019274

07 08 09 10 11 RRD 10 9 8 7 6 5 4 3 2 1

For my good friend Sharon O'Connell—
Mine's a pint

I have spread my dreams under your feet.
Tread softly because you tread on my dreams.

W. B. Yeats
Balscadder House, Howth

One

"A snake can't strike more than half its length."

David's talking in his sleep again. "Honey . . . ? You're lying on my hair." If I try any harder to reach the crowing clock, I risk whiplash. "David . . . ? Hey! Sleeping Congressman at six o'clock!" I whisper.

David grumbles and shifts almost imperceptibly. "I'll'mm nevermm be a mmmorning person," he mumbles. He's in the here and now, now: all nightmares vanquished or vanished. His arm, draped protectively over my chest, pulls me toward him.

"Listen, I'd love to snuggle all day, but you're doing a meet and greet at the Metropolitan Health Club at eight. Freddy will be waiting outside your place at seven-thirty with the black car to take you there. So up and at 'em, chief!"

Congressman David Weyburn blinks open his sleep-encrusted lids and rolls over just far enough for me to switch off the alarm clock. How do some men sleep through that kind of noise? But heck, they sleep through arguments and filibusters on the floor of the House of Representatives, so I suppose nothing should surprise me. "What the hell time is it, Tess?"

"6:04. You could have grabbed some extra z's if you weren't perpetually freaked out about someone learning that you've been sleeping with your head speechwriter. For three years." I lean over and kiss him gently on the mouth. Screw morning breath; we both had it. "Keeping separate apartments all this time is your idea, remember?"

David grunts his acknowledgment and swivels his feet onto the hardwood floor. "I've never been a morning person," he sighs.

"Take your shower here; it'll help wake you up."

He shakes his head. "I'll only have to do it again when I stop off at my place."

"Why?" I slide over and kneel on the mattress, kissing the back of his neck. "It's important to start the day off right, which, in my book, has very little to do with eating breakfast." I caress the planes of his chest and lean over him, the better to snake my hand down his body. "What do you say we hit the showers?" I murmur.

I feel David stiffen beneath my hand. "You're a very persuasive woman, Tessa Craig."

"Isn't that why you hired me?"

Following a highly satisfying sojourn in my bathroom, I kiss David good-bye with a "See you at 7:45; don't forget your bathing suit and a pair of flip-flops" and send him down to the street, where his driver's town car whisks him off to his own apartment, three-quarters of a mile away.

I sip a glass of iced coffee as I dress in a simple skirt and knit top—innocuous personal appearance uniform number 4a—and apply minimal makeup, since I'll be exercising in a swimming pool in just a couple of hours. Then I double-check the contents of my gym bag and take my coffee into my home office. Seating myself at the desk, I remove my daily journal and my favorite green pen from the center drawer. Pathetic how chewed the end of it is. I should be ashamed of myself. I glance at the print facing me on the opposite wall, a lithograph of Frank Lloyd Wright's Four Organic Commandments: *Love is the virtue of the Heart; Sincerity is the virtue of the Mind; Decision is the virtue of the Will; Courage is the virtue of the Spirit.*

Absentmindedly, I gaze at the quote for a few seconds before putting pen to paper.

August 1

I've never been angling for a ring—once you've been married, somehow it seems like less of a Big Deal—but I figured that after three years of dating, David would have at least been amenable to cohabitating. Our professional life got personal after we'd been working together for two years and by now, I suppose I should know him well enough to realize that getting a commitment out of him might be tough. After all, he's a politician.

But he's irresistible. He's got the whole package.

Media pundits have characterized Congressman David Weyburn as having the charm of a Clinton (Bill, obviously—though I'd say it's a lot more like Cary Grant's), the charisma of a Kennedy (Jack or Bobby—take your pick), and the looks of a Clooney (George, of course, not Rosemary). They don't make 'em any more telegenic. Not only that, David Weyburn has the ethics of . . . well, come to think of it, neither a politician nor a movie star spring to mind as a template for David's ethics. What I'm trying to say is that he's got 'em. And not only is this paragon my boyfriend; he's also my boss. Everybody knows the latter part of the equation. No one knows about the former except our mothers, a few good friends of mine, and a couple of close friends of David's—plus his campaign manager, Gus Trumbo, and his limo driver, Freddy—all of whom have been sworn to silence. A couple of my girlfriends hate the idea of me being David's "dirty little secret," particularly since neither one of us has anything to hide. They call me "The Beret." And as time goes on, I've become less amenable to pretending that David and I are merely colleagues. I'm not asking for a round of tongue hockey in the Capitol rotunda—believe me, I understand the concept of discretion—but conducting this relationship entirely on his terms has become harder and harder the more I've come to care about him. I want to be acknowledged as his woman, without worrying about his poll numbers among females from eighteen to eighty-four. Sometimes I feel like Dracula, all hidden away until after sunset; and even then, if we go to a restaurant it has to look like we're still talking shop. Frankly, I'd like to step out of the shadows and into the light.

The Metropolitan Health Club is an all-purpose pampering hub just a few blocks from my apartment. Seven airy stories of state-of-the-art gym equipment, general exercise, Spinning, and Pilates studios, plus an in-house child-care center offering a variety of programs for infants and toddlers, a rooftop sun deck, a café for snacks and smoothies, an award-winning restaurant helmed by a famous chef, and a full-service spa. Urban heaven.

I arrive ten minutes ahead of schedule to make sure everything is in order, as the MHC is my turf, so to speak, and I'm the one who set up the event. Already waiting at the check-in desk to greet the Hon. handsome and hunky David Weyburn (as he was recently described by a prominent gossip columnist) are a gaggle of young staffers (male and female) and Janet Moreland, the gym's general manager. I notice she's wearing makeup for the first time in memory, and I've been a member of the MHC for half a dozen years. David's communications director and campaign manager, Gus Trumbo, is already there as well, speaking to the media about his boss's strategic initiatives for public education reform. I smile, recognizing the talking points as my own. Fox News has sent a crew fronted by the perkiest reporter in New York City, Suki Glassman. If her eyes sparkled any more brightly I'd swear she used belladonna.

"We'll be taking Kelly Adonis's aqua cardio class this morning," I inform Janet. "So I don't know whether you want to clear the lap swimmers from the other half of the pool." I glance over at the Fox cameraman. "Are your cables going to be okay on the pool deck?"

The shooter nods. "I've handled worse," he replies tersely.

David is fifteen minutes late, which is early in candidate terms. I shake his hand as I always do when we reconnoiter at public appearances. Affable as ever, he greets everyone who wanted to meet him, pressing the flesh with both hands, a gesture that always seems to convey interest and compassion. I prefer it to the classic, perfunctory single handshake, which too often, in candidate terms, telegraphs "I don't really want to be here, much less meet you, much *much* less touch you, and I'm just trying to get through the rope line as quickly as I can and still be perceived as warm and fuzzy."

"Mr. Weyburn, I loved that speech you gave on port security," says one woman enthusiastically. "My husband is in shipping."

"Thank you very much. I expect you're as sick and tired as I am with people who think that mentioning the issue is the same as addressing it," David replies. "And continuing to fight for the safest possible New York is at the bedrock of my agenda!"

"Ooh, you said it," gushes his new admirer. "Are you single? Because I would love to introduce you to my daughter."

"That's very sweet of you, ma'am." David chuckles noncommittally.

"And Laurie's a sweet girl, too," adds the woman. "Never even been in therapy, can you believe it?"

There is no graceful answer to that question.

There had been "Meet your Congressman" flyers posted at the gym announcing David's appearance, and he is indeed mobbed wherever he steps this morning; from the front desk to the key desk to the gift shop (yes, my health club has a gift shop), to, as I will later learn, the men's locker room.

Most of the participants in Kelly's aqua classes are women on the north side of sixty, who adore Kelly's snarky exuberance (though his six-pack ain't bad either, if you have to look at something while you bounce around a swimming pool for an hour). These women are of the ilk who were Peter Allen fans back in the day; they probably think Kelly's straight, too.

If Kelly's name is familiar, it's probably because you remember his death-defying diving prowess at the 1992 summer Olympics—death-defying being the more operative adjectival phrase—for the freak accident that shocked Barcelona and the rest of the world when he cut his head on the 10-meter board performing a backward 1½ somersault pike with a half twist. Bloody, but not unbowed, he miraculously came back in the next four rounds to end up with a silver medal.

No sooner was the Olympic torch extinguished than Kelly signed a big endorsement deal with a breakfast cereal manufacturer to pitch Heads Up!, the caffeine-loaded corn puffs, followed by a spectacularly brief stint as a lifeguard on an ill-fated sand-and-jiggle sitcom that dived to the bottom of the Nielsen ratings before its first half-season was over. With nothing but a silver medal, a SAG card, and a song in his heart, Kelly became—what else?—a top-flight fitness instructor. At the MHC, he is much beloved and his classes are always filled to capacity, especially his Monday morning Best of Broadway class, where participants bop away to a CD of show tunes, all recorded in the key of E-flat, with the same 4-4 driving disco beat. The latter becomes particularly amusing on waltzes, and is equally incongruous on soaring lyrical ballads like "Tonight" from *West Side Story.*

Heads turn (including Kelly's shaved one) when the congressman bestrides the pool deck like a colossus. David does have a good physique. Think JFK Jr. in his permanently immortalized prime.

Some of the participants are already in the pool when we arrive, jogging in place to keep warm in the water. When they see the candidate, their faces light up as though a film star has entered their midst. They bounce over to him, eager to shake his hand through their neoprene webbed gloves, and assure him, without being prompted, that he can count on their vote come November. This year David is a second-term incumbent, running unopposed by anyone else in his party, so there is no need for a September primary. All these appearances are a run-up to the November general election where he will face off against Republican billionaire pet store entrepreneur Bob Dobson.

"Okay, girls, let's show Mr. Weyburn how we stay fit!" Kelly yells, as the music swells. "Don't worry, Congressman, I'll lead you through the choreography!"

"Choreography?" David shouts to be heard above the thumping bass track of "One Night in Bangkok."

"You'll catch on quickly, don't worry," I shout back. "Be thankful you didn't choose to come on one of Kelly's Fosse-only days. *Those* moves are great for your hips, but they're *really* hard to do in the water!"

To the title song from *Camelot* (don't forget the hard-driving 4-4 beat), Kelly calls out "Swing your broadswords. Double-handed! Smite that knight! Two hands, people! I didn't ask for an épée! Give me a basket-hilted Claymore!"

Poor David is a bit bemused. "It looks to me more like he's swinging a baseball bat."

"That's what the Tuesday night instructor calls the same exercise," I admit. "Baseball bats. Kelly is rather more theatrical."

"I'll say!"

For all the show tunes, it's quite an intensive cardio workout. To my astonishment I learn something new that morning. It has nothing to do with resistance exercises featuring foam barbells and neoprene gloves. It's this: Congressman David Weyburn knows the lyrics to every single song on Kelly's CD. I mean, I do, too, but it strikes me that this mutual interest has never surfaced in three years of being lovers.

"Sing out, Louise!" Kelly shouts to his class. "When you sing, you remember to *breathe*!"

And so we jog or execute jumping jacks, and do flies and curls with the weights as we sing along at top voice with "Oklahoma!" (there are a couple of regulars who have the yipioeeays down pat), *Annie*'s ever-optimistic "Tomorrow," and about twenty other numbers ranging in appropriateness for an aerobics workout from the sublime to the truly ridiculous.

David is more than gamely keeping up, and I can tell that the ladies in the class adore him for so unself-consciously getting into it.

"High kicks!" Kelly shouts, as "Send in the Clowns" begins to play. "Reach! Reach! Break the surface and touch your toes. Breathe, my little chorines! Breathe! Your breath is your friend. Use your core! Shoulders down. Suck in those abs. Nice work, Congressman. Everyone, look at Mr. Weyburn. See how *erect* he is!"

General titters all around.

"Isn't it rich? Isn't it queer?" David sings. He is working up a sweat. Something's wrong. The whole point of exercising in a swimming pool is that you don't sweat. Maybe it's just droplets from everyone's splashes as our toes break the surface of the water.

"Losing my timing this late—in my career."

I'm not following Kelly's lead, because I can't take my eyes off David. I see him grimace. Even the eighty-five-year-old Selma, an aqua cardio "regular" (three times a week), isn't struggling as hard with her kicks.

Somehow through the disco din I can hear a strangled gasp and David's face goes white. "David! Oh, shit! *Kelly!*" I shout, and by the grace of whomever, the instructor manages to hear me. A fraction of a second later, he's in the water, followed about three seconds later by the lifeguard, who took an extra sec to press the "stop" button on the CD player beside him. An eerie quiet has overtaken the pool. The ladies aren't even whispering among themselves. Every gaze is riveted on David's seemingly lifeless form, resting across Kelly's powerful forearms.

"Help me get him on the deck," Kelly commands the lifeguard, his voice dead calm; not even a hint of panic. I, on the other hand, am hysterical. If my heart were racing any faster, it would have sprinted out of my chest and been halfway to Cleveland already. "Tessa, call 911."

I don't want to leave David's side, but I dash around the deck to the lifeguard's chair and the emergency phone. "I need an ambulance immediately at the Metropolitan Health Club. The pool. Someone's having a heart attack." I don't know this for certain, but I'm not about to negotiate degrees of urgency with the 911 operator.

"Male . . . six feet . . . age forty-three . . . look, it's *Congress-man Weyburn*, for fuck's sake!"

"Don't you curse at *me*, miss!" snaps the operator.

Two

C'mon, sweetheart, hang in there. You can make it! I pray. *You don't want to die, baby; there's far too much to live for.* I'm too focused on the task at hand to cry. There isn't time.

By the time I reach David's body again, I am sure I already hear the siren. Kelly is on his knees, applying CPR, having ascertained that the lifeguard, though certified, has never actually had to administer the technique. He's giving David mouth-to-mouth and trying to keep the class at ease by making a jest, all the while working his ass off to save David's life. "I've dreamed about this day, but I always thought he'd be conscious when we kissed." Although Kelly's joking, the Fox News camera is still rolling, and Suki Glassman keeps encouraging the shooter to get closer, while I shout to them to get back and give Kelly the room he needs. Unsuccessfully, I try to cover the lens with my hand.

According to the giant time clock by the pool, EMS arrives

seven minutes after I'd placed the 911 call. They bustle in with their board and their gurney and immediately place an oxygen mask over David's pale face.

"I got him breathing again," Kelly informs the paramedics. One of them, a burly freckled young man who looks like he played right tackle at Fordham not too very long ago, shakes his hand. "Good job," he acknowledges, as he watches his team check David's vitals. "Looks like you got him stabilized."

"You saved his life!" I exclaim, hugging Kelly. "Jesus, do you mind?!" I shout at the cameraman. "He did save Congressman Weyburn's life, didn't he?" I ask the EMT.

"Let me put it this way. If the guy who looks like Moby hadn't administered CPR when he did, you'd be planning a state funeral, ma'am."

There's no time for me to get dressed if I want to ride in the ambulance to the hospital, which of course I do. I'm sure I make quite a picture when we arrive at the emergency entrance to St. Luke's, a damp white towel secured over my still-wet swimsuit, my feet shoved into a pair of cheap flip-flops. I don't even have my wallet; it's back in the gym locker. Oh, yes, I'm also wearing a black rubber bathing cap. So was David, until Kelly gingerly removed it after the EMTs worked their magic.

"Let me stay with him," I plead, but the E.R. staff, which has now taken over David's care, isn't buying.

"He's going into the CCU," a nurse curtly advises me. Her scrubs look like children's pajamas, with cheery-faced cuddly lambs and crescent moons stenciled all over them: fine for the pediatric wing, but for the cardiac care unit?

"How long do you think you'll keep him there?" My heart is thudding uncontrollably inside my chest.

"First we got to stabilize him. After that, it's up to his doctor."

I'm aware that David has never seen a cardiac specialist in his life. "Which doctor?"

"Whoever is on duty up there."

Damn, this is like getting into Fort Knox. "Give me his name—or hers; I want to check their credentials."

"I won't know the cardiologist's name until I get up there, miss. And every doctor who works here is a good doctor."

What a pain in my ass! "Do I have time to go back and get my street clothes?"

"Depends on how far you're going," she replies as I scurry alongside the gurney to keep up with her.

"Less than half a mile."

She nods. We arrive at a set of double doors marked "hospital personnel only." "You can't go any farther than this, miss. Check back in an hour or so, and we may have an idea of his condition then."

Having dressed and retrieved David's street clothes from a staffer who used a passkey to open David's gym locker, I sprint back to the hospital, drenched in sweat, since there are no taxis to be had, and I'm wasting precious time standing on a street corner in the sweltering heat trying to hail one for a mere eight-block ride.

"I'd like some information on a patient," I pant to the E.R. receptionist.

"You'll have to wait your turn, ma'am."

I lean in and lower my voice. "My *brother* . . . Congressman Weyburn . . . was brought in here about thirty-five minutes ago."

Her expression changes immediately. "Oh!" She checks the intake sheet on her clipboard and taps some information into a computer; the monitor is so antiquated that it's got a monochromatic DOS screen. She stares at the greenish glow for a few moments. "He's still in the CCU."

"How's his condition—Nellie?" I ask, reading her name tag.

She glances at the screen again. "Stable."

"Did they—"

"That's all it says here. I don't have no more information than that."

"I need to go back and see him."

"Family only," Nellie says.

"I told you, I'm his sister."

"I need to see some ID." I flash her my driver's license. "That don't say Weyburn, Ms. Craig."

"I'm married," I sigh exasperatedly, lying through my teeth. I can tell Nellie's deciding whether or not to buy it. "That's a great necklace, by the way. Is that a guardian angel?" Nellie beams. "I've got one of them hanging from my rearview mirror. I mean, you never know," I said, cracking a wan little smile.

"You need 'em a lot around here," Nellie replied resignedly. "CCU's on the fifth floor. Go through these doors and take the elevator straight at the back."

Pale as marble, David looks like a many-tentacled Frankenstein monster (sans neck zipper and still much handsomer, however), tethered by tubing to numerous machines recording a zillion statistics, such as heart rate, pulse, blood pressure, and then some.

I glance at the metal clipboard hanging over the railing. Dr. Magali Gupta appears to be the attending cardio. As I try to guess Magali's gender, a stunning copper-skinned woman in a lab coat approaches me. "I'm Dr. Gupta," she says extending her hand.

"Tessa Craig." Mercifully, Dr. Gupta doesn't ask for my relation to the man on the bed beside us. I hate lying, and it's no one's business that he's my lover, not to mention that the fact is more or less a state secret.

"He's stable for the moment, Ms. Craig, but we are going to need to do an angioplasty as soon as possible; there is a blockage in his coronary artery. It's quite a common procedure these days—we just insert a balloon catheter into the artery—but Congressman Weyburn has not been alert enough in the past half hour to sign a consent form. You are his next-of-kin, according to his medical records."

Good grief, I'd forgotten that! We've listed each other as such for a couple of years now because we're the ones we would most trust as a "first responder." In the "relation" box adjacent to "next-of-kin" we just write "friend."

"Are you asking me to sign off on the procedure, Dr. Gupta?" I see David blinking his eyes and trying to lift his hand (into which an IV drip had been connected) to say hello. I lean over to smooth his dark hair off his brow. "Honey, they want to do an angioplasty," I murmur, forgetting myself in the stress of the moment.

Dr. Gupta explains that the benefits of such a procedure far outweigh the risks and David tries once again to raise his right hand. "I'll sign it," he says groggily. His spidery signature on the consent form is nothing like the purposeful one his constituents see at the end of his monthly newsletters, but it's good enough for Dr. Gupta.

"Keep the media away," he advises me, his voice a low rasp. "I don't want this turning into a circus." He reaches for me and I clasp his hand.

"I'll be here when you wake up," I promise. "Or as near to here as they'll let me be." I run my index finger along the top of his hand, our code for "I love you." He wiggles his index finger in reply.

*　　*　　*

If there is a God, He—or She—or It—tends to listen selectively. First and foremost I had been praying for David's survival. I got it. Big whew! Not too terribly far down the list, I'd added, "Oh, and David—who would do it himself but he's under general anesthesia at the moment—asks that you keep today's events from becoming a media circus." God was evidently listening to Rupert Murdoch's orisons at that point, because the five-o'clock local news, which I caught on the TV in the CCU waiting room, led off with a Ringling Bros.-style spectacular.

"New York's favorite son rushed to the hospital for emergency heart surgery!" announces Monica Terwilliger, one of the anchors. "We open tonight with the shocking news. Forty-three-year-old Congressman David Weyburn, whose parents survived the Nazi holocaust, and whose constituents on the Upper West Side of Manhattan often describe him as having the looks of JFK Jr. and the vision of Barack Obama, suffered an apparent heart attack during a campaign appearance in his district earlier today. We go to Suki Glassman with the report. Suki, what happened this morning?"

The newscast cuts to Suki standing right downstairs from me at the hospital's emergency room entrance. "Well, Monica, it started out like any other campaign day for Congressman Weyburn: a meet-and-greet with a number of his constituents. But what at first seemed like a walk in the park, or should I say a jog in the pool, turned disastrous, and nearly fatal, for the handsome politician who many think may someday call the White House home."

There is a cut to a couple of seconds of footage of David signing autographs and pressing the flesh at the MHC front desk, followed by about ten seconds of Kelly's class.

"Congressman Weyburn was participating in a popular exercise class in the swimming pool at the Manhattan Health Club when the mood suddenly went from buoyant to bleak. In the middle of the aqua aerobics class, choreographed to popular show tunes by former Olympic diving medalist Kelly Adonis, Weyburn apparently began to experience chest pains."

And wouldn't you know the sound bite Suki's editor had selected was of David singing his handsome heart out during "Send in the Clowns," just as he began to grimace.

"*. . . Isn't it rich? Isn't it queer? Losing my timing this late—in my career . . .*"

"Congressman Weyburn was rushed to a nearby hospital, and we have just learned that he underwent surgery this afternoon to repair a blockage in one of his arteries. We have also learned that the 911 call was placed from the poolside by Congressman Weyburn's head speechwriter Tessa Craig, herself a member of the Metropolitan Health Club. Now, according to one of the EMS responders, the credit for really saving the politician's life more appropriately goes to that famous former Olympian, Kelly Adonis."

They cut to an interview with the big beefy EMS guy I had seen that morning. Apparently his name is Kevin McMillan, and he has a Brooklyn accent as thick as a pastrami sandwich from Junior's. "Yeah, the fitness instructor pretty much had 'im stabilized by the time we got there. If he hadnuh known what tuh do, things wolduh come out a lot different."

This pithy quote is followed by an interview with Kelly. It had been shot right by the pool, while Kelly was still shirtless, his pecs and six-pack abs a veritable commercial for regular exercise. I was sure the set-up had been deliberate, and although Kelly is certainly proud of his torso, I'd bet the instructions came from Suki Glassman's producer.

"Do you think you're a hero?" Suki is asking him, her pupils dilating as she shoves a phallic-looking mic right up in Kelly's face.

"Sweetie, you're a bit too close with that thing. You don't know me that well," Kelly jokes. "Never mind me, it's just left-over nervous energy. Do I think of myself as a hero? No, I don't. Saving someone's life is a double no-brainer with no twist." I bury my face in my hands. This is a disaster. Kelly is always "on," which is fine when he's encouraging (at top volume) twenty-five doughy figures in spandex to step up the pace, but not in a nightly news interview.

"Did you ever think you'd be saving a congressman's life?" Suki asks him. God, what a fucking moronic question!

"Well, Suki, I consider myself a patriot, and I'm just happy to have been able to have served my country today. I've dreamed about getting that close to Congressman Weyburn; I'm just sorry it didn't happen under happier circumstances."

By the end of Kelly's interview I am in such pain that I consider checking *myself* into the hospital.

Three

Following several hours of post-surgical observation in the recovery room adjacent to the O.R., David is admitted to a private room on the cardiac care floor, which is where I am reunited with him. A uniformed NYPD officer is stationed outside his door and requests ID from me before he'll permit me to enter. Before he was wheeled into surgery David had left a short list of visitors' names with the head nurse, and this information has made its way into the policeman's pocket. I tell the cop not to let anyone else in until I leave, and then close the door behind me.

Looking somewhat drained but otherwise alert, David is watching one of the eleven-o'clock newscasts.

I lean over and kiss his lips. They're dry, so I hand him the plastic sippy cup of water. "How do you feel, sweetheart?"

"Like Howard Dean," he mumbles. He doesn't need to explain or expound. A mere couple of clicks on the TV remote control confirm the reason. David's exuberant baritone on the

Stephen Sondheim couplet from "Send in the Clowns" is featured on the late-night news of every major network. Dean's Iowa yowl was better suited to the chorus of "Oklahoma!," and it's safe enough to say that the media's lurid love affair with the sound bite was a factor in the tanking of his 2004 presidential bid.

The Fox News producer must have made the determination to share his team's footage of David's singing and of Kelly's subsequent poolside resuscitation with the competition. Highly unusual not to treat the "event" as a scoop, unless there were an ulterior motive for making the tape available to their rivals, but it doesn't take an Einstein to guess what that motive might be. Fox's conservative bent is notorious, and David has long been a thorn in the right wing's side; not because he's a dreaded (to them) "liberal," but because his personality, his integrity, and his pragmatism have made him such a uniter that on most issues he has a solid base among voters on both sides of the ideological debate.

"I'd say you've had better days," I say, switching off the TV. "You've seen enough for one night. I don't want you to suffer a relapse. America needs you. *I* need you."

"C'mere." David pats the bed and I perch on the mattress beside him, fearful of disturbing any of his tubing. "I don't know what I'd do without you, Tess. Do you have any idea how special you are?"

Oh-so-gingerly I try to lie beside him. "I haven't the vaguest," I murmur. "Tell me."

He chuckles. "Contrary to popular opinion, I'm not a trained seal; you know I tend to bristle at performing on cue."

Some politician. I get off the bed and pull up the chair. "Thanks for your honesty."

"Now don't get like that, Tess."

"Like what?"

"You know what. You never actually pout, but—you should see yourself sometime—it's like you curl up inside your clam-shell and shut yourself down when you don't hear exactly what you want to."

This conversation is stressing both of us out. I rise from the chair and shoulder my purse. "Maybe I should let you get some rest. Do you think you'll be back on your feet in a week? You're scheduled to announce the Cruise Ship Accountability and Culpability Act in front of Pier 90 next Monday."

David reaches out his hand and waves me toward him. "Don't leave, Tess. Please. Okay: you're the most amazing woman I know, and that includes my mother, and I'm incredibly lucky to have you. And, yes, I'm still intending to go through with the cruise ship dumping speech. Did I vet the latest draft?"

I nod. "Though I still think it could use some tweaking. I'd like to rehearse a Q&A as well, even if we have to do it in the car on the way to the pier. And you need to decide whether you want to go with the provocative open, which is guaranteed to get bleeped on the news."

"Perfect. The very fact that something's being bleeped will grab people's attention. It's also a funny first line. Once every-one is chuckling, particularly my detractors, their defenses are down, and they'll be more receptive to the announcement and to the bill itself."

There's a knock on the door. "Don't get up, I'll get it," I joke. I open the door a crack. "Yes?"

A nurse is standing there holding a little plastic cup. "I have to give Congressman Weyburn his medication, miss." She goes over to David's bed, takes his temperature, and notates the readouts on each of the machines to which he is attached. "Visiting hours are over," she admonishes.

"Can she stay the night?" David asks.

The nurse frowns. She's all business. "It's against hospital policy."

David tests the waters. "But can she do it anyway?"

"Where's she gonna sleep? That chair? I don't want no trouble."

She's right about the chair. There's no alternative, unless I ask if they can bring in a cot for me, and we've determined that my presence at present is already against the rules. "Perhaps I should go," I say, noticing a dried bloodstain on the floor and hoping the DNA isn't David's. The linoleum looks like it hasn't been cleaned since the first term of the Giuliani administration. "I'll be back first thing in the morning," I assure him, and wait for the nurse to leave first. "I'll see if I can find out how long they're planning to keep you here." Now I'm wishing I'd gotten Dr. Gupta's pager number.

David asks me to bring him a set of clothes when I come by tomorrow. "I arrived in my swim trunks, and while I'm sure the media would love to film me leaving in them, I would prefer not to give them the freak show they're craving."

But the circus is already in town, and it's awfully hard to get the elephants out of the living room. The headline on the morning edition of the *New York Post* splashes IT TAKES A VILLAGE PEOPLE all over the front page, with a photo of David in the pool, bare-chested, caught mid-move in a posture that resembles the choreography of the seventies' disco hit "YMCA." The article on page 3 includes an interview with Bob Dobson, the Republican challenger for David's congressional seat, saying, "Do I think he's gay? It's none of my business, of course, but as long as you asked me, I won't avoid the question. I'm just wondering if he's got something to hide; that's what crossed my mind at first—what with this passionate kiss between him and the fitness instructor—and Kelly *Adonis's* sexual orientation *certainly* isn't a secret. So what sets me wondering is, whether Congressman Weyburn has something to hide, and if he's hiding it, with all due respect, why is he too ashamed to come out, as they say, and admit it. After all, he's built his reputation on integrity."

"With all due respect," my ass. And *"passionate kiss"*? It was mouth-to-mouth resuscitation for Christ's sake! What an outrageous twisting of the facts! This is an obnoxious and slimy smear, and it boggles the mind that the press even printed such trash. Dobson had invented a can of worms and then opened it with a flourish in a public news forum. David may never want to leave St. Luke's when he reads this.

I try to dodge the camera crew waiting outside the hospital. They ask me about David's condition and I reply simply that I know as much at this point as they do, which frustrates them, of course, but it happens to be the truth. Then they ask if David plans to have any comment on the *Post* headline and on Bob Dobson's remarks in the accompanying article. "I think Eleanor Roosevelt put it best when she said 'Great minds discuss ideas. Average minds discuss events. Small minds discuss people.' Kelly Adonis was administering mouth-to-mouth resuscitation to the congressman. Nothing more. He saved his life. It's sad that Congressman Weyburn's opponent feels the necessity to attack him when he's recuperating from major surgery, and sadder still that you guys are giving his remarks any credence."

But if I have any hopes of putting the issue to rest with my brief recitation of the facts, I am sorely mistaken. The event had been framed and Bob Dobson was wasting no time in gilding that frame with toxic paint.

* * *

David remains in the hospital for another day—another news cycle devoted to several replays of him singing the "isn't it queer" lyric, snarky comments about whether the words about "losing my timing this late in my career" will prove to be prophetic, and increased appearances by Bob Dobson wondering aloud whether David Weyburn is a closeted gay, and if so, isn't it time to take himself out of mothballs.

"Maybe you should let me accompany you home," I suggest to him, but he balks.

"It's bad enough they've invented a personal life for me; I don't want them sniffing around the real one. We'll put the fiction to bed and move on with the campaign. If we comment on it, they'll print or air the comment and it's just adding fuel to Dobson's auto-da-fé. You know what I really want to do when I get home?" I shake my head. "I missed 'The Glorious First,' because I was under anesthesia."

"The first thing you plan to do after arriving home after heart surgery is setting fire to *L'Orient* in your bathtub?"

"Yup."

"You're a piece of work." I chuckle. "Don't forget to tuck up the shower curtain. Sometimes I think you Nelson Society members take things to the limit."

David's favorite hobby is building model ships, something he's been doing since he was about eleven years old. Over the years he's built several very intricate replicas, and there are a handful of colleagues on Capitol Hill, including his mentors on both sides of the aisle, who have received these lavish, lovingly handcrafted gifts. His hero, and the one who tops David's parlor game list of the ten people he'd most want to dine with, is Horatio Nelson. Every summer David builds an inexpensive replica of Napoleon's 1798 flagship, *L'Orient*, and each year on August 1, he destroys it in his bathtub to commemorate Nelson's victory in the Battle of the Nile. To date, no one has complained to the building's super.

David's admiration for Nelson began when he was a child and his favorite uncle, Morris Weyburn, gave him a Young Adult version of the one-eyed, one-armed English admiral's biography. Although the one-eyed, one-armed part came later, little David was impressed by master Nelson's ability to overcome adversity (Nelson was a runty little guy, and young David suffered from acute asthma), bucking all expectations to the contrary to eventually command respect from every quarter. Even Nelson's detractors never begrudged his remarkable leadership qualities (Nelson realized early on that one has to give respect to earn respect) and his uncanny abilities as a military strategist. David most admires Nelson's principles of Mission Command, where every participant in an action knows precisely what his commander expects of him and is entrusted to execute his responsibilities with the commander's full confidence in his skills. Everyone's at the table when the assignments are made; everyone's in the loop. Kind of like King Arthur. And David operates the same way. People always feel like they're working *with* him, not *for* him, and yet none of us forgets he's the boss. It does make for a rather vast swath of gray when it comes to my relationship with him, however. I've never entirely made my peace with his calling the lion's share of the shots with regard to our personal life, something I've confessed to numerous times in my journal.

"You're welcome to come over later—with your briefcase, of course—and watch me blow up the ship," David says. "We can celebrate with classic English fare; order fish and chips from that little pub—you know, the one that delivers—the Pot o'Gold, or whatever it's called. What, Tess? What's with the wrinkly nose?"

Utterly bemused, I shake my head at him. "You've just had

heart surgery, my love! Deep fried fish is Public Enemy Number One when it comes to your arteries. And even if the dish were on your diet from now on, fish and chips isn't the kind of thing that survives a trip any longer than the fifteen-foot distance from the Pot o'Gold's kitchen to your table. But I will happily hold the fire extinguisher while you extinguish Napoleon."

"Roast beef and Yorkshire pudding?"

"Stop it."

"Steak and kidney pie?"

"Okay, now I *know* you're putting me on."

"Does this heart thing mean I have to eat nothing but Salade Niçoise for the rest of my natural life? I'm a guy: I want real food!" David suddenly winces.

I panic. "Are you in pain?"

"Just the thought of suffering through that sound bite again and again. But I can't ignore the news. It's part of my job to stay informed."

He declines my offer to walk by his side as he's wheeled out of the hospital, where the media are there to greet him, shoving a phalanx of microphones in his face. I'm with Dr. Gupta, following about eight feet behind. Someone has produced Kelly Adonis, who steps forward to wish David well. The men shake hands, as it would seem ungenerous not to do that at the very at least; after all, Kelly ostensibly saved David's life. The news photographers snap away and someone shouts out, "Hug him!"

David doesn't.

"Are you gay?" someone else shouts. "Are you denying it?"

David plays deaf as the orderly helps him out of the wheelchair and into Freddy's town car, there to whisk David home. Several reporters begin to follow the car like tin cans tied to a newlywed's bumper.

The *Post*'s late city edition on August 3 contains an article snidely headlined WEYBURN'S NEW HEART-THROB? once again running a photo of Kelly giving David mouth-to-mouth resuscitation, although the article primarily refers to David's release from the hospital with Dr. Gupta's excellent prognosis for his full recovery from the angioplasty.

I arrive at David's apartment that evening with the most recent version of his speech on the unregulated sewage dumping by cruise ships. Following a roast chicken dinner—which he somehow found the energy to cook—only the most insane overachiever *does* this after heart surgery—and after destroying *L'Orient* in the bathtub, we curl up together on the couch and go over the text of the speech.

"You smell good," he murmurs, snaking his hand across my back. "You know what I forgot to ask Dr. Gupta—in confidence, of course?"

I place the pages of the speech on the coffee table and snuggle beside him. "What did you forget, sweetheart?" I look into his dark, intelligent eyes as he traces a finger along one of my laugh lines. "God, you're gorgeous."

"And here's looking at *you*, kid. You're not only the best damn speechwriter in the country, you're also the prettiest."

"So what did you forget?" I ask him after a prolonged and extremely enjoyable kiss.

"I forgot to ask her when I'll be fit enough to make love. I mean, part of me most certainly is—as you can tell. But I want to be sure my heart's into it, too." He kisses me again.

"So do I, honey. So do I."

Four

"I think hitting the 'bad neighbors' angle is a good one," Gus Trumbo says, juggling the pages of David's speech and his cup of coffee, trying not to let it splash all over his clothes as Freddy navigates the potholes along Eleventh Avenue. He speed-reads the text aloud. "'Do any of you know that cruise ships are exempt from the Clean Water Act, our nation's water pollution control law? They're getting a free pass when it comes to pollution emissions. Why? Because officially, they're not U.S. "citizens" like all the other companies that operate in this country. Even though this multi-billion-dollar industry does business with travelers from all over the United States and in American waters, they are permitted to register their vessels in places like Panama and Liberia in order to avoid paying any taxes. Imagine a *municipality* getting a free ride like that.' I'm liking this, Tess. 'Cruise ships cheerfully take your money when you visit one of their shops and purchase their goods and services, but have zero accountability when it comes to disposing of your trash, whether it's human waste, food garbage, or the chemicals used in dry cleaning and film developing, not to mention the detergents used in keeping the ship itself clean, from the kitchens to the decks to the swimming pools to the engines.' Good stuff. Walks the fine line between substantive and wonk."

"Yeah," I chuckle. "It's a real tightrope sometimes."

"And the fact that Alaska, California, Washington, and Hawaii are on top of this, but *we* still have no cruise ship waste law plays well, too. This is a nice bit: '*New York*, which is home to one of the country's largest cruise ship ports, and certainly the most populous in terms of density, is not even in the picture. Do we have to wait for an *Exxon Valdez* type of disaster before we do something to protect our waters, our marine life, and the residents of New York? We've been missing the boat here, people.' Yeah, make them think a little."

"Gus, watch that elbow. That was my fifth rib." I try to readjust my position in the cramped back seat. "I love the perspective that David brought to the three-mile limit. That was all *his* actually; I didn't contribute that—just cleaned it up is all."

Gus shuffles the papers. "Where is that?"

"It's the black-water section." David takes an icky-looking container from his jacket pocket.

"You're not planning to *open* that jar, are you?" I ask him.

He gives me a withering look and recites from memory: "Now, let's get back to this three-mile joke-of-a-regulation for dumping black-water. This stuff is pretty repellent, right? Totally toxic. The jar I'm holding up now is literally full of shit. If you got on the Seventh Avenue subway line, the '1' train, at the 110th Street station and took it down to the 50th Street station, just a few blocks from where we stand, that's three miles. And it would take you all of sixteen minutes to make the trip.

Now let's imagine that you're a load of crap that's been released into the Hudson River at the equivalent of 110th Street. It wouldn't be terribly long before the current carried you down river and you were floating right past us."

Gus nods approvingly. "You're right. Never underestimate the gross-out factor."

"Gross-out factor plus perspective that any New Yorker can relate to," I add. "Let's run through a quick Q&A. Congressman Weyburn," I say, affecting a TV news reporter voice. "You're lobbing a lot of missiles at the cruise ship industry for not being regulated, but in truth, they're not the ones who make the rules. So, since they're not beholden to the Clean Water Act, how do you suggest they become 'good neighbors'?"

"I'm glad you asked that question, Ms.—or is it Miss— Craig."

I shrug off a grin. "Just answer the question, David."

"Ms. Craig, the cost of updating the waste systems on board these giant floating cities is approximately two million dollars per vessel. A drop in the bucket, so to speak, when you consider that this is about the same sum as *one-third of the incidental expenses spent by passengers on a single week-long cruise on a five-thousand-passenger ship*. A few years ago, a cruise ship carrying five thousand passengers could pull in $7,875,000 in a week in onboard expenses alone; this figure doesn't even take into account the price the tourists have paid to the cruise line for their passage. Heck, the cruise industry's annual *advertising* costs are over half a billion dollars. They can easily afford to fix the problem and become good citizens and good neighbors, but it's more than evident that they need powerful, take-no-prisoners legislation to compel them to comply."

"Have any of these cruise ship companies ever been caught in the act in New York waters, Congressman?"

"Excellent question, Mr. Trumbo. Yes, they have, as a matter of fact. According to the Department of Justice, way back in 1994 and 1995, the ship *Song of America* was fined three million dollars on two felony counts for false statements related to the presentation to the Coast Guard of a materially false Oil Record Book, and on two felony violations of the Clean Water Act for the discharge of pollutants, among them photo- and dry-cleaning waste, into the coastal waters, including the Port of New York." He reaches across my chest for Gus's cup of coffee. "Give me a sip of that."

"It's got Nutrasweet in it."

David makes a face and settles back, javaless, against the seat. "You know what pisses me off? Well, there are a number of things, but I'm referring to illegal cruise ship dumping. What pisses me off is that H.R. 1636—the 'Clean Cruise Ship Act of 2005'—was introduced on the floor of the House of Representatives back on April 14 of that year, and has been tied up in committee ever since. It was cosponsored by a number of west coast legislators and one congressman from Virginia. I am ashamed to say that there wasn't a single northeast representative among the bill's sponsors. I should have been among them and it's time to make amends. 1636 does call for tighter restrictions on cruise ship companies, but it doesn't go nearly far enough. In fact it doesn't even look that good on paper because there are so many loopholes in the bill. I would have insisted on toughing up the legislation. Reading it is a bit like peering through a slice of Swiss cheese. A rather thick slice, of course, since we're talking about Congress; the bill is dozens of pages long."

The town car pulls into the parking area by the pier. "Out and at 'em," Freddy announces. "And take your coffee cups and muffin wrappers with you. I had to fire the busboy."

"You gotta love Freddy," Gus mutters, peeling himself out of the automobile. "I always feel like I need a good massage after being all scrunched up with you guys."

"You *always* feel like you need a good massage," I quip. I notice that the podium and all the trappings for David's speech are in place, just as Gus has requested. "Hey, don't you just love it when everything you asked for is actually all set up when you arrive? How rare is that?"

After a last minute huddle, we're good to go. "Knock 'em dead!" I tell David, and he approaches the podium to the staccato rhythm of clicking camera shutters. I all but bite my lip in anticipation; I can't wait for their reaction to his opening line.

"We're going to talk about a lot of shit today, folks."

Damn, I love press conferences! I grin as the reporters at Pier 90 look momentarily stunned. Their realization that the very first sentence of David's speech will need to be bleeped results in a mass deer-in-the-headlights reaction.

"I knew that would get your attention," David continues brightly.

Suspended behind David, a big DON'T TRASH NY banner catches the breeze.

"I'm here today to announce that when Congress reconvenes next month, I plan to introduce the Cruise Ship Accountability and Culpability Act. For those of you who are fond of acronyms, yes, it's the CACA bill." He hits the point about cruise ships being beyond the reach of the law and adds, "An average-sized cruise ship housing three thousand passengers and crew members generates seven tons of solid waste every day, much of which is being dumped untreated into our waters. CACA will set up much tougher standards and regulations to protect our waters and our wildlife. Each year, millions of animals become trapped in cruise ship debris or become poisoned by it. Not only that, in order to maintain safe operating conditions, ships discharge ballast water back into the ocean, which means that water taken on in one geographical region is usually eliminated in another. The result is that very often serious diseases, red tides, parasites, and non-U.S. species of marine animals, are carried into our waters from ballast waters. Non-native species are the nation's number two cause of biodiversity loss, costing the American economy $137 billion every year."

David holds up the same glass jar he showed Gus in the car on the way to the pier. It's filled with something resembling a viscous semiliquid sludge. "This stuff is known as black-water—which contains raw sewage—and which can be dumped between three and twelve miles offshore, so long as it's treated with something called a Marine Sanitation Device—which is really just a fancy name for a sieve." He gives them the three-mile-away subway stop perspective, and I notice a lot of reporters jotting it down. Aha—something simple that tabloid readers can sink their teeth into.

"In a recent survey of black-water sewage treated by MSDs, sixty-eight out of seventy samples flunked their health test, and some of the gray-water samples exceeded the federal standard by as much as *fifty thousand* times the limit."

David swaps the black-water jar for another, only marginally less scary-looking, one. "*This* stuff is called gray-water, and it includes everything that comes out of the kitchens, the dry-cleaning facilities, the beauty parlors, and the photo shops. Paint, batteries, fluorescent lights, and oily bilge water get discharged into our waters as well; and plastics make their way into the ocean when incinerator ash is released, and when plastic products go down the toilet or through the pulpers in the galley. Believe it or not, cruise ships can discharge gray-water—which is totally untreated—anywhere at all, including just a few feet from where we're standing."

A heckler shouts out, "Congressman Weyburn, do these guys ever get caught?"

"The unfortunate answer to that is 'rarely.' On occasion over the years, these cruise companies have been fined for illegal dumping—when they're caught doing the nasty in American waters. *When they're caught*—which is, according to industry insiders, a very small percentage of the time, since the dumping occurs with obvious regularity." He mentions the *Song of America* fines and adds, "The industry considers itself self-regulating, but too often the honorable whistle-blowers suffer repercussions for exercising their consciences and their integrity. Many of these reported discharges are also labeled 'accidental,' and most of these 'goofs' never reach public attention. We can't allow the multibillion-dollar cruise ship industry to behave like a giant-sized bimbo and get away with a mere 'Oops, I did it again.' By the way, do you all know that most of the current cases of violations are by self-reports from persons on the ships themselves, because no one is monitoring the industry? No one. There is *zero* governmental oversight of this multibillion-dollar industry, these floating cities and casinos that are raking in our residents' money and giving shit back—literally.

"CACA will also close the loopholes that permit contaminators to continue to dump illegally even after they have been fined for doing so. My bill contains provisions for fines to be paid upon issuance and held in escrow pending the inevitable appeals. It also sets forth a time period for compliance with the new, more stringent standards regarding the disposal of waste substances and materials into our waters. Regular inspections will be conducted by fully staffed and adequately funded teams comprised of members of the U.S. Coast Guard along with NIH scientists and marine biologists."

"Yeah, but let's say they don't comply. Won't they just laugh at the 'punishment'?" the same heckler wants to know. I try to see what he's wearing, which might give me a clue where he's from, but he isn't sporting a Save Our Oceans tee shirt or a similar sartorial tip-off. Still, he's probably from one of the environmental groups.

David is well prepared for the question, however. "Not if the 'punishment,' as you call it, is strong enough, sir. Non-compliance with the retrofitting timetable and with any citations issued by inspectors will result in a ban from U.S. waters and ports, something none of the cruise ship companies can afford. It's time we did something serious about flushing out the offenders and passing some strong legislation to get the cruise ship industry to clean up its act."

The end of the speech is greeted with resounding applause, and, interestingly, a couple of wolf whistles.

"Any further questions?" David asks the reporters. "Yes, in the pinstripes."

"Ed Wilson, *Wall Street Journal*. Congressman Weyburn, how do you think tighter regulations will impact the cruise ship industry here in New York?"

"Mr. Wilson, cruise ships are the only unregulated partner in America's multibillion-dollar travel industry. A significant number of their passengers come from the New York area. As I said, no cruise ship company can afford *not* to comply. With the money that many of these companies make *just in incidental expenses* on a single week-long cruise of just *one* of their vessels, *exclusive* of the money they make from each passenger on the price of the cruise itself, they could afford to bring *three* ships into compliance with federal regulations and environmental standards. My colleagues on the other side of the aisle are notoriously anti-regulation because they claim it interferes with commerce. What it really interferes with is *profit*, and cruise ships already reap plenty of that, and pay no taxes on it. Cruise ship companies are lousy neighbors who have been getting a free ride for decades at the expense of our health and our environment. If they want to enjoy the benefits of citizenship, then it's time we made them play by the same rules as everyone else. They've got to do their civic *duty* by cleaning it up.

"Yes, Suki."

"Suki Glassman, Fox News. Congressman Weyburn, first let me say that I think you really look great. A lot better than the last time I saw you, about a week ago at the Manhattan Health Club. Can you tell me whether you'll be seeing any more of Kelly Adonis?"

"I'm not certain what that has to do with the Cruise Ship Accountability and Culpability Act. But I won't be joining that gym, so the answer is no. Any real questions? Yes, you in the purple polo shirt."

"Hi, Congressman, I'm Jon Jennings from the *Blade*. You have a really nice singing voice, by the way."

"Thank you, Mr. Jennings. What's your question?"

"Was your singing that Stephen Sondheim lyric so loudly a subliminal way of outing yourself?"

"Mr. Jennings, the volume on the CD was very high and there was a lot of splashing in the pool. I sang *all* the songs very loud, including 'There is Nothing Like a Dame' and 'Tomorrow.' If I'd been caught on camera crowing at top voice that the sun'll come out tomorrow, would you be asking if I harbored secret ambitions to be a weather man?"

"I have a follow-up question, Congressman. By your non-response just now, does that mean that you feel you have something to be ashamed of? Are you saying that people who are gay should feel ashamed of their sexual orientation?"

"No, I'm not, Mr. Jennings, but *you* seem to be saying that.

The subject of my sexual orientation is not the subject of this morning's press conference, nor should it be a matter of consideration, or an issue, in my re-election campaign. New Yorkers care about electing the most qualified person for the job regardless of what he or she does in the privacy of their own bedroom."

"The lady doth protest too much," shouts Jennings into his microphone.

"I welcome any questions on the Cruise Ship Accountability and Culpability Act. If all you want is salacious tabloid fodder, we're done for the day, and a sad day it is for the fourth estate." David steps away from the mic, and Gus Trumbo and I walk alongside him into the mercifully air-conditioned passenger ship terminal.

"Well, that was a fucking zoo," Gus says in his characteristically blunt way. He undoes his bow tie and pops open a soda can. "Anyone want one?"

"Dobson will be celebrating another field day, no doubt," said David, slumping into a chair. "As long as he can keep a ball in play that avoids any of the issues in this campaign, he wins the day's hand."

"Don't mix your metaphors, David," I groan.

"That's why you're my speechwriter, Tessa."

"My radar is usually pretty good, but I never thought this 'is he or isn't he gay' thing would survive so many news cycles. They're like a starving dog with a bone, aren't they? Except for the eco-heckler and the guy from the *Wall Street Journal*, they seem almost completely disinterested in reporting anything substantive, even when New Yorkers' health is potentially at risk."

"It's obscene," Gus agrees, removing his baseball cap and mopping his perspiring pate with a blue bandanna. He dabs at his brown brush mustache as well. "But just because the media is inviting you to mud wrestle, it don't mean you should climb down into the pit with them. We've got to stay on message and stay above this are-you-gay bullshit. But we've also got to be careful about trashing the media to their dirty little faces—even when they deserve it—because then they'll start gunning for you on their own. They won't need a directive from Murdoch or whoever, to smear you at every turn."

"Where's Freddy with the car?" David asks, holding an ice cold soda can to his forehead.

He looks pale and drained. I think he may have taken on too much too soon after the angioplasty. I walk over to his chair and murmur in his ear, "You want me to ride home with you? Get you into bed, or at least onto a recliner, with a glass of something cold. Did you take your antibiotic this morning?"

As if the gesture is something of an effort, David waves me away. "Even forty-three-year-old congressmen can have those days where they wish they could just crawl back under the covers."

"Want company?" I whisper. "We can just cuddle."

David shakes his head. "I just want to be alone for a while. I'll call you later, okay?"

I let my finger graze the top of his hand and he wiggles his forefinger in reply. "Talk to you then, then."

By the time I leave the passenger ship terminal and hail a cab for home, the reporters and camera crews have dispersed. But I am *not* looking forward to the evening news.

Five

 August 3

There's a large part of me that always feels the need to fix everything. To make it right. I hate injustice and I hate to see people hurting. And right now David is a victim of both. I feel powerless because what I'm able to do, personally and professionally, hasn't been helpful and I don't know what else to try. He gave a terrific speech this morning on his home turf, raising an issue that has all but been ignored by most of his congressional colleagues and predecessors, and it seemed to fall on deaf ears. As his lover, I want to be able to be here for him in every way; I'm his biggest, most devoted fan, and I hate being incapable of chasing the demons away.

August 4

No word from David. He didn't call me yesterday after all. I just left a message on his answering machine asking if he's feeling okay. It's still so soon after his heart surgery, who knows, maybe something happened.

August 5

Okay . . . if I keep calling him, I'm a nag. And God knows, that's not in my nature; never has been. I've already left "How are you" and "Just wanted to say hi" messages, and my calls haven't been returned. I suppose I can call David to discuss an upcoming speech, but there's nothing on the front burner, so it would seem like a pretty lame excuse. On the other hand, why do I need an "excuse" (or even a "reason") to call my boyfriend of three years? Lovers e-mail each other and talk on the phone all the time without requiring a reason. I'm too old to be stressing over this. I've been married, divorced for longer than I was wed—by this stage in my life I shouldn't expect every day to be filled with hearts and flowers. This is teen angsty stuff I'm going through—the anxious heart palpitations, the rationalizations for why he hasn't called. Dead? Under a bus? Too busy to send an e-mail or leave a message on my voicemail? Maybe we never get past it—the anxiety. Maybe it's just part of being human. We feel so much more than we say most of the time. I suppose it's a form of self-defense, in a way. Emotional armor.

The following day, David phones me. I always screen my calls, so when I hear his voice, it's with no small degree of trepidation that I pick up the receiver. Why do I feel nervous? This is silly. "Hi, baby."

"Hi, Tess." He sounds a bit weird.

"Is everything all right?" My heart is still inexplicably thudding in my chest. *Can he hear this over the phone?* I wonder.

"I've had better days."

"What's up?"

"Tess, we need to talk."

The last four words of his sentence are the worst four words a woman can hear.

"Okay," I reply weakly.

"I'd rather do it in person. Have you got any plans for this evening?"

"No," I hear myself say in the same tiny, deflated voice.

"I'll be over around seven then."

"Seven it is."

There's a long pause during which it seems terribly clear that neither of us has anything else to say.

"See you later, David."

"Bye, Tess."

He arrives at my duplex with a bottle of cabernet. "I think you'll probably need this," he says, uncorking it and heading to my china cabinet for a pair of wine glasses. "Tess, I'm just not good at this," he says suddenly, the words tumbling out of him. "I care about you deeply, I'm immensely fond of you, I think you're a stunning woman, and God knows you're the smartest one I've ever known . . . but I . . . I want some time alone."

If he had cracked me in the head with a baseball bat, I

couldn't have been more shocked, nor could it have hurt any more than his last few words.

"Wh-when did *this* happen?" I say, too shaken to sit.

"I've been doing a lot of thinking lately. In fact, it's just about all I've been doing for the past few days. It's not you, Tess, it's me," he says as soon as he sees the tears begin to roll down my face. "You're wonderful. But I just don't think I can be in a relationship right now."

"You don't *think* . . . ?"

"I was trying to go easy," he sighs. "I know this kind of blind-sided you."

"True. I sure as hell didn't see it coming." I sniffle, hunting for a tissue. "Look, David . . . if you want some space . . . some time off from 'us,' yes, sure, take whatever time you need." I wonder if I even mean this. But I can't exactly say to him, "No, you *can't* do it." And I know I wouldn't mean *that*.

"It's not a matter of space . . . or time . . . something temporary . . . I mean, I just don't want to be . . . I don't . . . I want to be on my own, Tess. From now on."

"You're breaking up with me." The words aren't much more than a gargle in my throat. "You *are* . . . aren't you?" A Pinter-esque pause follows. "Oh, God" escapes my lips as a strangled sob. He might as well have sucker-punched me.

"There's so much going on right now . . . my plate just feels too full, Tess." He pats the sofa beside him and I perch. Part of me wants to be near him and part of me wants to be on another planet. "There's this whole bullshit with the 'gay' accusa-tions—"

"But isn't that *more* of a reason to assert *our* coupledom?" I posit, wiping my nose. "Show the world that all the mudsling-ing is particularly ludicrous because you happen to have a long-term girlfriend?"

"I swore to you from our first kiss, Tess, that I would never drag our personal life into the spotlight, nor would I allow anyone else to do so."

"But that was then; this is now. I do see what you mean—your personal life—and mine—are nobody's business, but I give you full permission to 'out' our relationship. David, we've been lovers for more than three years now. I love you and I'm proud of us."

"But it compromises both of us as professionals because we also have a working relationship."

"I am sure we're not the first. Look, do you really believe that it's better to allow Bob Dobson and the media to continue to propagate a pack of lies at the expense of revealing the truth?"

"Tess, call it my Achilles' heel, but my integrity will not allow me to let them run this campaign on their terms. My personal life is sacrosanct and always has been, and fiercely guarding my privacy in the past has never been an obstacle to getting elected. Whether or not I'm gay, straight, single, married, have a steady girlfriend or am unattached, has nothing—nothing—to do with any of the issues in this campaign. The minute I put *one toe* over that line in the sand, Dobson has dragged me all the way into the surf."

"But no one is talking about the *issues* because they've still got their teeth sunk into this dish of scandal. *And* the scandal is an utter fabrication, to boot! It's not as though you were caught redhanded—well, so to speak—with your cock where it didn't belong and then tried to construct an elaborate denial for the obvious. Of *course* there's no shame in being gay, but you're not. End of story." You know how with some people, the angrier they get, the calmer they sound? Well, it's a very strange combination, but the more emotional I become, the more pragmatic I get as well. "Remember how the media refused to leave Mike

Piazza alone about the same subject until he held a press conference and issued a flat-out denial. Yes, it was humiliating; true, it should have been unnecessary, but it finally put a period on the thing and people shut up about it—apart from the half dozen news cycles about the press conference itself."

"You know me better than that, Tess. To think I would ever capitulate. If I hold a press conference to announce, 'Hey folks, there's nothing wrong with being gay, but it just so happens that I'm not,' and add that I've got a girlfriend—and you know what the next question will be: 'Who is she?'—I've lost control and forfeited the upper hand to my opponent."

David takes me into his arms. "I am so sorry, Tess." I try not to ruin his linen shirt with my tears, then think *oh, screw it*, and let 'em rip. After all, he doesn't care about breaking my heart; why should I give a damn about his designer shirt? "I've got to focus every ounce of energy on the re-election campaign," he continues. "Suddenly, it's not the walk in the park I had anticipated. And I *do* want you to be by my side for that. In fact, I don't think I can win without you."

"You—what?" I think I know what he means by this last remark, but I still can't believe my ears. "Are you really . . . you really have the balls to say to me right now . . . just after you tell me you want to break up . . . that you don't have room on your plate, or your agenda, for a girlfriend—though you seemed to do just fine with one—me, I mean—during your *last* re-election campaign—but you want me to keep writing your speeches for you. That is what you just intimated, isn't it?" I break our embrace to witness his red-faced acknowledgment. Love and pity ebb from my heart as though someone had just yanked out a stopper.

"My timing is horrid, I'll admit, but you're the best damn speechwriter I've ever had, and one of the best in the business.

We've been a team for years. You know how I speak, how I think; you're my other brain."

"If I were, I wouldn't have just dumped me."

David releases an enormous sigh. I can see that he's in pain, too. This isn't easy for him either. "There's nothing you could have done to change things, Tess. It's me. I just can't handle being in a relationship right now. I want time alone. Indefinite time. I'm not going to ask you to wait for me, because that's another kind of cruel. It gives you hope when the truth is that I can't give you any guarantees as to when, if ever, I will feel ready to have a lover again. You're wonderful. You couldn't be 'better' or 'different' in any way, expecting that might change things, because it's not about you. And even if it did have something to do with your behavior in some way being incompatible with mine, people shouldn't tie their personalities into pretzels because they think it's who their partner wants them to be."

"You want to walk away from 'us' but you still want me to *work* with you nearly every day? Do you really think my heart can handle that? Seeing you all the time and not being able to kiss you any more, make love, feel your arms around me at the end of the day? Right this second I think it would be impossible."

David takes my hand in his, which serves to further reinforce my words. His touch, the feel of his skin against mine . . . never to experience that again feels huge right now; it trumps everything else.

"Will you still work for me?" David asks softly. I find myself unable to slip my hand from his. I imagine it's like knowing that you're drinking a goblet of poison but it tastes *sooo* delicious that you can't toss the glass aside. "You're the best. Certainly the best for me."

A tiny, breathy snicker escapes my nostrils. "Best speechwriter, but not good enough to remain your lover. I know you said that your decision to end our relationship has nothing to do with me and everything to do with where your head is at, but right this minute it's hard to really process and accept that." Several moments of tense silence elapse. "I'll have to hand you back your own words: I need time. And space. And after I take all the time and space I need—and I have no idea how long or how much that will be—I can't guarantee you the response you want to hear. I haven't entirely compartmentalized my personal and professional lives where you're concerned. It started out that way, but by the time we were lovers for a while, the edges of everything became blurred, and black and white started bleeding into shades of gray, which is probably very unhealthy, except that I know that while I give my best to every client I've ever had, I love writing *your* speeches just that much more, in part because I also happen to love you. And . . . when you hand me wonderful gems of perspective like the subway stops from 110th Street to 50th Street equaling the three-mile cruise ship dumping limit, call me madcap, but I love you all the more." I will myself not to burst into tears. "I love you because you see things the way I do—and I love you because you see things in ways I don't."

We rise from the couch, and David gently kisses my forehead. I've always found that gesture terribly patronizing. "Take the time you need to reach a decision," he says quietly. "Except that you know how fast the campaign has heated up, and I have a feeling Dobson is going to throw as many logs on the fire as he can afford. And the man's a billionaire."

"You just squashed my heart like it was a cockroach, okay? I may be loyal but I've always felt that *genuine* loyalty is tied up with deep feelings for the person or cause that someone is loyal to. Please ignore that grammar," I add, using the back of my hand to brush away the symmetrical floods of falling tears. "I'm not made of granite, David. Do me a favor," I say, escorting him to the door. "Stay out of touch for a bit. Don't call me. Don't e-mail, don't text me, don't send me a letter. If I hear your voice or read your words, it will make my decision that much harder."

He leans in, as if he's thinking of kissing me on the cheek, but I reel back slightly, avoiding it. If he touches me one more time, it will seem damn near impossible to piece together all the tiny shards of my shattered heart.

I watch and wait until I can no longer hear his footsteps on the stairs. As I close my apartment door, it feels for all the world as though I've shut the book on a chapter of my life. History . . . her story . . . my story.

I kick off my shoes and head up to my bedroom, throw myself onto the bed the way I did when I was a brokenhearted adolescent, and sob into the pillow as if someone very dear to me had just died.

Hours later, long after daylight had turned to dusk, I am still fully clothed, lying face down on the duvet, though I've swapped my pillow for the drier one on the side of the bed that used to be David's. I give myself permission to wallow in depression; after all, it's healthier to grieve, to mourn the demise of a three-year relationship, than to soldier on as if nothing major has happened, right?

When I awaken, still in my skirt and top, the sun and the exceptionally voluble birds on the tree outside my bedroom window mock me with their cheeriness. My mood is a lot more Ebenezer Scrooge than Little Mary Sunshine. About the only thing that would make me feel better this morning, apart from a few cups of strong black coffee, is a trip to Venus.

Six

Olivia deMarley is happily single and a bona fide heiress. She is also the only one of my four college suitemates with whom I have remained in touch all these years. She was known as "Livy" to her family and friends, but when she chose to turn her back on her trust fund in order to try an experiment in living the way she decided "real" people do, she took a nom de guerre for her day job—or rather *night* job—with which she put herself through Harvard, with a nice little nest egg to spare.

"Venus" deMarley was born, not quite on a giant scallop shell—more like twined around a pole—at an unmarked boîte in Waltham called Pandora's Box, where those in the know would pay a $35 cover with a two-drink minimum to see a rather striking array of exotic dancers, all culled from the dorm rooms of Boston's nubile coeds. She brazenly began to call herself "Venus" full time after her father, a self-made millionaire with a heart condition who also owns a minor league baseball team—the Bronx Cheers—announced that she was dead to him. She continued to dance—heading out to Vegas for a while, and then moving from one upscale exclusive club to another in New York—until about eight years ago when she decided she'd had enough: enough gyrating in five-inch platform shoes (and not much else) for so many years, and more than enough money.

Venus has the kind of looks that make grown men weak at the knees and give every female within a five-mile radius a severe case of Venus envy. She's a whisper under six feet tall with a body like Julie Newmar in her Catwoman days and blazing red hair that nearly reaches her waist. She has never needed Botox and is in better physical shape than most Marines. I love her because with me she has always been down to earth and has never pulled her punches. She's the most sympathetic friend I've ever had, but also the most honest, with no qualms about telling me when she thinks I've blown something, whether it was my physics final, or attempting to convince a very drunk Paul Wilson that we were distantly related, which is why I couldn't possibly date him. Pompous Paul and I, who were, of course, no relation to each other whatsoever, ended up going out for three weeks and four days of my junior year. I'm a terrible dissembler.

"You sound like shit," she says bluntly, upon hearing my voice on her answering machine. "Is everything okay, T?"

"Not exactly." Suddenly I burst into tears. Venus listens and patiently waits, knowing I will eventually say something once I manage to pull myself together. After about three to four minutes of gut-wracking sobs, I tell her about my conversation with David. "August sixth. It's a bad karma date, you know. Remember Hiroshima. And the airline losing my bag on the first day of our big European vacation, remember: August sixth, 1986."

"But you said you didn't expect David to drop that bomb on you yesterday? In retrospect, were there any signs? Any clues?"

I think about her question for a moment. "Nothing. He's been a bit wired about the 'gay' flap in the press, but so am I. Look . . . V . . . are you busy today? I really don't want to rehash everything over the phone." I glance at the model ship sitting atop my dresser. "And I can't stand looking at this apartment. It feels like I haven't been able to leave the scene of the crime."

Venus sighs apologetically. "I'm having the duplex painted, T. The place is covered with dropcloths and Poles."

I'm nonplussed at this comment. "V . . . you're not turning your apartment into a private strip club, are you?"

Venus laughs heartily. "Not poles. *Poles*. With a capital P. They're the painters." Suddenly she exclaims something in a foreign tongue.

"Are you talking to me, V, because I don't speak whatever that was?"

"I'm sorry, sweetie," she replies, and I'm still not sure if she's talking to *me*. "I just told Ignatz, 'Watch that roller; you're dripping onto the floor.' My Polish cleaning lady taught me a couple of important words and phrases when she found out that the workmen were from Lodz. Now they're my new best friends. I discovered I really like the language—lots of shushing sounds—so I ordered the Berlitz CDs."

This bizarre conversation is at least entertaining. It's taking my mind off my own *mishegas*—which reminds me—I owe my cousin Imogen a call. Whenever I talk to Imogen she always seems to be enmeshed in some sort of imbroglio. I have never known a woman to have so many life crises. Imogen has a way of magnifying a bee sting into a four-star disaster.

"Tell you what," Venus proposes. "I'll come by this evening

with a DVD and a bottle of something really good—make that two bottles. You supply the popcorn and the Chinese take-out menu." Her cheer-up-Tessa tone shifts into sympathy. "Really, tell me if you're not okay and I'll send the Poles home. Can you hold out until this evening?"

Suddenly I'm crying again. I was doing fine until she went back to being softly solicitous. "Yesh." I snuffle. "I'b okay. Ride as raid."

"You're not okay. You just lost your m's, n's, and t's. Blow your nose, sweetie. I'll wait." Dutifully I reach for a Kleenex and comply. "Say something, T."

"I'll see you this evening?"

I can almost hear her smile. "Good girl. You didn't say 'evenig,' so you've dried those tears. Any objection to Mouton Cadet?"

"Why didn't you *call* me?" Imogen whines.

"Actually, Imogen, I *am* calling you."

"Wait, let me put you on speakerphone." I do. "*You* know what I mean," she says, her volume adjusted so she can multi-task. "Sorry, I've got a professional makeup artist here, and she can't do her job while I'm holding the phone to my cheek."

"Oh. Cool. Do you have a special event tonight?"

"Nah . . . I'm going to get new passport pictures taken this afternoon."

"Imogen!"

"What? You have to *live* with that photo for *ten years*! But we were talking about David. Why didn't you call me as soon as he left the house last night?"

"Because I didn't have the strength," I sigh. "You tend to be something of a force of nature."

"I know relationships," she announces. "Do I know relationships or do I know relationships?"

Being married for over twenty years might mean she knows something about her *own* relationship, but she *didn't* know much about David and me, in fact. I tried to keep the two of them as far away from each other as possible. Imogen has never stopped talking about what a dish David is, what a catch; and how gorgeous our children would look. David considers Imogen to be just about the shallowest, most annoying person on the planet. Half the time I don't know why I have anything to do with Imogen, but she's my only relative who is more or less my age. In one way, we've sort of grown up together because we had no one else to play with at family gatherings like weddings and seders; but on the other hand, more often than not I feel like she and I are operating on different planets. At age twenty-three she married a Jewish guy—a wealthy periodontist from Great Neck—and squirted out three kids: Shauna is now about to enter Brandeis, and the twins, Jacob and Emily, are about to be bar/bat mitzvahed. Imogen's philosophy is that marriage is the cure for all ills; she is the self-proclaimed poster child for wedded bliss.

I did give it my best shot, though the outcome was wildly different. At age twenty-six I married an Episcopalian scientist researching Down syndrome (sadly, the disease ran in his family) at the NIH until his program was drastically de-funded in 1991. We picked up everything and moved to Köln because Rob received a sizable grant from the University of Cologne. After a year there, despite my advanced degrees in history and poli-sci, I still was unable to get a decent job. The best I could do, having extremely limited German (the foreign language tapes just wouldn't stick in my head), was a day job as a waitress at a Konditorei, hazardous duty, in fact, for it damaged both my waistline and my marriage.

The language barrier and the capability of contributing only

meager funds to our marital coffers took its toll. Soon, my dis-
illusion was in real danger of becoming full-fledged depression.
We never had kids because Rob was worried that they would
end up with Down syndrome, and it broke his heart to see
those poor babies and their families suffer so. Spending day
and night in his university laboratory, his goal was to isolate the
gene and find the cure. It was noble to say the least, and I
wished him the very best (still do, actually); but there was
nothing in Germany for me. I never saw him, had no kids, or
even a pet, to care for, worked long hours on my feet for a pit-
tance, and was developing a pot belly from noshing on nothing
but pastries—not what I had envisioned doing with my Ivy
League education.

Rob and I began to quarrel regularly, mostly about money
and my unhappiness with living in a country where I couldn't
get a job in any area remotely resembling my fields of study and
past job experience. So with regrets, we agreed to legally call it
a day, but I've been divorced for a decade and we still e-mail
each other every now and then to say hello. Rob, marriage, the
NIH, and Cologne now seem like another lifetime ago.

"Why don't I come into the city and cheer you up?" Imogen
offers. "I could leave Sid with the kids and we could just have a
girls' night in. I tell you, I am so fried with the bar and bat
mitzvah plans. Jacob wants either a basketball theme or something to do with *Lord of the Rings*. I told him the first was out of
the question: The Musikoffs have already booked Madison
Square Garden that weekend for Ben. Emily wants an eques-
trian theme, but we were thinking of renting the Temple of
Dendur at the Met and they won't let you bring horses into the
museum. They're trying my last nerve! I'm at my wits' end.
How am I supposed to settle on a venue when I can't get the
two of them to agree on anything? And by now, it's impossible

to get it together. You need time to plan these things. We started talking about it three years ago, like everyone else does, and somehow, the clock just ran down, and here I am with two squabbling twelve-year-olds who can't even agree on a menu. I've hired a party planner but after months and months of wrangling we still have no venue, no theme, no caterer—at this rate I may have to print the invitations off the computer. It's far too late to get something engraved. I'll never live this down. You've never had kids, Tess, so you can't understand my mortification. How am I going to show my face at the country club?"

"Why don't you just throw a luncheon by your pool after the synagogue service?" I suggest.

"What, are you kidding? You're kidding, right? When was the last time you've been to a bar or bat mitzvah?"

I give it barely a second's consideration. "Shauna's probably."

"Well, you remember what that was like? And *no one* rents out the *Intrepid* for bar mitzvahs anymore. That's been passé for years."

"What do you care what anybody else does?"

"You are kidding, right?" I really hope this isn't her new catchphrase. Imogen tends to find a new one every six months or so. "I have to be on the Upper West Side late this afternoon anyway. I have an . . . appointment."

"Venus is coming over this evening," I counter, knowing the two of them have never quite seen eye to eye on a number of subjects.

"Oh, great!" Imogen crows. "I've been thinking about her lately. Do you think she would teach me how to pole dance? I saw a piece on the news—it's supposed to be a hot new exercise craze. One of the women in my Torah study group swears by it.

She lost thirty-five pounds and got her husband back after he'd been having it off with one of his paralegals. Whoops, that's my other line. Gotta run! I'll see you around seven-thirty!"

August 7—Day 1 A.D. (After David)

In madcap movies there's always one main character who remains the straight man, the centrifugal force about which all the zany characters spin and dazzle and do their thing. All my decision making seems to have been taken out of my hands this week. My closest friend and my self-absorbed cousin are calling the shots today. David called the shots yesterday. Actually, I really need to admit, right here on paper, that David has been calling the shots, emotionally, ever since we first became romantically involved. How did I let that happen? And for so long? I've always thought of myself as independent, resilient, and relatively forthright about my needs. Do I see a different me than others do?

I want a man to take me in his arms and tell me he can't live without me; that he thinks about me several times a day; that he can't wait to come home to my smile and the scent of my skin, or anticipates with heart-thudding happiness the moment when I'll cross the threshold and step into his arms. I want to hear him say that I make him laugh; that he's not afraid to cry in front of me; that he doesn't want to spend another day apart if he can help it.

David never said he loved me. In all those years, never in so many words. What "so many"? Three. But he never actually said them. That secret finger gesture he would make in response to mine really meant "me, too." Not the same thing as articulating those three monosyllables. As his speechwriter, perhaps I should have scripted them for him. Now, that was snarky, Tess. But I feel angry and sarcastic right now and I think I have a right to vent. Besides, this is my journal; who's going to see it?

Seven

"Would you just go off to Italy like that if your husband cheated on you?" With both eyes still on the TV, Imogen reaches for a fistful of popcorn and chases it with a gulp of wine.

"Faster than you could say *pronto*. And I'd put my trip on his credit card," Venus adds. "God, that's gorgeous," she says, pointing to the television. "Ahhh, Tuscany," she sighs. "I love this movie."

"Funny how it has almost nothing to do with the book," I say. "The book is about the house, almost as a metaphor for where she's at emotionally, and the movie is all about a romance with a younger man as the road to fulfillment—even if it tanks. And the central character in the book hardly resembles Diane Lane."

"They always do that when they make the movie," Imogen says. "Would you want to spend two hours of your time watching a frowsy woman of sixty fixing up a farmhouse?"

"Don't diss frowsy women of sixty. With any luck, we'll all get there ourselves one day." The decidedly un-frowsy Venus stretches her long legs and releases a cramp in her instep. "Has either of you ever gone out with a younger man?"

"Nope," I reply immediately. "They've never done anything for me. Different tastes in music, different . . . I don't know . . . men always act so much younger emotionally than we do, that I think you're really letting yourself in for it when you get involved with a chronologically younger one. It would be like dating your son or something."

"Surely you exaggerate," Venus purrs.

"Surely I don't. But I wouldn't know. Since I have no experience in that realm."

Venus gives me the sloe-eyed look that has sent countless men to their knees. Or reaching for their wallets. "Surely you do, T. Exaggerate. *Trust me.*"

Imogen is uncharacteristically silent. Venus and I both stare at her until she feels compelled to contribute to this particular conversation.

"Well . . . I've been happily married for so many years that I wouldn't . . ." She studies the inside of her wine glass, then decides to replenish the contents, filling it almost completely. "What the hell. I left the car in a garage; I can always crash here tonight, right, Tess?" My cousin takes another sip of wine, and Venus and I watch as her features begin to soften, and her eyes take on a glow that seems to light them from within, as if there is an ironically kinder, gentler Mr. Hyde being released from the wellspring of her soul. "Younger men . . . listen to you. They treat you like you're some kind of special, precious creature. They don't take you for granted. You know how fantastic that feels to a forty-three-year-old mother of three teenagers, one of whom is a nubile young girl about to go off to college? Younger men don't think you're fat just because you've gained a pound or ten since your twenties. There's something to be said for that 'in praise of older women' thing."

I'm too surprised by this odd confession to do more than remark upon the concept in the most generic sense. Inside I'm thinking, *My God, Imogen, after years of holier-than-thou goody-two-shoes blather about how great marriage is, you've been knocking it off with some young stud??* Instead I say, "It's not that a younger guy's not as smart as I am, but—unless we're referring to someone just a couple of years younger, which is still more our less our age, then I can't imagine what we'd talk about. I mean, what would I say to a twenty-two-year-old guy?"

"*Fuck* me!" Imogen looks like the Cheshire Cat.

I laugh, and the sound suddenly strikes me as coming from someone else. Hyper-aware for a moment, I recognize it as David's laugh. And I've been doing it for years. When did I stop sounding like me?

Imogen, too, bursts out laughing, spilling her wine in her lap. "Oh, shit. Sorry about that, Tess." She fixates on the remainder of her wine. "You don't know what you're missing," she suddenly giggles drunkenly. "Oh, damn, now I've given myself the hiccups."

"Is there something you'd like to tell us?" I ask her, trying very hard not to leer, which somehow seems a more preferential attitude to take. Utter shock (knowing my cousin) is where my brain is really at, but since Imogen is releasing the heretofore unseen racy side of herself, I figure I'd get more details if I acted more salaciously curious than judgmental.

My cousin looks as though she can't decide whether she needs another fortifying glass of wine, or whether her little mishap was an indication that she's had quite enough. "Every Thursday I drive into the city for a massage. Well, that's what Sid thinks.

I've told him time and time again there are no good day spas in Great Neck."

"You're having an affair with your masseur? God, that's classic!"

Imogen fixes Venus with a withering gaze. "You must think I'm a real 'Desperate Housewife.' You didn't let me *finish*," she whines. "I'm not even getting a massage every week. Well, not from someone at Bliss or someplace like that." She lowers her voice conspiratorially. "Okay . . . you'll never believe this . . . it's the party planner! For Jacob and Emily's bar and bat mitz-vahs!"

I frown, thinking something doesn't quite tally. "You must have found the only heterosexual male party planner on the eastern seaboard."

Imogen shrugs happily. "Sid thinks Roger is gay, too. Which is fine by me."

Mentally I kick myself for jumping to stereotype. After all, David is 100 percent straight, and ever since the swimming pool incident, the New York press and his political opponent have been making as much hay as they can out of hinting that he's a closeted gay.

"*Ladies* . . . you can't believe how creative this man is! I'm telling you! He made me see stars." Imogen's eyes are like saucers.

"Well, I'm all for great sex," Venus says, raising her glass.

"No, I mean he showed me what we could do with a plan-etarium theme. Jacob's been thinking lately about being low-ered into the catering hall in a spaceship, although Roger thinks the theme's been done to death; you know, from 'Today I am a man' to 'One small step for man; one giant leap for mankind.' So we're considering the possibility of trying to alter the gravitational field in the dining room. Something like that. To make it really special. Though it might cost a bit extra. All those spacesuits and oxygen masks for every guest. Gets a bit pricey."

"And orange isn't my color," I add. "Besides, where's the crime in having a bar mitzvah be a religious celebration? Without rocket ships and DJs and zero gravity. And if you're going to spend fifty grand on a kid's thirteenth birthday party—double that since you've got twins—what do you do for an encore? For Emily's sweet sixteen? Or for their weddings?"

"I'd rather hear about the hot young party planner," Venus says.

Imogen grins. "A triple-threat." She lowers her voice to a conspiratorial whisper. "He's twenty-seven, hung like a bell-pull, and he listens to me."

Imogen never talks this way. It's because Venus is here that my cousin is getting down and dirty. By her own admission, Imogen lives in "a very quiet cul-de-sac, not on Wisteria Lane." Her racy talk is an attempt to compete with a glamorous heiress who has seen—by virtue of her former career—plenty of men of all stripes. "Did you ever stop to consider," I posit, "that he listens so well because you're paying him the cost of feeding a moderate-sized developing nation just to stage your kids' bar and bat mitzvahs?"

Imogen looks wounded. "God, Tess, it's not like I'm paying Roger for sex!" She places her wineglass on the coffee table and begins to pout—the same look she's been perfecting since we were kids. "I wouldn't be throwing stones if I were you."

"Yikes!" If she weren't my relative, she wouldn't be my friend. Not tonight, anyway. I wonder if Sid even suspects his wife's infidelity, or if he's too deep into other people's gum tissue to notice. "How'd we get on this topic anyway?" I ask tipsily.

"Jetting off to Italy after your husband betrays you," Venus answers. This is the woman who, in addition to the wine, had also brought over a gift-wrapped copy of *It's Called a Breakup Because It's Broken*. "I know that's not how it ended with David but I still think you should take a leaf from Diane Lane's book—well, her character's. Go to Italy to clear your head from him: from his body; from his campaign promises to you; from his asking you to continue to write his speeches—which as far as I'm concerned is the ultimate act of chutzpah and insensitivity, no matter how much he really *does* need you—for that, at least. If men had a clue how that kind of thing sounds, and how much it hurts, and how lousy their timing is, they wouldn't say it. Bask under the Tuscan sun," she commands me. "Recharge your emotional and spiritual batteries. Meet a younger guy who murmurs words of *amore* in your ear that you don't understand but which sound wonderful and make your soul wet. Have wild sex. Drink terrific wine. Meet his family. Fall in love. You know the drill. It'll be good for you. You need a change of scene. Manhattan may have every material dream at your fingertips but this thirteen-mile-long strip of skyscraper-planted schist has a way of beating a vulnerable person down even further."

"I don't have the energy," I groan.

"Don't have the energy for a vacation?"

"That, too. I mean for Italy, V. I think I remember how to ask where the bathroom is and how to say 'no cheese, please' on my pasta, but after that I've exhausted my vocabulary. I don't know how to say things like '*Prego, signore*, please take your hand off my thigh.'"

"Why would you want to?" Imogen finds this hysterically funny. Mr. Hyde-the-salami has emerged in full regalia. She's in no shape to drive home, that's for certain. And I really don't need her sleeping on my couch because she can be a real pill when she's hung over. Not to mention—as much as I did want to live with David, which is different because he was my long-term lover—I do covet my privacy. Imogen snoops.

"Well, if you're not up for someplace where there's a language barrier, pick another venue. Trust me, you do need to cry in your beer somewhere other than New York City, T." Venus's lovely face lights up as she has an epiphany. "That's it! Beer!"

"Ireland?" For the past twenty years or so we've had the ability to complete each other's thoughts and sentences, something Imogen and I, despite our blood relation, have never been able to accomplish. I let the Ireland idea sink in for a bit.

"Think of those lovely musical accents; oh-so-fascinating rogues with sparkling eyes—which just might be the whiskey talking, come to think of it—who'll charm the pants off of you, tell a grandly entertaining yarn, and speak your language. Of course they won't marry you until their mothers die," she adds somewhat ruefully, then raises her Eire banner once more. "All the fish and chips you can eat; oh, and if the Guinness is too strong for you, ask the bartender to toss in a shot of cassis— black currant liqueur."

"I know what cassis is, Venus. I used to drink it with vermouth when I was sixteen."

But she ignores me. "Inexplicably magical encounters with leprechauns and the sí; indescribable mystery; glittering pots of gold at the ends of breathtaking rainbows. Great music, good food, no snakes, fabulous walks—"

I point at Venus's mane of red hair and laugh. "Enough! You sound like an ad from the Irish Tourist Board." And somehow, before I can come up with a reason *not* to visit Ireland on the spur of the moment, Venus has convinced me to log on to the computer and book an airline ticket and a room—in a charming-looking, if somewhat pricey, little hotel on St. Stephen's Green.

This is what I get for being rather squiffy on champagne when the minutes have ticked well past midnight. I feel like Cinderella with two fairy godmothers as the three of us pull an all-nighter, planning my traveling wardrobe, doing last-minute laundry, nestling David's model ship into a cardboard Fresh Direct box which gets shoved onto the top shelf of my coat closet, and getting me packed and ready to go.

The next afternoon, over glasses of drinkable pinot at the nearly empty Boathouse Restaurant in Central Park, I give David my decision. Well, sort of. I could have left a message on his answering machine, but part of me felt that would be too cold, and another part of me really wanted to see him, even though I'd asked him not to contact me. In his favor, he'd kept his side of the agreement and allowed me to make the overture. There's also a part of me that wants to look at him again, be in the same room with him, to prove to myself that it's over and that I am capable of inhabiting the same space without still wanting him, a way of convincing myself that I'm getting over him. Now that I'm sitting across from him in a clean, well-lighted place, I ask myself, *Who am I kidding?*

"I told you the other night that I'll need time," I reiterate. My gut tells me to say, *You must be out of your tiny fucking mind to have the gall to ask me to continue to work for you after you've just chucked me, much less for no apparent reason, or for one so vague that my sensibilities are still parsing it out.* That's more or less the eloquent version. But I go with the promptings of my brain instead. "At the moment, David, the breakup wounds are raw and un-sutured, so I'm incapable of behaving with anything remotely approaching professionalism. I can't turn on a dime or switch gears and behave as though we're nothing more than colleagues—and it's even worse than that, because you're my boss. Believe me, it wouldn't be doing either of us any favors. Which brings me back to needing time. And space. I'm heading out of town tonight—"

"Where to?" He looks surprised.

"Ireland. Because it's there, because I've never been, because Venus talked me into it, because I want to try a pint of Guinness drawn properly, and because I want to clear my head someplace that's far, far away."

"When will you be back?"

"A week." I hold up my hand to silence his inevitable response. "David, I know Dobson and the media have got you in the hot seat, and that you need to put the focus back on the issues, before your constituents think that a man who made a mint running a leash and flea collar company called Pet-o-Philia is more fit than you are to sit in the House of Representatives; but I can't give you what you want right now. What you need. You've got other speechwriters. *Gus* is a terrific—"

"He's not as good as you are, Tess."

I place my wine glass on the table and dab the corners of my mouth with the linen napkin, suddenly feeling naked and vulnerable without the prop to hide behind.

David sighs. "I do understand, you know. I know you feel that my decision seemed to come out of left field. And I know you're hurting. I'm not insensitive to your feelings. It wasn't easy, Tessa. It was just . . . the right thing to do."

"For you, maybe." David isn't sure what to say to this. Clearly, right now he could use a speechwriter. Ironic, isn't it, how some of the most articulate people you know are lost without a script. Feeling angry and resentful I begin to tear up, but stifle it immediately when I catch the waiter looking in our direction. I'm in a public place with a public figure, and throwing crystal and cutlery isn't my style anyway. This meeting is self-consciously civil. I'd love another glass of wine, but in my psyche's present condition, I'd end up flying hung-over. "I'll give you my final answer when I return from Ireland. You'll just have to wait a week or go with Gus. He's not exactly a slouch, and he served you quite well as a speechwriter before you met me."

David frowns. "It's not that."

"What is it, then?"

"You know what it is. You know better than anybody. *I hate to lose.*"

"Well," I sigh, "even Admiral Nelson had his bad days."

Eight

 Much later that night, I board an overnight flight bound for Dublin.

The plane is packed to the gills with travelers, of both the tourist and homebound variety, many of whom seem to have exceptionally large, young, and noisy families. I'd been hoping to get some sleep, but that seems unlikely in this airborne day-care center.

Right after I ensconce myself in my window seat as cozily as I can manage and fire up my laptop, hoping to squeeze in some last-minute work (notes to myself, mostly) before takeoff, a large turbaned gentleman sits beside me, taking up an extraordinary amount of my personal space. I try to become absorbed in my typing, but I can't manage this without my left elbow touching him. He seems to enjoy it. So I try to keep my arms as close to my own body as possible, but I can't work this way, so I store the laptop and take out a novel to read instead. For some reason, every time I need to turn a page, I am having the same close encounter with his ample torso. I know the quarters are cramped, but he seems to be purposely invading my territory, such as it is. I try to convince myself that his too-proximal behavior is a cultural thing, and that therefore, I should give him the benefit of the doubt. It's a long and crowded flight, and we all need to be respectful of one another or it's going to seem even longer.

He tries to engage me in conversation. A little light banter.

"Do you have a husband?" are the first words out of his mouth. Glancing over at him, I shake my head.

"Do you have a son?"

Why does he want to know this? Oh, never mind, the issue isn't worth deconstructing. I simply shake my head a second time.

"Me, no wife and no sons."

"Daughters?" I hear myself ask.

He laughs into his beard. "No, no. No daughters. Do you have a husband?"

I could swear we just covered this terrain. "No, I don't," I say pointedly, hoping it will be a firm indication that I don't wish to converse with him at the moment. To emphasize my point, I return to my book.

"No wife, no sons," he repeats, then asks *me* about sons again. I'm stuck in an endless loop with this man.

"Please excuse me, sir. I would like to read now," I say, but this does not deter him. By this point, the flight attendant has come down the aisle offering drinks. My new pal asks for two scotches and two cans of Diet Coke, then mixes himself two repulsively lethal cocktails of aspartame and Johnnie Walker Red. When the attendant comes back the other way, my row-mate purchases two more mini-bottles of scotch.

Four drinks in about fifteen minutes' time, and he becomes even more expansive. And of course he's expanding in my direction, and not in the direction of the vacant aisle seat to his left. "Wouldn't you be more comfortable on the aisle?" I ask diplomatically. I'm dreadful with direct confrontation in these situations.

"Oh, no," he assures me, taking my hand in his and giving it a squeeze. "I'm very happy."

I pull my hand away. "Please don't do that again," I say firmly. I politely ask the fellow to move aside so I can get out of my seat, and instead of sliding into the aisle and standing up, he forces me to climb over him. It's impossible for me to achieve this feat without many of my body parts making contact with his. I feel dirty and disgusting; totally violated.

Locating a flight attendant I quietly inform him that I would prefer not to spend the night getting manhandled by the gent in 28J. The attendant, Gary, is both sympathetic and appalled. "Do you want me to bitch-slap him?" he inquires energetically. I can sense that Gary would actually be up for this, so I politely decline his offer while asking if there's another seat to which I might relocate for the remainder of the flight. "It's practically standing room only in coach," Gary says, scanning the section. "I feel terrible about this. Let me see what I can do."

He confers with two of his colleagues for a minute or two. Breaking their huddle, he approaches me and says, "Collect your personal items. If you've got anything in the overhead bins, I'll take it forward for you. We've got a couple of empty seats in business class." I make a mental note to write to the airline to commend the staff of flight 107 on their graceful way of handling the situation.

Cheered to spend the rest of the night flight unmolested in a reclining seat, with the added ability to order champagne at will—not that I *will* at 2 A.M., but I love the idea that I *can*—I begin to settle into my new seat, when . . .

"Is that *you*—wait, don't tell me your name—*Jess?*" A tall, broad-shouldered man with streaked blond hair unbuckles his seat belt and rises to his feet. Dick Elgar. A speechwriter for the enemy. I made the mistake of dating him briefly about a decade ago. Dick and I are what would happen if Carville and Matalin didn't work out. "My God, I almost didn't recognize you! You've lost weight," he adds appraisingly. "You look great . . . thinner . . . taller . . . maybe it's your hair . . ."

For the record, I have weighed a steady 117 pounds since college. I am still 5'6" and my hair has been a bit below shoulder length, medium brown with subtle caramel highlights, since Clinton was in the White House. "You need to work on your pick-up lines, Dick. And my name is not Jess."

"Not Jessica? Are you sure? Wait—what does it begin with?"

"T."

"Tammy? T-T-torpedo? Debbie?"

"Debbie doesn't begin with a T." I address the other residents of business class. "What does it say about me—or him—that I *slept* with this guy—more than once, in fact—and he can't remember my name?"

"I do remember her name," Dick says. "C'mon, Tess, I was just teasing you. You used to have a sense of humor."

"That was because your candidate was a buffoon. Everything he said made me laugh."

"C'mon, sit here," he says, indicating a vacant seat adjacent to his own. "Let's have a drink and catch up for old times' sake. Damn, you look great. You look really trim. Are you sure you haven't lost weight?"

"It must be all the Pilates," I reply tartly, wondering why I engaged at all. I should have sidestepped this conversation several words ago. *"Dick,* you sure know how to worm your way into a girl's heart," I say, aiming for just the right amount of sarcasm. "I'm sure you're giving Casanova a run for his money. But I would prefer to *sleep,* all things considered."

I tuck into my new seat, and like a little girl with a birthday party "loot bag," open the business class complimentary Dopp kit to see what goodies I've landed. Slipping on the abbreviated socks and donning the eye mask, I slide myself toward slumber.

Day 3 A.D. August 9 for the rest of the world

I've spent the afternoon in the company of Socrates and Plato, Bacon and Milton, Dean Swift and Oliver Gold-smith, Homer and Shakespeare, Newton and Locke, Cicero and Aristotle—and Jane Austen's first love—Tom Lefroy, who eventually became Ireland's Chief Justice. I wish I could tell her he didn't turn out to be much of a looker in his old age. These venerated souls are further im-mortalized in marble busts that flank the length of Trinity College's Old Library. What a magnificent place! I could move in there tomorrow. Twenty-thousand of the college's oldest volumes reside in the Long Room with its cast-iron spiral staircase, the barrel-vaulted ceiling a subtle hint to the visitor that she is in a cathedral to literature, a biblio-phile's wet dream.

The lush lawns of the Trinity College Green appear to be the perfect place to take a nap, which is exactly what I did, after arriving at my hotel before my room was ready. Leaving my luggage with the bellman, a congenial Austra-lian, I whipped out my laminated street map and hit the pavement.

I suppose the first stop for any first-time Dublin tourist is the Book of Kells. In our age of the computerization of everything, the very fact that every single aspect of this treasure was made by hand, from the vellum to the pigments to the illuminations, is staggering when one considers the years of painstaking workmanship involved. Having been introduced to Ireland through the experience of this gorgeous dinosaur convinces me that here indeed is a kind of special magic, the ultimate value placed on craft and beauty.

I want to be in love with this city.

I want it to change me. That's why I came here.

I've already mailed postcards to Venus and Imogen and scarfed down a portion of Burdocks's fish and chips, licking my fingers while admiring the gothic façade of Christ Church Cathedral. Alas, even on an enforced vacation I still seem to be multitasking.

I often find myself making fun of tourists in New York who, oblivious to traffic of all varieties, put themselves at risk of bodily harm, or worse, by looking up instead of looking out. So far today, my romantic gawking at any architecture older than my grandmother has nearly gotten me run over several times. And Dubliners seem even more bullish than New Yorkers when it comes to crossing major intersections: the pedestrians fording the avenues opposite Trinity College Green just put their heads down and charge.

Wandering the streets, I am struck by how much Dublin reminds me of home in so many ways: a similar cosmopolitanism to New York with its myriad restaurants of relatively obscure ethnicities, people of all shades, their accents and speech reflecting a polyglot community rather than the homogenized one I had anticipated. Where are the red-headed colleens, the freckle-faced boys with their tousled strawberry blond hair? The statue of Molly Malone, known to the locals as "the tart with the cart," seems a lot closer to the silhouette I expected. Bosoms over-flowing her bronze bodice, to me the wench epitomizes the feisty spirit of the Irish working class. I realize I have sunk into stereotype of sorts, even though the stereotype in my mind is one I view as positive: the quaintness, the charm, the folkloric. Bronze Molly, too, is a relic of an ancient age.

However, my hotel, situated in a Georgian townhouse, satisfies my craving for old-world charm. The wallpaper (a muted floral), a roomy four-poster, late eighteenth-century furnishings, a giant claw-foot tub, fluffy towels, lovely little amenities such as lavender toiletries, and a window overlooking St. Stephen's Green soothe the savage breast of this stressed New Yorker. Volumes of Joyce and Behan, the plays of Shaw and Sheridan, of Wilde and Synge and Yeats and Beckett, as well as Maeve Binchy's latest novel, stand like paperback soldiers on the mantel-piece, waiting for me to call them to action. I wish it were cool enough to ask one of the staff to light a fire for me . . .

I can't believe I fell asleep in the middle of writing in my journal.

I awaken a few hours later; in the interval the sky over St. Stephen's Green has morphed from vivid blue to the color of dusty coal. What time is it? The alarm clock, an anachronism in this chamber of Georgian charm, informs me in digital carmine numerals that it's 9:13 P.M. I've slept through dinner. Jet lag has exacted its price.

Downstairs, I approach the sweet French graduate student slipping tomorrow's breakfast menus into cushiony leather folders. There doesn't seem to be an official concierge in this hotel, at least not during any of the hours I've come and gone; guests seem to rely on the first visible staff member to answer any queries.

"I'd like to visit a real Irish pub," I tell Justine, realizing how silly that sounds. "Which one would you recommend?"

"Do you like James Joyce?"

"Sure."

Justine directs me to Davy Byrne's not five minutes' walk from the hotel. "Very famous," she says, "but maybe not quite so much . . . atmospheric . . . as you would like. But there are several pubs on Duke Street. Why not try them all?" she suggests, shrugging with extreme Gallic joie de vivre.

"I'm tempted," I reply with a wink.

"You are on holiday," she says, which I interpret as a license to overindulge. "In *Ireland*."

When in Rome . . . or Dublin, as the case may be.

Davy Byrne's is terribly modern. In other words, even though Joyce drank here (which is a bit like an old American hostelry advertising "George Washington slept here") and his fictional Leopold Bloom consumed a mustard sandwich within these walls on June 16, 1904, a lot has changed in a hundred-plus years. I am disappointed. And I don't even like mustard. Nevertheless, I immediately learn that it's impossible for an unescorted female to look around a pub (what am I supposed to say? "Just checking out the décor"?) without being invited to join someone for a pint.

A trio of ruddy-cheeked mates are sharing a joke, and of the three invitations I receive within my first half-minute inside

Davy Byrne's, I opt to join the crowd, rather than either of the two solo imbibers. Safer on a couple of counts, I expect.

"What'll you have?" asks the oldest of the three, a wizened gent with a shock of white hair who looks like he's worn the same tweed jacket every day, rain or shine, summer or winter, since Eamon de Valera entered Parliament.

I'm actually not much of a beer drinker, something I will not admit to on Irish soil. And if I do plan on exploring more than one pub tonight, I reckon I'd better start slow, so I order a glass of Harp, thinking a "glass" will contain less than a pint. Oh, well, at least the lager is lighter than a stout. Guinness has always seemed to be more of a meal than a beverage. Then of course, if the Guinness were too strong, I would feel like a real puffball asking this bartender to smooth it out for me with a shot of cassis, per Venus's coaching.

Conlan is my benefactor, a former parliamentarian himself, so maybe my hunch about the age of his sport coat isn't far off the mark. His drinking buddies ("We come here every day after work since 1974") are Tim, who the other two call Gogo and who owns a plumbing concern, and Joe, the youngest, who is a journalist. Within a half hour, I know all their life stories from snatches such as:

"You know, Joe's da tossed him out on his arse when Joe confessed that he thought he might be a queer. He was all of fourteen at the time, but it torned out 'e was just experimenting, Joe was."

"Gogo's wife left him for his business partner."

"Good riddance, I say."

"I'm not disagreein'."

"Ach, Conlan's been a widower so long the statue of Molly Malone has been looking good to him lately."

"Aah, you're both full of shite. It doesn't work anymore

anyway! At my age I'd rather have a pint than a woman. At least I *know* I can lift me *forearm*."

"There is something to be said for staying out as late as you please without fearing a tongue-lashing when you come home."

"I niver missed Abby when she left. Had the last laugh anyway; me partner had the clap off a woman he met on a business trip to Paris and passed it on to her. Sorves 'er right, the tart."

I marvel at how their accents turn such misogyny into music. And how some of the things I did expect from Dublin are proving to be true. Yet I am somehow comfortable here, a lone female amid the easy camaraderie of three men I didn't know an hour ago.

I finish my pint of Harp and decline another, as Gogo buys the next round. "This may be terribly irreverent, but I'd like to visit another place that . . . well . . . fulfills my imagination's fancy of a typical Dublin pub."

"You're wanting the oak paneling, then?" says Joe.

"The stained glass partitions?" adds Gogo.

"A cozy little snug?" concludes Conlan.

I nod.

"Do you like music?"

I grin.

"O'Donoghue's, over on Merrion Row, is where The Dubliners got their start back in the sixties," Gogo says. "Sometoimes we tree head over there after a few pints here. Anyone can sit in if they've a mind too. Conlan's quite a good'un on the whistle. They've always got a local band playing there. Doesn't matter who; it's all the same to my tin ear. But fine, fine music."

"Oh aye, O'Donoghue's is a good one, but it doesn't have the atmosphere that—"

"Tessa," I remind them.

"Tessa. Are you Irish, then? Used to be a music hall singer

named Tessie O'Shea. You're not an O'Shea, are you?" Conlan looks hopeful.

"Craig. Tessa Craig's my name."

Joe frowns. "Sounds Scots."

"Well, that was my married name anyway. My maiden name is . . . Goldsmith."

"Ah, well then! You *are* Irish!" The delighted look on Conlan's's face says it all.

"Jewish, actually," I admit, ever so slightly self-conscious.

"At the height of the troubles in the seventies, a man walked in here on a St. Paddy's Day," says Conlan, "and he begins talking to the bartender over a pint. And the bartender says, 'I've never seen yiz before; are ya new in town?' And the man nods and says, 'Just arrived today.' And the bartender, a proud Cat-lick himself, asks the man, 'Are yiz a Cat-lick?' The man shakes his head. 'A Protestant, then?' the publican says darkly. 'No, not one of those either,' says the man. 'I'm a Jew.' The bartender picks up a glass and begins to dry it, then he takes his cloth to wipe down the bar, momentarily lost in thought; something about the man's reply still unsettles him. And torning to the man, the bartender asks him, 'But are yiz a *Cat-lick* Jew or a *Protestant* Jew?' "

"That joke's so old the cavemen told it to the dinosaurs," Joe groans. As Conlan dismisses this criticism, Joe tells me that if it's old-fashioned charm I'm after in a pub, my best bet is Blackpools. He draws a map on a cocktail napkin and wishes me the best of Irish luck. Thanking the three of them for their generosity and hospitality while declining yet another round, I head out once more into the night.

Nine

As I wend through Dublin's dark streets following Conlan's chicken-scratched treasure map, I am conscious of not being frightened. Would I advise a slightly inebriated female in search of further entertainment to wander through Manhattan alone in the late evening clutching an ink-stained cocktail napkin as a Baedeker? Hell, no! But tonight my body senses that I have a greater chance of getting lost than of getting mashed.

Blackpools is off the beaten path, at the fecund apex of a cul-de-sac, sandwiched between an Ethiopian restaurant and an internet café. At first glance the pub seems so crowded that patrons are spilling into the street, but then I realize that the sidewalk loafers are smokers, banished, as in New York, to the great outdoors. As a nonsmoker myself I rejoice in this exercise of civil obedience. But, ah, the irony of it. Oh, yes, happy is the day when imbibers can enjoy their alcohol without fear of succumbing to the dangers of second-hand smoke. Give me liver disease over lung cancer any day of the week.

Squeezing past the knot of tobacco-addicted drinkers, I cross the threshold of Blackpools to find it just as advertised: the cozy snug, the warm glow of lamplight on richly stained glass, the oaken paneling, and the faint lilt of folk music, scarcely audible above the din, for the pub seems to me a giant indoor block party. Laughter tinkles over the clink of glassware, punctuated by the occasional blare of an outright guffaw. A cluster in one corner has burst into song. A knot of football fans of myriad ages, genders, shapes and sizes (all loyally sporting their team's jersey) parts like the Red Sea so that I can belly up to the bar.

A sign over the huge gilded mirror reads WORK IS THE GREAT REALITY, BEAUTY IS THE GREAT AIM. "Quite a crowd you've got tonight," I say to the bartender, an attractive guy who I'd peg to be about my age.

"What'll it be, miss?"

I had been operating under the impression that Irish bartenders were the embodiments of conviviality. This one is an anomaly, all business, a taciturn fellow in a sea of mirth.

"Guinness . . . I guess," I reply, hoping I don't require that shot of black currant. This pub feels like the right place to sample my first pint of stout.

"Coming right up, then." He pulls my pint and places it in front of me. I leave a few euro on the bar.

"Is it always this busy in here?"

"Most nights."

"When isn't it, then?"

"When we're closed."

I feel like I'm talking to a salt-and-pepper-haired New Englander instead. "Forgive a stupid, and rather forward, question from an American, but I was wondering . . . do you like your job?"

"Now, why do you ask that?"

"Well . . ." I gesture behind me. "Everyone seems to be having such a blast, and you don't much look like *you* are—and the bartender is kind of the host of the party, isn't he? Is there something else you'd rather be doing?"

"*Fish*, if I had me druthers. I'm not one for the small talk, miss. If it's sparkling repartee you're after, it's my brother Jamie you're wanting to meet."

The foam is soft and sweet on my lips as I taste my first pint of Guinness on its native soil.

Suddenly a voice just next to my ear says, "I bet you expected it to smell like sweat socks."

I turn around to encounter the greenest eyes I've ever seen, twinkling like emeralds on a rajah's sarpech. I could swear they weren't there a second ago. "Excuse me! Smell like what?"

"Sweat socks. That's what all American women say about Guinness. Uneducated palates, all," he tsks-tsks.

"And how did you know I was an American?"

Green-eyes smiles. Damn those Irishmen and their dimples. Venus was right. "The way you took that forst sip. Tentative. Only Americans do that. And you confirmed my suspicions with the very forst words out of your mouth."

Now I'm smiling too. "Are we that predictable?"

"Nah, not really. It was your accent," he confesses. "It's charming."

"My *American* accent is charming?"

"Irresistible. In fact it's what made our Da fall arsey-farsey over our Ma. Isn't that right, Niall?" The bartender nods acquiescently. "So you've met my brother, Niall. Not much of a talker he is, but he can't help that. Have yiz seen John Wayne in *The Quiet Man?*"

"I have, in fact." There's something about Green-eyes that makes me want to laugh—in the best way. Just because it feels good to do it.

"Well, our Niall here is the original Quiet Man. But like I say, it's not his fault: forst-born runs the family business, no matter whether he wants to or no. That's Doyle primogeniture for yiz. Forst-born takes over the pub, second-born—that's me—is the fisherman—though I have to say I can't abide the smelly critters, and it's lonely as shite sitting in a little boat all day with nothing but the mermaids to flort with."

"Oh aye, if you're going to flort with the American, yiz might as well begin by introducing yerself, Jamie," mutters Niall, as he sets up the glasses to pull three pints at once.

"Ach, I must have left me manners in my skiff." Green-eyes extends his hand. "Jamie Doyle."

"Tessa. Tessa Craig."

"Craig?" He frowns. "Scots?"

"It's—was—I'm divorced for years now—my married name. My maiden name is Goldsmith."

"Ah, yiz *are* Irish, then!"

"Actually, it's Jewish."

"Many years ago a man walked in here on a St. Paddy's Day— stood right where you are, in fact—and orders a pint from me great granddad, who looks 'im up and down with a wee bit o'suspicion. 'Yer a stranger to Blackpools,' says me grand-da. 'Are yiz a Cat-lick?' "

"I've heard that one," I smile. "About an hour ago, in fact."

"Ahh, but it's all in the telling," Jamie replies with a wink. "Would you care to join me someplace a bit quieter? The snug does not appear to be occupied at present. Do ya know why snugs were built, Tess?"

"A more private place to snog? Snogging in the snug?"

"I like the way you think, woman, but I'm afraid you don't win the cigar. What part of New York are ya from, by the way?"

"Manha—how did you know? Manhattan."

Jamie graciously motions for me to precede him into the alcove, then slides in beside me. The glow through the stained glass panel separating the snug from the rest of the pub turns our little haven into a boozy cathedral, a truly *spiritual* experience. "Snugs were built so that a lady could have a quiet place to enjoy a pint or a dram without being considered vulgar for drinking in the company of men. How did I know you were from New York? Me ma, Maureen, grew up in Inwood. Do yiz live far from there?"

"A few miles south. The Upper West Side."

"St. Luke's Hospital. Do ya know where that is?"

Suddenly I am reminded of David and wonder how he's doing. Suddenly I miss being kissed. "Yes, I do. I live not far from there."

Jamie lights up like the Rockefeller Center Christmas tree. "I was born there! Niall, too, two years earlier. But with the two of us still in nappies and a third'un on the way, our da, Eamon, decided that we couldn't all survive in Manhattan, even in Inwood, on a cabdriver's earnings, so we came back to the auld sod, as they say. Da's a sixth-generation Dubliner."

"Wow. Did James Joyce drink in Blackpools? Brendan Behan?"

"Gorl, there's not a pub in Dublin that Brendan Behan didn't drink in."

Jamie insists that I order the fish and chips, something I'd kind of o.d.'d on already today, having grabbed my lunch from Leo Burdock's. "It's all fresh every day, cortesy of yours truly. I'll be personally insulted if ya don't sample my handiwork. It's a lonely job I've got, jouncing out there all day, but it's how I earn me keep, so to speak, so if ya torn me down you'll be guilty of seriously damaging my self-worth." He winks at me. "I'm only half-kidding, though." He gestures in Niall's direction. "I get me jollies being around people all the time and tryin' to make them happy. I would be in clover if Niall and I switched jobs, but Da would never hear of it; t'would give him a coronary. Now, yiz ever hear of Burdock's? Most famous fish and chips in Dublin, yes? Or so say the guidebooks. Well, they might as well be Mc-Donald's compared to the fish and chips at Blackpools." He waves at one of the waiters, a ginger-haired young man who almost has to push his way through the crowd to reach us. "Patrick, meet Tessa Goldsmith Craig. Forget the Craig part, she's divorced, and I have yet to determine whether she's a Cat-lick Jew or a Protestant Jew. Tessa, this is another one of me brothers; he and his twin, Michael, wait tables here when they're not makin' us all deef with their head-bangin' din."

"We play in a local band . . . different pubs over in Temple Bar so far. Jamie's an old dinosaur. Forty years old and he acts like he's eighty-two. He doesn't understand alternative music, Tessa," says Patrick. "I take it yiz are forcin' the fish and chips on her. Actually, it's really good," Patrick admits. "It's just that I've smelled, eaten, and—well, never mind—it nearly every day since I was fourteen, and our ma and da set Michael and me to bussing tables and washing dishes after school. But don't let me spoil your appetite," he grins. "Can I get yiz a refill before I go?"

"They're on me," Jamie says. "Mind if I have a taste of this?" he asks me, and I permit him to take a sip of my Guinness.

"Just checking. Good gorl! Ya didn't ask Niall for the shot of black currant. Oh, don't look at me all shocked and surprised. We know all your American tricks."

"It tastes a whole lot better over here than it does in the States, that's for sure."

"No preservatives. Yiz didn't take the Guinness Brewery tour yet, did ya? Cuz yer welcome to, of course, but they don't actually make it there anymore. How long are you in Dublin for, then?"

"A week. I just got here today, in fact."

"Where yiz stayin'?"

"Boynton's, over on St. Stephen's Green."

Jamie's eyes widen. "Very posh."

"That it is."

"Here on business?"

"Pleasure. I hope. Expect." Patrick returns with the next round, and I wonder if I can get through a second pint of Guinness, especially after the pint of Harp I downed over at Davy Byrne's.

"You're traveling alone, then?" Jamie really takes me in for the first time.

Looking back into his deep green eyes I sense that he can read me entirely: my thoughts, emotions, sensibilities. And I suddenly become exceedingly vulnerable, naked to this loquacious handsome stranger. "Are you all right, Tess?"

"I don't know," I reply, deliberately focusing my gaze on my beer glass. "Just now I felt like you knew a whole bunch of things I haven't said yet."

"It must be the Vulcan mind-meld. My sisters think I can do that, too."

"Funny, your ears don't look pointy to me. I could never get into *Star Trek*. Never understood the allure. 'Star *Drek*' I always call it. I had a friend who used to love it, but I couldn't even get through a single episode."

"Those old episodes are *classics*, ya know!"

"Sorry to disappoint, but I just can't relate to it—that whole *Star Trek* cult fanaticism thing."

Jamie places his hand on top of mine. "I'm afraid we can never be married, Tess," he says solemnly. After a somewhat pregnant moment he briskly adds, "So tell me, what is it you don't like about *Star Trek*, especially as you've never actually seen it enough to form such a prejudice against it."

"I suppose it's all that polyester," I muse. "All those cheesy jumpsuits. Now, with all the homegrown folklore right here, you tell me why *you're* a Trekkie."

"You don't know then? Polyester nothwithstanding, *Star Trek* offers a highly romantic view of the world. A very hopeful one. It's idealistic about the nature of the human race, despite often overwhelming evidence to the contrary."

And then it all pours out. I tell him about my career as a speechwriter, my relationship with David, its abrupt termination, and the tipsy suggestion of my cousin and my former college roommate to decompress for a week in the land of leprechauns. I try not to feel sorry for myself, though I am indeed about to cry into my beer. Jamie offers me his handkerchief. Not only is it pristine, but it's the first time a man has ever offered me a hanky.

"That's a very romantic gesture—for a Vulcan." I dry my tears and clutch the cotton square to my chest.

"Well, actually, I'm more like Deanna Troi than Spock."

"Who?"

Jamie looks embarrassed. "Never mind. I shouldn't have expected you to have hord of her." He grows momentarily thoughtful. "I'm sorry you got hort, Tess," he says softly. And just then, as he's about to touch my shoulder to comfort me, Patrick arrives with the fish and chips.

"Am I interruptin' a 'moment'? If you're going to be makin' the patrons cry, Jamie, I'm goin' to have to toss you out on your arse," he adds cheerfully, in an effort to lighten an awkward moment. "Is my brother bullying you, miss? We can't have that at Blackpools. It'll spoil our reputation."

"Be off with yiz, Pat," Jamie says, sounding like the typical older brother. He scribbles something on a paper napkin which he carefully folds and stuffs into the back pocket of his jeans. "Sorry to be rude for torning away from yiz jist now. I was jist writin' meself a note."

Blackpools's fish and chips is indeed as advertised. Burdock's was good, but bland by comparison. This is spectacular. Jamie watches me with evident amusement. I realize, though, that there is no way I will finish the second pint of Guinness. And boy, that stuff can pack a bit of a buzz. I don't think I've drunk this much beer in a decade.

Jamie insists on getting the check for the fish and chips—"particularly as I talked yiz into it." He holds out his hand for me to grasp as I slide out of the snug, and I rise, only to feel as though the floorboards have turned to mush since we sat down, and that someone seems to be pulling them out from under me. "How were yiz planning on getting back to Boynton's?"

"The ssame way I got here, I ssuppose." My s's are slightly slurred. "Walk. I've got my trusty map. Though maybe I should have left a trail of bread crumbss. Bessides, I need air. Fresh air." I also need the ladies' room.

I return to the snug, self-consciously placing one foot in front of the other, navigating the still-crowded room. No matter how earnest my efforts to conceal my level of inebriation, it is abundantly apparent to my supper companion.

"May I see yiz home? If you don't mind my sayin' so, yer in no condition to be walking back to St. Stephen's Green alone at this time o'night. You can ask me brothers to vouch for my gentlemanly character, if yer afraid I'm some kind of masher."

As a New Yorker, my radar is always alert for creeps, but there has been nothing in Jamie Doyle's demeanor to set it off. Stepping into the night air, I stumble, and he catches me by the elbow. "Steady now. Look, there's a cab right over there!"

"That's a hansom cab, Jamie."

"Yes, I know. Have you any objections to riding home in a carriage?"

"Price. I don't know what they cost here, but in New York, it's ssomething like thirty-five dollars the moment you climb into it."

"This one's free."

"I don't believe you!"

"I haven't lied to you yet, Tess. It's me younger brother Liam. Oi, Liam!"

The carriage pulls up to Blackpools. "How many brotherss have you got?"

Jaime counts on his fingers. "Niall you've met; he's the eldest, then after me there's Liam—the thord Doyle son is always a cabdriver. Remember, forst-born runs Blackpools, second son is the fisherman, thord-born is the hack driver—our da was one, but he was drivin' the taxicabs in New York—and after that, God willing, we leave the rest to Providence! You've met one half of the twins, so that's Pat and Michael, and finally there's Seamus. He's the youngest. He's a student at Trinity College. Comparative Literature." He hands me up into the open carriage. "But you haven't asked me about the gorls. Mary Margaret is now a ma herself, with twin girls, Enya and Fiona, and Brigid is about to start the second year of her candidacy at the Sisters of St. Joseph." He chuckles. "My littlest baby sister . . . a nun-in-training. And Molly Bloom is the dog. Are yiz warm enough, Tess? Y'are? Good, then. I wouldn't want yiz to catch cold on yer forst night in Ireland. Boynton's Hotel, Liam!"

Liam clicks and the horse begins to trot out of the cul-de-sac. Though the night is still warm, Jamie arranges the mohair blanket around my feet. "I don't suppose you'll be wanting a tour guide for the rest of your stay?" he asks expectantly.

"You mean Liam?"

"No, no, not Liam. I mean me. I rise before dawn to hit the water, but by midmornin' after I deliver me catch to the pub, I'm a free man for the remainder of the day. I'd be more than happy to show yiz the sights . . . that is, if yer wantin' any company." He jots down his mobile number on a Blackpools business card.

I had intended to spend the week by myself, alone with my thoughts. And I have *a lot* of thinking to do. Big life questions about where I'm going now, who I am, what I want out of this thing called human existence. This trip is meant to be a journey of self-discovery. It's tempting to spend more time with Jamie, and I would certainly get more out of the sightseeing aspect of it with a native guide. Yet I wonder if it's possible to truly discover oneself in the company of another. So I am about to decline Jamie's gracious offer.

"As you barely know me from Adam, you're welcome to think my opinion is worth shite, but sometimes it's easier to find yourself when you're not doin' it all by your lonesome."

I look into the oddly omniscient malachite of Jamie's eyes. "This Vulcan mind-meld thing is scaring me, you know," I tease, and he understands in an instant that I'm only half-kidding.

Liam pulls up in front of my hotel and halts his horse, which releases a complacent snort into the night. Jamie alights first, then lifts me down. Satisfied that I've got both feet steadily on the pavement, he presses my hand. "I'll meet you in the lobby at noon." Turning my hand over, he gently kisses my upturned palm. "Now order some orange juice from room service and drink that, along with a big glass of water before yiz go off to bed, and you'll be fit as a fiddle come morning. And get a good night's sleep, Tess. You've orned it."

Ten

Day 4 A.D. (the wee small hours of August 10) . . . having just accepted the offer of a cappuccino from Boynton's late-night concierge, a nice young man from Barcelona

I met an interesting man tonight. His intelligent eyes blazed with an internal flame and he smelled a bit of fish. And I'm angry. Not that Jamie Doyle wasn't pleasant . . . he was very nice, in fact, but he sort of wormed his way under my skin and robbed me of the ability to stand up for myself and express my needs. And that's what this trip was supposed to be all about in the first place! I didn't ask for a tour guide of Dublin. Don't want one, really. I'd rather be alone and see less, or not even know why the hell what I'm looking at is important, than have someone steering me by the arm, leading me by the nose, telling me where to go and what to look at. I want to do this trip my way.

The other night, when I was still back in New York entertaining Venus and Imogen (or was it the other way around?) I heard myself laugh and it sounded foreign to my ears. It wasn't my laugh. It was David's. A snicker not my own. I'd even allowed my lover's laugh to inhabit my body and displace mine. Did I laugh tonight with Jamie? I think I did. Whose was it? I don't remember. My God . . . I don't even recall the original sound of my own laughter. Oh, shit . . . I just spilled orange juice all over the place. [A brief interval while I mop up the damage.] I hope the stickiness doesn't encourage literary cockroaches (Don Marquis's Archie comes to mind) to read my journal. Yuck! My reflexes are a bit fuzzed from the beer.

Damnit! Why didn't I tell Jamie Doyle no? Why didn't I just say, "You've been very kind, and it's a generous offer, but I need some time alone. That's why I came to Ireland. To get away from all the everyday everythings except myself." Yes, that's it. "I came here to find myself, Jamie. So . . . and I mean this in the nicest way . . . hello and good-bye."

"I . . . I want to be alone, Jamie." It's 12:05 P.M. and we're sitting on the striped silk divan in Boynton's cozy parlor. A shaft of sunlight bounces off the window sash, illuminating the fireplace like the metaphorical presence of God in seventeenth-century religious paintings.

"All right then, Greta Garbo." I can see that he's disappointed and trying to make light of the situation. "Niver let it be said that Jamie Doyle twisted a woman's arm. Even if she's a fascinating American who's always secretly wished she had a dog. An Irish setter would be an excellent choice. Or an Irish wolfhound—though it might be the size of yer entire flat. I hear real estate is tight in Manhattan."

I *have* always wanted a dog. But couldn't think of keeping one in my apartment. He's right on both counts. This is weird. Did I tell him last night, in the course of spilling my guts about my career and busted love life, that I'm a mutt-owner manqué? I couldn't have: I haven't thought about getting a pet in years. "I think you're a witch, Jamie Doyle. Or warlock, I guess."

"I thought you were seeking the supernatural. Fairies camped out under toadstools to shelter from a sudden downpour. Leprechauns clutching pots at the ends of rainbows. The mysteries of the sí. *Giants*—it's too bad you're only here for a few days; I'd show you the Giants Causeway. Too many American visitors to Ireland check their imaginations with their luggage and then the airlines lose it. All they see is a bunch o'boulders. But Tessa Goldsmith Craig would embrace the legend. At least I thought she would. I guess I was wrong. It was lovely to meet you, Miss Garbo." Jamie extends his hand. When I don't shake it, he shoves it into the back pocket of his cords. "Hello and good-bye, then."

He turns and walks into the vestibule. The wind chimes herald the opening of the hotel's front door, and I hear it close as I stare into a fire that doesn't exist. Then I glance out the window in time to spy Jamie walking toward Grafton Street.

Well . . . if the decision is my *own*. A wiry man in a spattered white cap and coveralls is painting the wrought-iron railing in front of the hotel, and I inhale a whiff of the oil-based fumes as I trot past his bucket. "Wait, Jamie!" I dodge a gauntlet of bemused pedestrians as I rush to catch up with him. Managing to grab a handful of his denim workshirt, I bring us both to a halt. One of the carriage horses lined up opposite St. Stephen's Green, a dapple-gray, whinnies at my success. "You win, Jamie." He turns to face me. "You've . . . bewitched me. I don't know how you did it, but . . . I surrender. You want to show me

Dublin, you can, okay? My travel agenda is at your disposal."

The corners of his mouth curl upwards in an impish smile. "I'm so glad Aer Lingus didn't lose *your* imagination." He links my arm through his own. "Thank you, Miss Garbo."

"Now that I've given up—kicking and screaming, I'll have you know—on being alone all week, you're not entitled to call me that anymore."

Jamie smiles, and, off my guard, I am struck by its warmth as well as its wattage. Then I remind myself of Venus's description of Irish men "charming the pants off" me and I gird myself in an extra layer of emotional armor.

Can Jamie sense my sudden defensiveness through my arm when he suddenly says, "Now, Tessa Goldsmith Craig, you can put on all that New York toughness you've a mind to, but I'll be a good host and tell yiz before it's too late to truly enjoy yourself that it's ineffective in Ireland." I burst out laughing. "Aha! There's the spirit!"

"That's not why I'm laughing. Your little psychic victory . . ."

"Why then? Oh, don't tell me you won't let me in on the joke."

"You pronounce the name of your country 'Oyre-land.' Are you *sure* you're not *Jewish?*" This—my turning of his countrymen's joke on me on him—is something Jamie finds hysterically amusing. He flings his arms about me, and in a split second I am lifted off my feet and his lips—soft, sweet—are making contact with my own, giving my brain no time to edit the action of my lonely hormones. I give back as good as I get. After all, he's being such a good host; I wouldn't want to appear an ungrateful guest.

"I . . . barely know you," I murmur as he relinquishes my lips and my feet are returned to the pavement.

"What better beginning?" He smiles winsomely, and I make

a quick mental note to e-mail Venus and tell her I'm a drowning woman and it's only my second day of vacation. "Now, I know you've seen the Book of Kells and Ireland's oldest harp, so we don't need to go back to Trinity unless you want to amuse me by blending in with the students."

"Flatterer."

Having determined that there were a number of highlights I didn't see yesterday, Jamie is determined to hit the ground running, cramming in as many sights as humanly possible. Actually, he has so much stamina, I begin to wonder if he is, in fact, 100 percent mortal. We spend the afternoon traversing Dublin until my feet are begging for mercy: the Dáil (Parliament), the National Museum, the Abbey and the Gate Theatres, Dublin Castle and City Hall, a variety of pubs so that we can catch some refreshment along with our breath—and with all of it, the history of the city in a nutshell, from the Vikings and Brian Ború to the IRA's cessation of hostilities. I try to process it all, but I beg Jamie to slow down, pleading extreme sightseeing overload. By dinnertime all I can remember is that "dubh linn" means "black pool." I can't recall fatigue figuring in Leopold Bloom's progress throughout the city, but not being a fictional character, I need to rest.

"Boy, you should see Central Park. *This* is so . . . manicured," I say, as we lie flat on our backs on one of St. Stephen's Green's pristine lawns. Dublin parks are meticulously landscaped, in contrast with New York green spaces, perhaps a metaphor for our respective national characters. I think of all the acres of untamed undergrowth in Central Park, or in Prospect Park out in Brooklyn. "Your parks are very European, Jamie. Very . . . well behaved. Our parks wouldn't stay looking like this for more than two seconds."

"Ach, this is nothing." His hand meanders across the inches

of lawn that separate our bodies and finds mine. As our fingers entwine, I feel a sense of warmth spread through my arm as though my hand had been kissed by a sun god, and I am consciously aware that my body is relaxing, sinking into the cushion of cool grass while the left side of my brain warns the right side to stop editing and just enjoy each moment, for they won't come again. A breeze brushes my forehead. "You like gardens, then?"

"Always wanted to have one of my own, actually. But I have a black thumb." Eyes closed, my words drift upon the air into Jamie's ears.

"I'll show you Powerscourt. Some of the most beautiful gardens in Ireland."

"Is it far away?"

"About as far from here as Scarsdale is from Manhattan," Jamie replies, displaying a surprising knowledge of New York geography. "Maybe a bit farther. I never clocked it, exactly. It never occurred to me to do so. But why do you care?" he adds, evidently amused. "Are yiz in a hurry to be somewhere anytime this week?"

"N-no . . . but . . . Actually, Jamie . . . I don't want to sound ungrateful, because you've been wonderful today, but . . . I'd wanted time alone this week. I need it."

"So you've told me," he says softly. "I didn't mean to impose."

And yet I can't bring myself to disengage our fingers. How much can I really want to be alone when I won't let go of his hand?

A late dinner ("I hope you fancy sausages") is at a pub in Temple Bar called The Missing Link, where Patrick and Michael Doyle and their band, Devil's Kiss ("the name is shite, don't

you think?") are scheduled to perform. Having sampled a few
of the other Temple Bar cafés and pubs, I begin to feel that
nearly everyone in Dublin, especially in this vibrant neighborhood, is roughly half my age. I've never seen so many twenty-
somethings in one place. Acknowledging that their technology
has passed me by, for the most part, and that I may never "get"
their music, I am myself a relic of another era, well-preserved
thanks to the good graces of God and Estee Lauder.

"Ahh, you're a good soldier, Tess," Jamie tells me. As I am
unable to hear his words through the music, he writes them on
a paper napkin.

"You're a good *brother*," I try to reply above the din. The
musicians are accomplished enough, so far as I can tell, but
Devil's Kiss could wake the dead, and this wasn't what I had in
mind when it comes to enjoying "traditional Irish music" in a
local pub. The young performers are enjoying themselves
though, and most of their audience, contemporaries, appear to
know many of the lyrics and sing along. "I wish them well . . .
but . . . it's been a long day for me, and I think I've still got a
bit of jet lag."

At a break in the second set, Jamie pays the tab and we make
for the tiny raised stage to congratulate his twin brothers, who
are presently sky-high on life from their peers' reception of
their performance. "Patrick told me that Jamie had met someone," Michael says. He's wearing more jewelry than I am: numerous leather and metal bracelets on each wrist, and both of
his ears sport small gold hoops. "Has he told you yet that he
loves you?" Blanching, I glance at Jamie, who colors quickly.
"Ah, well, then, it's only been a day, hasn't it?" Michael adds. He
clasps my forearm for balance and leans forward to whisper in
my ear. "Jamie has the most open heart in Ireland. But it's not as

strong as it should be. And I'm not discussing his *health*, in case you don't take my meaning. You're leaving within the week, yes? Going home to your fancy life in America?"

I nod my head. "Though it's not as fancy as you imagine."

"Don't you go horting my big brother." Michael's words are as much a plea as a warning.

Jamie walks me back to Boynton's and we end up having a late-night cappuccino in the buttery. As the only two guests in the graciously appointed room, it's easy to imagine that it's two hundred years ago and we own the place.

"Refreshingly quiet," I whisper.

Jamie's smile relaxes into a huge grin. "I've got me a headache to beat the band, I do."

"I'll bet it's the band that gave it to you." I reach into my purse and take out a pillbox, offering him a range of over-the-counter pharmaceutical remedies.

His hand encloses mine, which encloses the pillbox. "If there's anyone who can cure it, it's you." In the gentle light from the votive on our table, his Irish eyes are indeed smiling. "I'm so . . . drawn to you, Tess."

"But you barely know me."

"That doesn't change things. It just makes me want to know more. Your energy, your beauty . . . it's a good beginning right there." His smile sags a bit. "I'll take those aspirins, now."

I parse out the pills. "Your brother Michael seems to be really looking out for you."

"Mickey fancies himself a mobster, he does. Too many episodes of your American telly over here," he chuckles. "Tony Soprano and all. Your American tough guys give a young'un with a large imagination and the secret of a pint-sized ego a chance to dream. But I'm not in a mood to talk about Mickey. I want to kiss you, Tessa. Just as soon as the gremlins in me head stop doing the Tarantella."

"Not a jig?"

"Never!" Jamie rises from his chair and sidles beside me onto the upholstered banquette. Our lips meet, and tongues, tasting of coffee and foam, explore the new and wonderful terrain of each other. He snuggles me into his arms, and my soul feels happy. Out of the corner of my eye I catch a flash of the late-night concierge, the Swede who had served us the cappuccino, slipping discreetly back into the shadows. The frissons of passion zing like crazed electrons along the length of my spine.

"I . . . really should go upstairs and get some sleep," says the voice coming out of my mouth, the voice my brain evidently sent, the voice my brain decided did not want to make love with Jamie tonight. Another voice inside me begs to differ, but not loudly enough, and Jamie, for all his uncanny sense of intuition, doesn't hear it. He only hears the one that expressed the wish to retire for the night alone.

He slowly disentangles his limbs from mine; displaces his left hand from the center of my back, then his right hand, the one that had been exploring the contours of my neck and shoulder, and sits back against the banquette. Not daunted or deterred or disappointed, he runs the hand that had been so lately an intimate of my breasts, through his light brown hair to return it to its customary appearance of slight tousledness, for my own curious hands have sent it every which way. "I'll be looking forward to tomorrow, then," he says affably.

"Why tomorrow?" The still, small voice inside me is loud enough to berate parts of my brain for breaking the embrace, and perhaps the mood as well.

"Did you say you enjoyed gardens?"

"Did I?"

He nods. "Splendid ones. I'll be here at noon to take you out to Powerscourt. Now don't go upstairs and be peeking in your guidebook ahead of time. It'll be high noon, as you Americans say, before ya know it."

He makes me laugh. "New Yorkers don't say 'high noon'; in fact I'll bet no Americans at all have used that phrase in several decades."

"Ahh, but Tessa Goldsmith Craig, dontcha jist long for the past?" His cadences make his words sound like music played on a golden pennywhistle. If he's the Pied Piper of Dublin, I'm beginning to suspect I'd follow him over hill and dale into a magical dell, safe from the grasping and dishonest, the corrupt and the ignorant, that make up the worst of the world.

Eleven

 Day 5 A.D. (August 11, sometime after midnight)

I seem unable to resist Jamie Doyle, at least in the short run. I am having such fun in his company that I'm neglecting the reasons I flew across the Atlantic in the first place. The third day of my weeklong vacation is about to begin and I still crave the chance to be alone with my thoughts for more than an hour or so at a time. And the idea of a man I barely know wanting to do things for me without expecting a quid pro quo, asking for nothing but my presence, and then wanting to do more for me, is alien, and occasionally irksome. This holiday is not proceeding as planned. While I delight in the adventuresome aspect of my new acquaintance, I despair that my time here is slipping out of my grasp, out of my own control. Why can't I simply say "go away!" to Jamie? "Thanks, but no thanks." "I don't need this right now." "It's not a good time for me."

Babble from a vintage 1970s feminist movie pops and sputters inside my memory, begging to be given valid consideration, only to be replaced by the voice of Venus inside my head laughing at me and cajoling me to follow the path of the more fascinating rainbow. "For God's sake, girl, go with Alan Bates!"

David. I'm not over him yet. Not by a longshot. How can I even consider getting involved with anyone else now, even if—or maybe especially since—I'll be leaving the country in a few days?

"It's too soon for this," says the voice of reason. "You're not emotionally ready, Tess."

I don't feel like warring with my inner thoughts tonight. Out of habit, I turn on the television, looking for something that will serve as "white noise" while I get undressed and prepare for bed. Jamie wasn't kidding about the invasion of American programming. Nearly every channel has one of our exports in syndication. A flash of spandex catches my eye and the banner below the image tells me I have landed on an episode of *Star Trek: The Next Generation*. Might as well, with one eye and half an ear, find out why Jamie is a Trekkie. Brushing my teeth I catch sight of a pretty brunette in blue, a character they call Deanna Troi, and until I rinse and spit I wonder why the producers didn't name her Helena instead.

Then I recall that Jamie had mentioned that name, insisting that he was more like Deanna Troi than the oh-so-logical Vulcan Spock. Aah . . . now I will pay closer attention to this television show that continues to elude both my imagination and my heart. But by the time I crawl under the covers, and slide the cool smooth sheet past my hips, reaching for the remote to send this program to a galaxy far far away, I learn that Deanna Troi is an "empath," with the capability of intuiting, understanding, and deeply feeling the emotions of others—their rapture as well as their pain. And if I don't "get" the allure of *Star Trek* any better than I did half an hour ago, I do understand a lot more about the man called Jamie Doyle.

Once outside the city, toodling along the roads in Jamie's little yellow Mini Cooper, I begin to see the Ireland of my imagination's fantasies, the emerald hillsides studded with sheep and dotted with wildflowers which morph into the huge granite outcroppings that I can easily envision as the celestial destination of Jack's magical beanstalk: surely there are giants within these hills. I admit that I find the little villages charmingly rustic in a fairy-tale way, and realize I probably sound like an idiot in search of the improbable. "Just don't go referrin' to the residents as 'quaint,'" Jamie cautions.

"I'll stuff the inclination," I promise. I want to stick my head out the window like a dog and enjoy the wind's caress through my hair, to breathe in the aromas, both sweet and savory, of Irish country living. Passing through Enniskerry, I bite my tongue to refrain from remarking that it looks like an advertisement for the Irish Tourist Board, ready for its postcard close-up. I am about to make a comparison to New England, but catch myself before I do, wondering if it's a uniquely American thing to see something of our own everywhere we go, in an effort to lay claim to it somehow.

"Pretty, isn't it?" Jamie says, his hand on my knee. "Ya can see why we're so house-proud. There's no place like Ireland on God's green earth—and we like it that way."

The road from the village into the Powerscourt estate proper is shaded by old, old trees which command both awe and respect, not just for their beauty but for what I perceive as their wisdom. And then the surface turns to gravel as we rumble up to Powerscourt itself, a grandly Italianate villa, and I blush to admit that the first thing that catches my eye is the sign for the gift shops. Followed by the one for the ladies' room.

Acres and acres wait to be explored. And here we are, Jamie and I, in Ireland's lush countryside amid a united nations of botany: the Italian Garden, the Japanese Gardens, the North American trees rising toward the sky in Tower Valley (the centerpiece of which is a tower modeled after the design on Lord Powerscourt's pepperpot), and the two majestic winged horses built of zinc by a nineteenth-century German professor.

And I want to run and skip and laugh through every hectare of it.

Here I am, snapping digital photos like a modern-day Margaret Bourke-White. I am in love with the obligingly photogenic winged horses, wishing we could mount them so that we could soar across the stately Triton Lake and into the pines beyond.

Then suddenly the heavens open and the giants weep—whether from sorrow or joy I'm unsure—and Jamie and I run down the pebbled pathways in search of shelter, finding it (more or less) in the Grotto within the Japanese Gardens, a mystical-looking sanctuary thanks to the petrified sphagnum that covers its every surface in shades of green and gray.

And hungry with emotion I kiss Jamie Doyle with a mouth full of ardor and happiness. Kissing and kissing, as if we've just invented this delicious pastime and require as much experimentation as possible to perfect it before announcing our discovery to the world.

And the firmament stops leaking, sending a gift between a break in two clouds, one resembling a dragon and the other a giant briar pipe . . . a rainbow worthy of chasing to its end.

And, sodden clothes and squishy shoes notwithstanding,
we clasp hands and follow it where it leads, leaving us in
Powerscourt's Pets Cemetary, a necro-garden of sorrows,
where the once-and-always beloved four-legged friends of the
wealthy and well-connected, have an unparalleled eternal vista.
Perhaps I, too, could look at those undulating mountains forever.

And I weep for the loyal that lie beneath this earth and for
the dog that Jamie knows I always wanted. Maybe he knows,
too, that the reason I never did get a pet wasn't my stated one.
It wasn't really that it's too hard to keep a dog in a Manhattan
flat or that I spent too much time out of town. Those were my
excuses. But my *reason*? That I never wanted to experience its
death. I have yet to master the precepts of mortality and most
likely never will.

"I know what will cheer you," my companion says as we
stroll back toward the house. As one looks out from the steps
of Powerscourt, the vista over the gardens to the mountains is
spectacular, and the view heading toward the opposite direction is no less grand. A breeze riffles through my imagination,
and suddenly Jamie and I are in a Merchant-Ivory movie,
though I have yet to determine its plot.

"Are you reading my mind again?"

He steers me straight for the shops. "*You* tell *me*."

From the array of unusual semi-local crafts, the Irish souvenirs one might find in any gift shop in the country, and a smat-
tering of kitsch, I select gifts for Imogen (a book on famous
Irish Jews) and for Venus (*Speak Gaelic!* CDs and a sachet of
lavender-scented drawer liners). I find myself feeling somewhat
guilty when I'm drawn to a fluffy white terrycloth bathrobe
with the word *Herself* embroidered in gold thread above the
right breast. "A bit self-indulgent, don't you think?"

"Oh aye, but *Herself, Himself,* they're some of my favorite colloquialisms. Sweet and tart on the tongue. They're expressions often used to refer to someone putting on airs and pulling an attitude as though they were the lady or lord of the manor—but it's not without a degree of affection, ya see. We all need to feel important and special sometimes, don't we?"

Jamie insists that I try on the robe (he calls it a "dressing gown"), and though it's unlike me to make such a spectacle of myself, he asks so endearingly that I have to oblige him. "What do you think?" I say, appraising my image in the gift shop's mirror.

"Tworl around so I can get a better look."

There are other tourists watching me now, evidently amused, and I think the joke's on me. "The sleeves are kind of long, aren't they?" Until I start rolling them up I look like a little girl modeling her mother's—or maybe her dad's—jacket.

Jamie grins. "I'm a betting man, and I have a feelin' you'll grow into it."

Once the voluminous sleeves have been adjusted to my proportions—the "one size fits all" label isn't kidding, evidently—it's like wearing a big hug: safe and cozy. I feel warmly confident. "Isn't it grand?" I crow giddily. My embarrassment gene suddenly slips into recessive mode, and I succumb to the urge to twirl and prance about the gift shop like a heroine in a 1950s musical comedy. *Herself.* It's me. Or the me I wish I was—or could be. You gotta love it. Purchasing this bathrobe has just become what Imogen would term a "moral imperative" in the realm of retail. I proffer my credit card to the rosy-cheeked old-age pensioner at the cash register.

"It's quite yummy, isn't it?" she says, as she wraps the robe in tissue paper. "And you look darlin' in it." She leans toward me, and adds in a conspiratorial whisper, "I wouldn't be a bit surprised if you got lucky this evening. Your gent seemed quite taken."

"He's—" I decide not to explain. Better to just play along. "From your mouth to God's ears," I reply, giving her a little wink.

Okay, so now I've spent exponentially more on myself than I have on my friends, and Jamie counsels me to stop feeling guilty over it, because Imogen and Venus would understand. He's right, I suppose. Venus has a huge warm heart and this entire trip was her idea in the first place, so I'm sure she'd want me to feel okay about treating myself to a pricey memento. And Imogen is so acquisitive that she'd never think twice about buying a present for herself, no matter the cost.

And so back we head to Dublin through the picturesque vales and around the hillsides. Although I spy grazing sheep and lazy cattle who eye us with only the mildest of interest, there's nary another soul in sight; it could be almost any year in eternity. "You know, I feel a bit gypped that we didn't find a pot of gold at the end of that rainbow," I tell Jamie. I know it's a legend, but I do actually feel disappointed.

"We found the gift shop. Doesn't that count? Maybe you did find a pot o'gold, but you didn't recognize it. Sometimes folklore arrives in metaphors, y'know."

"You just made that up!"

His irresistible grin spreads from dimple to dimple. "I know!"

We motor up to Boynton's front door, a no-stopping zone. After several awkward moments, Jamie inquires as to my dinner plans.

"I really need some time to myself this evening," I tell him truthfully, "though it's been a gorgeous day, and I did have a wonderful time in your company." I've been neglecting my journal, and though the handsome new friend by my side is infinitely more compelling than an inanimate book of observations, so much has happened in the past couple of days—I think I'm beginning to have feelings for Jamie, for starters—that I really need to step back and get analytical, at least for an evening. Right now I feel like Alice falling down the rabbit hole, and I need to don a pair of crampons and slow my descent before I really end up way over my head. I'm supposed to be *un*complicating things on this vacation, and Jamie Doyle presents a massive, albeit charismatic, complication in my life right now.

"I'll try to stop by Blackpools later," I assure him. As I ascend the steps to the townhouse, we slip into an Alphonse/Gaston routine: he seems to be waiting until the door closes behind me before he motors off, and I am waiting until he drives away before I enter the hotel. Even this little good-bye is a difficult one, which further messes up my head. I "blink" first and head inside, to the emotional safety behind the royal blue door.

Yet something, a sixth sense, if you will—or it could have been my desire to look out of the nine-foot-high windows in the little parlor to see if Jamie is still there, sitting in his mini, trying to see inside, past the drawn striped silk drapes, guessing that I would have entered the charming sitting room for just that purpose, before going up to my room—something makes me poke my head into the parlor. Are my eyes deceiving me? Or maybe it's a trick of the light. A man is sitting on the sofa, the sumptuous, cushy kind of couch that envelops you, even cradles your tush as you sit. He is sipping a cup of tea. His silhouette, the strong back, broad shoulders, the full head of dark brown hair, naturally wavy, is horrifyingly familiar. Of course it could be anyone sitting there, I tell myself. But it isn't anyone. It's David.

There are a half dozen things I want to say, but the first thing that comes out of my mouth is "You broke your promise."

David turns around, still holding his teacup. "I know. Can you forgive me, Tess?"

"Not unless there's a very good reason for your following me across the Atlantic and interrupting my vacation when I expressly asked you not to contact me."

"I'm sorry," he replies, hitting just the right note of contrition. "I thought all bets were off when you asked me to meet you at the Boathouse the day you left." He gently places his cup on the pretty tray atop the coffee table.

"*My* contacting *you* doesn't count. It's your not contacting me that was the bargain we struck. I told you I needed time alone. To think. Sort things out. And I haven't yet been able to give any serious thought to whether I can continue to work for you. With you. So we'll have to start the clock again, I'm afraid."

"I wanted to see you, Tess. I've missed you. Really missed you. And I know I broke our agreement, but I had to come here to tell you that." It's probably the most romantic thing he's ever said to me.

Suddenly I become fearful. "Are you feeling okay . . . I mean . . . how the hell are you, David?" *Oh, God, he didn't cross the ocean to tell me he's only got four days to live or something?*

"I'm fine, Tess. Perfectly healthy, if that's what you're asking. Don't worry." David rises and holds out his hands to me, and guided by a force stronger than my conscious willpower I accept them and drink him in. He's as handsome as he was a few days ago, as tall, as confident in his skin, but his face appears a bit more careworn; the recent stresses—both physical and political—are already exacting a price from his princely looks.

I feel as though I've gone, emotionally, in the past five minutes, from the proverbial frying pan into the inferno. It would be inhospitable for me not to invite him upstairs to my room. Besides, my skin is still atingle from his wildly romantic statement of a minute or so ago. He must have been anticipating how things would play out, at least at the beginning, because he shoulders an overnight bag and follows me up the stairs, our collective tread noiseless on the thick Persian carpeting.

And the big question I haven't voiced yet is the next one to escape my lips. "How did you know I was here?" Only two people were aware of my travel plans, and I'm relatively sure that one of them wouldn't sing, now matter how much pressure was applied.

"Your cousin was reluctant to tell me at first, but she still thinks we might have a happily-ever-after in our future."

"It figures." Imogen is going to hear from me. It doesn't count as a head-clearing vacation if your ex-boyfriend appears, rather literally out of the blue, to muddy your thoughts even further. "Do *you* think we have a happily-ever-after?"

He doesn't reply, and I know not to push. Do I even want to get back together with him? We have a history. It's safe and comfortable because it's familiar, but does that mean it's healthy? And then there's Jamie Doyle. A vacation flirtation? Perhaps it is only that. I'm emotionally vulnerable, and Jamie is more than willing, evidently, to make me feel good about myself, even if it's just for a week. A confidence-restoring fling. Maybe he makes a habit of beguiling American lost souls, making each woman he enchants feel special, sending her back stateside with a rejuvenated sense of self-worth. Sensitive Samaritanism.

I'm thinking too much about Jamie.

Twelve

I need to deal with David now. He's behind me on the stairs, his hand on the small of my back comfortable and reassuring. It's been less than a week since he decided to end things, and I've missed his touch more than I've been willing to admit to myself. After all, it wasn't *my* idea to end our relationship.

Once inside my room, David admires its décor, its view, and its appointments—particularly the fireplace and the marble bath. And then . . . (had I been expecting him to take me in his arms and kiss me? Tumble me onto the bed?) . . . he says, "You look good, Tess."

"Sightseeing agrees with me, I suppose." I try not to sound disappointed. "So does shopping. Look what I bought this afternoon!" I untie the green ribbon securing the clouds of white tissue paper and lovingly unwrap my new acquisition, modeling the fluffy *Herself* bathrobe for David.

He chuckles. "Isn't that a little big on you?"

I guess I had expected, or wanted, him to be at least complimentary, if not enthusiastic. Then again, what straight guy gets
enthusiastic about a terry robe? "I . . . I guess I need to grow
into it," I say, now feeling very small indeed.

"So . . . may I take you to dinner? I understand there's a terrific restaurant—modern Irish cuisine, they're calling it—
tucked into a hotel on the Liffey."

I take a deep breath. "Is that where you're staying, then?"
Did he assume he was going to room with me? Do I want him to?

"I booked a room at the Shelbourne down the street."

Oh. "Dublin's grande dame. I haven't poked my head in
there yet. I suppose you'll blend in with all the local politicians
who apparently belly up to the bar every day. The Dáil is just
around the corner." Okay . . . he needs me, but isn't making
any assumptions that I will leap into his arms or throw myself
at his feet just because he tracked me down and took a transat-
lantic flight to be with me, instead of waiting a few more days
until I returned.

"Let me shower first and I'll be ready to go. Did you make a
reservation?" Through the half-closed bathroom door I can
hear him on the phone with the concierge, prompting her.
Boynton's is no stranger to a celebrity clientele, and if the
young woman from Berlin has never heard of American congressman David Weyburn, she's responded in the affirmative to
his charisma, which, when I hear my phone ring, is evidently
enough to convince the people at the Octagon to hold aside a
quiet table for two against our arrival this evening.

It's rather a strange dinner—not merely because the insanely
expensive food (which isn't dissimilar in menu or price to anything one might find at an upscale New York bistro) is served
up in infinitesimal portions which would probably make the
average Irishman apoplectic—but because our conversation is

awkward. We discuss what I've seen of Dublin thus far, how I find it, how the topography and weather compare to New York City, the much-vaunted friendliness of the Irish (I omit certain salient details there), and it feels like an odd sort of first date, rather than a romantic reunion. David has ordered a bottle of French wine. I find myself drinking too quickly out of anxiousness and in the expectation that the classic social lubricant will ease the tension.

And maybe it's a good thing that I'm still hungry even after devouring a tiny fruit tartlet masquerading as dessert. After all the fish and chips I've consumed thus far, a scant few inches of broiled halibut plated up with a couple of green beans is probably a gift to my digestive system, at any price.

"You don't seem to be having much fun," David remarks astutely, signing the credit card slip with characteristic authority.

I lean over the table to whisper to him over our cappuccinos. "This place is kind of cold, don't you think? The atmosphere, not the temperature. No 'Irish charm' whatever. It's so yuppified in here. We could be dining in TriBeCa, if it weren't for all the pub signs outside. They don't even have Irish Coffee on the menu!"

David places his hands over mine. "Then let's do a pub crawl! Tell me where you want to go."

"Authentic. Someplace authentic; that's all I know," I reply, thinking of Blackpools, which would in fact be the last place I'd step inside with David.

As we stroll through the narrow, crowded thoroughfares of Temple Bar, it feels a bit like the French Quarter of New Orleans used to, when it seemed like every fraternity house in the city had spilled out of its taverns onto Bourbon and St. Louis. David and I are in another demographic entirely; I'm just about the only woman not dressed in fraying hipsters and a belly tee.

I feel like such a grownup in my black sheath, pashmina, and pumps.

"There's a pub every few steps," David rhetorically notes. "Anything catch your fancy yet?"

I remember the men in Davy Byrne's mentioning O'Donoghues, which is right near David's hotel and mine, so I suggest we head over there. Once I dangle it as the birthplace of The Dubliners, David is sold, though we look rather incongruous in our dressy attire inside this dark, and highly casual, nightspot. And if it isn't old Conlan, sitting in on the tin whistle with Turlough, tonight's band, named after a seventeenth-century blind harper. I give him a wave and he tips me a wink as I scare up a pair of low stools to perch upon while David bellies up to the bar for two Irish Coffees. My craving must be satisfied.

We toast each other and sit knee to knee, as the band plays its trad tunes, toe-tappers all. In the low light, David's eyes become deep, beautiful pools in which I can see my own image reflected back at me, and I wonder if the distortion I notice is his vision of me, or my own view of myself through his eyes. Then I begin to think it's just the rather potent Irish Coffee softening and blurring the edges. By the time I've nearly finished my drink, licking the whipped cream moustache from my upper lip, I find myself placing my hand on David's leg and leaning closer, murmuring under the music, "I'm glad you're here. I wasn't at first . . . but I am now."

"I'm having a wonderful time," he avers, with a winning smile. "Care for another?"

"No more caffeine for me. But as I haven't had a whiskey since I've been in Ireland, except in the coffee, get me a Jameson's with a water back."

David gives me a surprised look. "You don't drink whiskey!"

"When in Rome," I shrug. "If I don't care for it I won't finish it."

But that old John Jameson knows his stuff: it *is* good going down, and the music is terrific and the spirit is within me and I want to get up and dance and not give a hoot who's watching. "Dance with me, David," I say, tossing back the rest of the whiskey, leaving the glass on the bar. And the David who was often game for anything, gets up and joins me. No one knows who he is, which is another reason not to care. So we're up on our feet, and then I spy Gogo and Joe, my other new pals from that evening in Davy Byrne's, and they rise to their feet and stamp and clap, and Gogo grabs the elbow of the woman who had been sitting on the bench beside him and they burst into a traditional jig, filled with joy and release. I try to emulate them and kick up my heels like a wannabe at the Riverdance auditions. David's head is thrown back in a laugh, and I grin until my eyes fill with tears because I am so happy.

Catching David's eye, the bartender pours another pair of whiskeys and we try to down them as we dance, then give up and clasp each other about the waist instead, standing by our stools. I tilt my chin to his face and our lips meet in a soft, familiar kiss. Can the Irish magic be giving me back my man? Is a renewal of our relationship the pot of gold at the end of today's rainbow?

"Remember where we were before our first kiss?" I ask David. "Earlier in the day, I mean. You were campaigning on the Upper West Side and there was an Irish pub on Seventy-ninth Street?"

"The Dublin House!" David laughs. "Boy, was that an old timers' place! The walls were brown from all the tobacco smoke that had built up over the years."

"And the locals complained because of the no-smoking law. They said they'd only vote for you if you promised them you'd do something about it. The Republican was a guy named Callaghan, as I recall."

"And that day you'd tipped me off that Callaghan was under investigation by the D.A.'s office, but you wouldn't tell me how you found out."

"Of course I wouldn't."

"No matter how much I tried to wheedle it out of you."

"Curiosity killed the cat."

"But you looked so beautiful as you denied me your source, and I was so thrilled to get the information that I could have kissed you on the spot."

"You almost did, remember? Everyone had gone home by then, and you locked the door and pulled down the shades on all the windows of your re-election headquarters and led me by the hand into the kitchenette. And you backed me up against the refrigerator . . ."

"And once I kissed you I couldn't stop. I remember that part. Very well."

"It was like all the pent up emotional *whatever* that had been going on throughout the campaign, and all the undercurrents between us . . . those began soon after I came to work for you, I seem to recall . . . all of that exploded."

David laughs and downs the rest of his second glass of Jameson's, signaling the bartender for another round. "That wasn't all that exploded. Remember looking around the kitchen for some soap?"

I, too, burst out laughing. "And having to use dishwashing liquid and wet paper towels to clean your Armani slacks. It made so many bubbles! And your little predicament made you even more endearing."

"You, too. On your knees scrubbing my whatdoyacallit."

"Your placket."

"My *placket*. That's a funny word: placket. Placket placket placket."

"Congressman Weyburn," I whisper, "you're drunk."

"So are you, Ms. Tessa Craig. Placket placket placket. It sounds like a duck. Quack quack quack. I never used to like Jameson's."

"We made love that night. At my place, actually. We took a taxi there like real people, instead of calling Freddy for the black car."

"And you had knitting stuff all over your bed. Yarn everywhere."

"I'd been inventorying . . . to see what I had enough of. I wanted to make a granny square afghan."

"Which I still have on my bed, you know." David takes my hand. I don't tell him that the ship he made for me has been shoved into a closet.

I'm feeling extraordinarily mellow right now. Well, of course I am: I've had half a bottle of wine with dinner, and since we've been at O'Donoghue's I've imbibed an Irish Coffee and am presently on my third whiskey. "I like knowing that," I murmur. "I like it a lot."

"I need you, kiddo," David tells me. We are nearly nose to nose, so close I can feel the energy coming off his body and bouncing off against my own. "You know this; I'm facing the toughest re-election campaign of my career. The gay flap thing won't go away, and to ensure that any frank discussion of the issues is continually evaded, if not tanked entirely, the RNC has loaned Dobson Len Avariss."

"Oh, Jesus," I sigh, "Len Avariss makes Karl Rove look like Mother Teresa."

David takes me in his arms. "I want you by my side for this, Tess."

"I'd like to be there," I hear myself say.

"Another whiskey?"

"No . . . I'm good, thanks."

"You are good, Tess. You're verygood. We're good together."

I rest my head, which suddenly feels like a lead balloon, on his shoulder. "Yes we are, aren't we?"

"*Yes* we *are*. Whatdoyousay we get someair?"

"Thassa goodidea. I could use someair."

The road alongside St. Stephen's Green is dark. "Are there anymuggers in Dublin?" David wonders aloud. He pulls me closer to him.

"Muggers? I haven't met any." Arms about each other's waists, we weave tipsily toward our hotels.

"Carefor a nightcap?" David asks, pointing to the windows of the Shelbourne's bar.

"Ummm. Tempting. But I think a glassofwater would be more the . . . thing."

"Water. Okay, water is good. Your minibar or mine?"

"I think you should see me home." I'm not even sure exactly what I mean by that, apart from the literal desire for David to ensure that I arrive at Boynton's safely. Do I want him to come upstairs to my room? My body must have asked him—perhaps the fact that I didn't take my arm away from his waist was the giveaway—because my mouth didn't form any specific request.

There's no concierge at the desk, so like giddy children playing hide and seek in a strange house, we start to tiptoe around corners, "exploring."

"Hey, where do you think this leads?" My stage whisper summons David around a narrow dog leg in the ground floor hallway. "Oh, lookit's an elevator! Who knew they had one? I've been walking up to the third floor this whole time."

There's barely room for both of us; the elevator being an obvious afterthought or else the compromise the hoteliers reached in combining modern sense with Georgian sensibility. It's one of those little cages where you have to close the gate like a brass accordion once you're inside the car or the lift won't lift you. "I've always harbored a secret desire to be an elevator operator," I whisper to David as I close the gate.

"No, wait, I want to work the lever." David edges me aside. It moves in a half-moon arc like the ones I remember seeing in the old Saks Fifth Avenue and Radio City Music Hall elevators during my childhood.

"You don't lookvery authentic," I tease. "Where are your white gloves? And do you call that a uniform?"

"On the floor of the House of Representatives, this suit, my dear, might as well be a uniform." David emits a slight hiccup, which sends me into a giggle fit. "Third floor: ladies' lingerie." He moves the lever as, snuggled together, we watch the arrow on the brass dial above our heads. After affecting a surprisingly smooth landing on the right floor, he opens the gate. "After you, Ms. Craig."

"Wait, we need to close the gate behind us or no one else will be able to sue—I mean use—the elevator. It'll be stuck on three. Wait—my turn." I close the gate and then start for my room.

"C'mere," David whispers playfully. I oblige, tottering a bit. I think my feet hurt from walking so much in high heels this evening, but I'm so tipsy that I can't really discern whether I am feeling any pain. My tootsies are just a bit numb at present. "Take off your dress."

"What?"

"I'm serious. Take off your dress, Tess. Don't worry. There's no one up here to see us." He puts his finger to his lips. "They're all asleep, see? Shhhh." He pulls me toward him into a kiss and while our lips dance he unzips my sheath, sliding the dress down over my shoulders. "Your bra, too," he insists, taking my purse out of my hand.

"What racy little devil got into you tonight?" I suppress a slightly nervous giggle.

"I am possessed by the spirit of John Jameson," David replies, affecting a spooky hollow voice. "Oooah-ha-ha-ha!"

"*Shh!* You're nuts!"

"C'mon, Tess. I dare you. Remember that time at the house I rented in Montauk?"

"Too well. You dared me to walk naked into the surf in a full moon. Knowing I'm scared shitless of sharks," I hissed.

"Well, there're no sharks here . . . so what are you waiting for. Just your thong and your pearls—and your heels, of course. From here to your room. You're the sexiest woman in Ireland, Tess, trust me. And the only person who's going to see you is me. The only thing you have to fear is fear itself." He unlocks the door to my room, and, standing in the doorway, holds out his arms as if I'm a toddler just learning to swim to papa.

Equally possessed by Mr. Jameson's spirit(s) I take the dare and saunter toward him with my best Belle du Jour attitude. And halfway to the door I hear the *whirr* of cables and gears and a *thumpf* and a bit of a clatter behind me, and instead of flight (toward David and the privacy of my room) I freeze like the proverbial frightened deer and turn my head toward the noise.

"Tess! You didn't stop by the pub tonight so I wanted to make sure everything was all right," blurts Jamie Doyle. Suddenly we all assess the situation, as, looking from man to man, I can see that David wonders who this Irishman is, I wonder what David is thinking of Jamie's familiarity in assuming he can pop up to my room, and Jamie's cheerful countenance dissolves as he processes the fact that he has just been speaking to a mostly naked woman, who is clearly entertaining another man in the vicinity of her hotel room.

"But . . . I see that . . . you're already . . . well taken care of." Stunned and wounded, he steps back into the elevator and shuts the gate with a resounding crunch of brass.

Do I hear the word *"shite!"* as the car descends toward the lobby?

Thirteen

"Who was that?" David asks my red, crestfallen face.

"Just . . . a new friend. With a penchant for spontaneity." My mortification is complete. I close myself into the bathroom, down a pair of aspirin and a couple of glasses of water in quick succession, and run the shower. I'm all sticky and sweaty from dancing. As I lather up, I hear a knock at the door.

"Mind if I come in? I need to . . . you know."

Well, we'd been a couple for three years, comfortably sharing the bathroom many times in the past, particularly when nature placed a personal call to the other one of us. I mean, you can't exactly be selfish under those conditions. And I confess that I'd always found our comfort level with that kind of bathroom stuff to be romantic in a way: a sort of emblem of domestic bliss at its most basic everyday level that reminded me how good it felt to be half a couple. And if David isn't squeamish tonight about using the toilet while I'm in the shower—and I know that exes can feel awkward about that kind of intimacy, although they never did while they were lovers—then I am hopeful that a reconciliation may be on the menu.

"Do you want company?"

The last time we'd showered together was the morning of David's heart attack. I can see his silhouette through the plastic curtain. He's already stripped to his boxers. "Only if you promise not to almost drop dead in a few hours."

"It's a campaign promise I promise to keep." He parts the curtain and steps into the tub beside me, immediately adjusting the shower head to suit his convenience.

"Hey! I'm not getting wet!"

"I'll take care of that. Stand over here and I'll wash your back."

My mind is a muddle. I had hoped to clear my head in the shower, but David's visit had thrown a monkey wrench into everything. It's a cardinal rule never to operate heavy machinery when you've had a great deal to drink, and I think one's brain can sometimes fall into that category. My judgment is certainly impaired at present and David's presence exacerbates the condition, especially when he caresses my back with his soapy hands. And I wonder to myself about Jamie . . . I am so embarrassed that he saw me tonight that I can't imagine facing him again. And I've kissed him . . . and what was that all about if what I really wanted was David back? But I never thought that would happen—I mean, who could have predicted that David would have shown up here? So . . . this kissing-Jamie-thing . . . was that like the romantic equivalent of the old "hair of the dog" adage regarding alcohol consumption? If you kiss another guy soon after you break up (or, in my case, are broken up with), is that supposed to ease the emotional pain?

And . . . oh, hell, there's no way to focus on my thoughts

with David's hand sliding in and out of some very sensitive southern areas.

"I think your back is pretty clean now," he murmurs. "Turn around and let me wash your front."

Reason and common sense now fly the coop entirely to make room for pure sensation and sensuality. I love it when David bathes me. And standing under the shower head I close my eyes and let the water massage my cheeks in rivers of freshwater tears.

I'm about to don my fluffy new robe when I step out of the tub, but David stops me. "I've missed your skin," he says. "Don't cover it up just yet."

And with the moonlight streaming through the window and the streetlamps along the edge of St. Stephen's Green contributing a glow of their own, we make love for the first time since David's surgery, and I trace the planes of his torso with gentle kisses, happy that the heart beneath it is healthy and beats for me once more. "Welcome home," I say huskily as I feel him enter me and my body rises to receive his in a dance that, while magnificently familiar, is filled with the joy of renewal.

"Thanks for still being alive," I tell him, resting my head against his chest in the satiated lull that follows our mutual expressions of ecstasy. There was never a doubt as to how much we wanted, desired, each other.

"I can feel you smiling," he whispers, stroking my hair.

I suppose this means things aren't really over between us, I muse silently. *After all, people break up and get back together all the time.*

I am awakened by the clip-clop of horseshoes. The hack drivers below my window are chauffeuring their first crop of tourists for the day, competing with the rush hour auto traffic for pavement. I reach for David but come up with a handful of bed linens instead. The man who is not a morning person is already dressed in his suit and is standing before the mirror adjusting his tie.

"Oh . . . I had hoped we'd go into the countryside today. Rent a car, or take a tour bus . . . I discovered the most magical gardens and I wanted to bring you back there."

"I'm sorry, Tess. I need to go check out of the hotel I never stayed in, and my flight leaves at noon. I've got to get back. You know the kind of schedule I have; I need to spend as much time in the district as possible while Congress is in recess for the summer. Somehow I didn't get the chance to tell you that I'd only be in town—here, I mean—for twenty-four hours. I . . . I came to woo you back."

"As your speechwriter, or as . . . ?"

David sits on the edge of the bed and gently places his hands on my shoulders. "Well, you're the best damn speechwriter anyone could have. There's no doubt in my mind whatsoever about that." He catches one of my silent tears on the tip of his index finger and drinks it. "About us . . . well . . . I really thought it might be possible to make a go of it again . . . please believe that I wouldn't have done what we did last night if I didn't think otherwise . . . I think you know me well enough to know I'm not an asshole . . . and I never had any intentions of hurting you, Tess . . . but in the light of day . . ." His voice trails off as he searches for the words and I sense the metallic chill of the executioner's blade, colder and crueler for my believing I had been granted a reprieve. "I have to be honest with you . . . things feel the same to my brain as they did a week ago. I love you, Tess . . . I do, but . . . you know I hate to make campaign promises."

"But you have done," I reply, trying not to sob. "Like the

story about the scorpion and the frog. It's in your nature." I hang my head and blink back the tears. Inhaling deeply, I steel myself. Funny—though hardly amusing—that he tells me he loves me in exactly so many words when the axe is falling for good. "I love *you*, David. I do, and, especially after last night I would love for us to be lovers again. But . . . I'm tired of being the frog. As far as working for you goes . . ." I take another deep breath. "I think it's probably best for both of us if I look for another job when I get back to New York. Hell, I've got a great résumé," I add with forced cheer. "It shouldn't be too hard to find someone else to write for."

On the mattress I rise to my knees and clasp David about the torso. "Good luck, my darling," I say, looking up into his dark eyes, and my tears return. His eyes, too, are moist. Neither of us is very happy right now, but I know I said what I had to say, did what I had to do.

Didn't I?

Day 6 A.D.—or maybe it's Day 1 A.D. redux
(August 12)

Campaign promises. Empty, hollow, shallow things that the "honest" politicians might actually believe at the time they utter them, but the result is the same either way. David didn't just make campaign promises to the voters; he made them to me, too. And this morning I finally realized— or maybe accepted—that to believe them was the emotional equivalent of moving into a sand castle during a hurricane. With campaign promises, there's always the offer of hope without the guarantee of fulfillment. And even if fulfillment of those campaign promises actually does mate-

rialize in some form, it's always the constituent who bears the brunt of them. No such thing as a free lunch. Sure you can have your playgrounds, your libraries, even your "free" lunches for impoverished school kids. I'm just going to have to raise your taxes so we can pay for them.

But I made a choice last night. I was operating on lust and hope. Although the alcohol anesthetized me against the possibility of further emotional pain, no one forced me to make love with David. I wanted to. I missed him, I wanted him back, I needed to hold him, to feel him inside me again. And whatever else David may be from time to time, he is a man of integrity. I do believe that at least for a few hours yesterday, softened by the rosy glow of nostalgia, emboldened by a tot or three of whiskey, and the sexy headiness of sharing a foreign adventure, he, too, supposed it was possible to change his mind and rekindle our relationship.

It makes it very hard for me to be angry at him. I'm sad . . . disappointed certainly . . . but not infuriated. I'm more emotionally numb than anything else right now.

I have spent the morning hiking the cliffs of Howth, having picked up my guidebook in search of someplace not too far from Dublin where I can see the sea. Water always has a way of calming me, of enabling me to turn my thoughts inward as I gaze out at its infinite blue. I have been sitting on a little rock. Way down to my right I can glimpse a lighthouse, the prize in the cosmic Cracker Jack box for walking this far along the cliffs; and far below me, the waves crash against the rocks, the white spray a dozen Naiads' salty tears. Even the sea nymphs weep for my broken heart.

How could I, by most accounts an intelligent, outwardly confident, "together" woman, have come to lose track of <u>me</u>

so badly? I'm forty years old. Why did it take so long for me to realize this? Why did I need to be hit with a metaphorical two-by-four for it to register?

As I sit here, embraced by a breeze with the occasional passing tourist (they all seem to be German) and a few wildflowers my only companions on this side of the sea, I begin to recognize that I had become deeply enamored of the image I was partially responsible for creating, the magical semi-fiction of Congressman David Weyburn that magnified his assets and obscured his flaws. And I begrudgingly begin to acknowledge that the "faster than a speeding bullet, more powerful than a locomotive, able to leap tall buildings in a single bound" superimage had the same effect on me, one of its chief architects, as it did on his constituents and on the rest of America. The image overshadowed the reality. No one got to see the real man, just the hyped-up version of him. The real David Weyburn is not an evil person, of course; he's just (it almost pains me to write this) a highly self-absorbed and—perhaps even this word applies—a narcissistic one. Perhaps those qualities contributed to his success as a public figure, but it sure makes it hard to be such a man's lover.

However . . . when all is said and done, like Pygmalion I fell in love with my own creation. There's been an odd transference occurring ever since our personal and professional lives began to blur. In order to effectively write David's (or anyone's) speeches, I had to get inside his head and become him, in effect; and I began to lose myself along the way. As a ghostwriter my own personality became a shadow in the service of others.

Funny, how I had to travel from one little, sometimes unreal, island all the way across the Atlantic to another isle where creating tales of make-believe and fantasy is a part of their culture, in order to realize how much I needed to become reacquainted with myself after such a prolonged absence.

I take my time walking back down to the village. Howth is postcard-picturesque, tourist-friendly, fisherman-friendly, cyclist-friendly, with a long mole jutting into the bay on which I stop to enjoy the view from sea level and turn back to marvel at the climb I'd undertaken. I had made another stop along my winding and rocky descent, pausing in front of a large cottage once home to William Butler Yeats. A discreet sign tells me I have come upon Balscadder House and underneath it a quote from the great poet and playwright . . . perhaps a gentle plea to literary critics and other potential detractors, both professional and personal: I HAVE SPREAD MY DREAMS UNDER YOUR FEET. TREAD SOFTLY BECAUSE YOU TREAD ON MY DREAMS. And my own "pilgrim soul" cries out in sympathy.

In New York City, people rarely strike up conversations with strangers. We're too much on our guard, too preoccupied with our own thoughts, too busy snagging a precious moment or two to ourselves to engage in banter just for the sake of common conviviality. But here, it's different. At the light rail station, a woman of a certain age asks me if I'm enjoying my ice cream cone. My affirmative reply sparks a conversation where I discover that her son lives across the street from where I grew up in the Bronx. He's a lay teacher at the parochial school I used to look out on from my parents' bedroom window. I don't tell her about the Hawaiian-shirted priest we used to watch climbing into a powder-blue Buick every Saturday evening, driven by an attractive brunette. "Father Luau," as we called him, would slide over so that he was in the center of the front seat and then drape his left arm over the woman's shoulder. I don't think she was a sister, in any sense of the word.

Back in Dublin, it's a short walk from the station to my hotel, but I decide to take a detour: there was a sweater that caught my eye a couple of days ago in a shop window on Grafton Street. Lucky for my wallet, all the popcorn stitching makes me look like a fat cow. And for the price of the handmade one-off (or so the shopgirl swears), I have a feeling I'd be better off just buying the wool at a local yarn shop and adapting an Aran pattern myself.

Focused on the exciting prospect of a new knitting project, designing sweaters in my head, I head into St. Stephen's Green and using my purse for a pillow, stretch out on the pristine lawn, gazing at the Georgian row houses peeking through the trees on the opposite side of the Green and pretend it's really 1807. The warm sun feels good on my face.

A passing cloud, briefly altering the temperature, awakens me from my nap, so I figure it's a sign I should go indoors. It does look like rain, come to think of it. After crossing the street to walk back to Boynton's, I sense a hansom cab accelerating its usual lazy pace, then stopping suddenly alongside me.

"Want a lift?"

I look up at the driver. "Jamie?"

"I swapped jobs with Liam today. I woke up and decided I couldn't stand another morning of wallowin' with the fishes without taking meself a bit of a break. Hop in, if you've a mind to."

I hesitate before stepping into the carriage. "That . . . was David you saw last night. And I'm sorry you saw quite a bit more of *me* than I'd bargained for. David flew all the way from New York to . . . try to talk me into staying on as his speechwriter . . . as it turned out. I hadn't expected any of what happened last night . . . to . . . happen . . . but it did . . . and now . . ."

"It's none of me business, gorl."

His words are curt; clipped, but I find them comforting in a way, refreshing and reassuring. "Thanks for not being pissed off at me. I don't think I was very fair to you. So . . . for what it's worth, I'm really, really sorry, and I can hop out of this thing at Boynton's and you can tell all your mates about this fickle and confused American career woman you met."

"Get up here, woman." Jamie pats the box beside him. I descend from the carriage and clamber up to join him. "Forst of all, yiz owe me nothin'. If all we had was a flortation, I can live with that and be happy knowing that yiz had as good a time of it as I did. We're both adults here. And there's one philosophy says that what a bloke does on holiday don't count. Getting drunk as a dormouse, modeling lampshades, talking shite, kissing strangers . . . I'd lay money that more people than you know act goofy on their vacations, as you call 'em, specially when they began 'em with messed-up heads like you did."

"How'd you get so wise, Jamie?"

"Philosophizing's a time-honored Irish pastime, my girl."

"He's gone, you know. Might as well tell you that. This time I'm certain it's over; last night . . . and this morning," I say, recalling the painful reality of the situation and the pragmatism I applied as a plaster. "They were the unexpected coda. The David Weyburn chapter in the Book of Tess has been closed. D.C. al fin, exeunt ex-inamorata for good."

"How're you doin', then?"

"As well as can be expected," I sigh. "This much I know: I don't want a drink. I had enough last night to float a barge, and besides, I'd rather not medicate myself over it. In an odd way I think I feel kind of relieved. Before . . . when he first told me he wanted to end our relationship, I was hoping his feelings were only temporary—even though he said they weren't. But then he showed up, and I found myself dwelling in hope again, residing in a kind of romantic purgatory. But now that it's pretty clear that I should stop hoping, I feel relieved to no longer live in limbo. I know I should feel sad . . . and I do . . . but I keep thinking perhaps I should feel sadder. After all, I was sure he was the love of my life."

The chestnut horse snorts. An editorial comment if I ever heard one.

Fourteen

August 13. 1:00 A.M., having determined that the "A.D." thing really isn't terribly emotionally healthy . . .

I refused Jamie's offer last night to have a late supper with him after he finished what was technically Liam's tour of duty. I stayed out of the pubs, too. After soaking in the tub for a half hour and summoning room service, I spent the evening in my Herself robe curled up with Yeats. Stumbling upon Balscadder House had spurred me to renew my acquaintance with some of my old friends like "Leda and the Swan," "Sailing to Byzantium," "For Anne Gregory," and perhaps dearest of all, "When You Are Old."

I read them aloud, and wept over the last, as I always do, mourning the fact that the man I thought was the one who would still be there to love me when I grow old and gray and full of sleep and who loved the pilgrim soul in me and the sorrows in my changing face was not that man after all.

Although I came to Ireland to reflect on a few major decisions, David's surprise appearance helped me to make them <u>now</u>, or at least illuminated the obvious, necessitating no further rumination—at least on where he and I stood professionally and what I was prepared to do about it. Having given him my answer, I no longer need to be alone so I can think things over.

I no longer have a lover. I am a free spirit. Tomorrow is another day. The first day of the rest of my life. Yadda yadda yadda.

Full of sleep in any case, I nod off with the volume of Yeats still in my hand.

August 13, continued: 11:30 A.M.

Back from a late breakfast and a bit of souvenir shopping. I decided to eat in Boynton's Buttery, though the prices for simple breakfast food are astronomical—but according to my guidebook they're known for their homemade breads, the basket of which more than lives up to its billing, as does their steel-cut oatmeal. Today feels like a new beginning, so the carb-hearty—and expensive—breakfast seems like the appropriately self-indulgent way to start it. In the same vein, since I figure in a couple of days I'll never see Jamie Doyle again anyway, I've decided to surrender to the sense of fun he instills in me and hang out with him until I leave for home. The balance of my holiday sightseeing plans is in his hands. Wallowing in self pity: bad.

*Spending time with irrepressible Irish new friend: good.
Whoops—there's the phone. Concierge ringing to tell me
Jamie's downstairs. Gotta dash . . .*

"I think what you need is spiritual renewal," Jamie says,
opening the car door for me.

"Since when are you *Father* Doyle?"

"I didn't mean to proselytize," he replies, pulling away from
the curb. "I could fancy meself a father, though. I think I'd be
rather grand at it. Teach 'em to play football—ours, I mean—
not that silly American game with all the armor." He chuckles.
"Teach 'em to *fish*. Oh aye, I could do *that*. Yiz ever want to be
a mother, Tess Goldsmith Craig?"

The guy's got a chutzpah gene, I'll give him that. "Yes," I quietly admit, "but that was another lifetime ago. It's too late now."

"Oh, don't say that, gorl. Why is it too late? You've got nothing wrong with yer plumbing, have you?"

I'm shaking my head and trying not to laugh. "Are you always so blunt with strangers?"

He honks the horn at the particularly elderly motorist ahead
of him, and gunning the engine, darts around three other cars.
"Yer calling yerself a stranger to me? After we kissed and all—
which was very enjoyable, by the way. If that's a stranger,
what're you like when you're familiar?"

"I was vulnerable," I say, knowing he's right.

"And you're full of shite," he replies warmly. "Ahh, you're an
enigma, Tess Goldsmith Craig. An enigma *code* I'm hoping
you'll let me crack. C'mon, I'll give yiz a chance to get even.
Ask me a deeply porsonal question."

"Why have you never married?"

"Oh aye, that's a good one. How do you know I've never
married?"

"Lucky guess?"

"You'd be right, though." He tilts his head as if it will better enable him to sift through his memories. "Never found a woman willing to put up with me," he lilts. "Haven't met one who'll take me in with all my *Star Trek* memorabilia. Don't know one who wants to marry a poor pub owner . . ."

"I thought you're a fisherman."

"By trade. And for the time being. But if I won the lottery and had me druthers I'd spend my life behind a bar. When I wasn't being a da. One of each I want, in case you're wondering. A boy and a gorl, maybe even twins, as they run in me family. I've even got the names picked out. For me kids and me bar. That's what I want from this life. My very own place. Decorated the way I like, with a menu of my choosing, shootin' the breeze with the regulars all day, talking poetry and politics and sports and any old rubbish that strikes our fancy. Have you any friends who want to be married to a man who gets his jollies pulling pints for a bunch o'drunks every night, and comes home to her, dog-tired from bein' on his feet all day, stinkin' of whiskey and beer whether or not he's had a few of his own during the night? Do yiz? Because if ya do, I'd like to meet them. Every woman I meet, she's got her own thing going, which is all very well and good for her, financially independent and all, but they've all got an attitude. Every one of them. 'Tisn't who *y'are* they're carin' about, but what you *do*. You can be a complete shite and a Lothario, yet if yer a brain surgeon they're falling over themselves to get to you. But tell 'em your dream is to open yer own pub and they're gone before they've barely taken the time to laugh in yer face. Because the minute a woman meets yiz, she projects herself into your collective future, and I can see just as well as she can in the crystal ball behind her eyes that for all her independence, deep down this financially successful woman who's worked hard to orn every euro she's got, doesn't want to be the primary breadwinner, working her arse off while she does the primary parenting as well, thinkin' all the time that being married to Jamie Doyle is like havin' *another* kid around the house. I'm not exactly the catch of the day."

"I take your point," I sigh. "And no, I don't know anyone who fits the bill for you. Sorry. So what's this spiritual renewal you're prescribing for my soul?"

"I'm bringing yiz to Glendalough."

"What's Glenda-lock? Sounds like a witch's wrestling hold."

"That's Glinda. And you'll see when we get there. Description ruins the magic."

"Spoilsport!"

"That's what *you* think!"

At first the road is the same one we took to get to Powerscourt, but then we pass the turnoff. The terrain begins to change from pastoral to dramatic, the rolling hills and conifer forests gradually disappearing in favor of a harsher, more primitive landscape as we motor through the evocative Wicklow mountains. In what would seem to be the middle of nowhere, Jamie pulls to the side of the road and insists we get out of the car to look around. As far as the eye can see, enormous boulders give the impression of having been tossed to earth by angry giants dwelling on the mountaintops above us.

Jamie comes up behind me and places his hands on my shoulders. "Pretty wonderful, isn't it? This is called the Sally Gap. Highest crossroads in Ireland."

"Why is it called the—"

"*Shhh*, mo cushla. Can't you hear the footsteps?"

"You're giving me the creeps. What footsteps?"

"Don't ya hear them? The tromping of heavy boots. The ghosts of redcoated soldiers passing through, along the Military

Road on the way to their barracks." I shiver involuntarily. "Oh, this place is full of lore. It's even passed for Scotland, something we Irish have a good laugh over. They filmed a lot of *Braveheart* out there in the high heather desert and bog land."

There is something eternal about it up here. Take away the passing cars and the blue jeans and we could be deep in the past—in almost any century.

Jamie presses his body against my back, and I try to turn my head to read his eyes. "Just protecting you from the wind. Here among the ancients, chivalry is still very much alive." I can hear the smile in his voice, imagine the twinkle in his eye.

"All right, why do they call it Sally Gap?"

Jamie presses his face close to my ear. "Once upon a time, there was a man they called Patrick. Famous for chasing the snakes out of Ireland and all, right? And when Patrick died—right where we're standing—the story has it that Oisín, another figure from Irish legend, came riding by on his white horse and scooped up Patrick and took him off to paradise. And the *gap in the saddle* between Oisín and Patrick was shortened over time to 'Sally Gap.' And there you have a bit of local etymology. Chilly?"

"It *is* windy up here," I admit, leaning my body into Jamie's. For warmth, of course. "But I like listening to your fairy tales."

"You've come to the right place, then." We get back in the car and continue toward Glendalough. "For we've got stories about the fairy folk who dwell up here—so if you don't take off your jacket and torn it wrong way out, they'll lead you down the wrong road even if you've followed the right signs. I could tell you tales about the Wicklow Mountains being filled with gold, a monster with the head of a horse and the body of a snake living large in Loch Tay, and of course the romantic entanglements of St. Kevin, who lived in these parts in early Christian times."

"Early Christians," I muse. "Wouldn't some people call them the first Reform Jews?"

"Very funny." His hand feels warm when he places it on my leg, so I decide to let it rest there. "It was in the seventh century, and St. Kevin was of course a celibate, which didn't preclude him from being a hottie, as you ladies say. In fact the name Kevin means 'handsome and beautiful.' He had his first hermitage in Wicklow—right around where we're drivin' now. Now, there was a young woman named Kathleen, gorgeous to behold and amorous of inclination, who took a fancy to our St. Kevin. And she chased him about and about the hills, hoping to lead him astray. But St. Kevin, though a man of religious convictions, wasn't much of a gentleman, for he thrashed poor pretty Kathleen with a bunch of nettles, and to be sure he would further avoid her sight, journeyed a bit further south. Following the instructions of a vision he received from on high, he relocated his hermitage and founded a monastery . . . guess where?"

"The vale of Glendalough!"

"Wait! How did you know that?!" Jamie appears genuinely gobsmacked.

"I'm right? Cool! I was just reading the *road sign*. I must let you know, though, that I am no longer inclined to be a fan of your St. Kevin, since you've told me he was, quite literally, a violent misogynist."

"Then why are you smiling?"

"Because we got here all right, without turning our clothes inside out."

"*Tsk-tsk*. I'll find one of the wee folk for you yet, Tessa Goldsmith Craig."

But there *is* something mystical about Glendalough, the "valley of two lakes." The centuries-old stone buildings, even in their various states of decay, built by generations of early medieval monks, commemorate the immortal power of Faith. And though I don't share their religion, I do indeed take comfort in the concept of Faith. I'm not even religious, but I have always found spiritual solace and renewal in Nature; and here in this ancient valley, as a summer breeze darts among the ruins, rustling the pines until they bathe me with their pungent scent, I understand why Jamie wanted to bring me here.

And I walk among the dead, stepping with gingerly respect over and around the gravestones of those who lived here hundreds of years ago, the monks and the laic, whose devotion, patronage, wealth, or influence earned them the perk of burial here, eternal sanctuary in this legendary soil. What did they wear? Eat? Die of?

Jamie and I walk along one of the hiking paths beside the lake until we can no longer see the round tower, a pointy-capped hundred-foot-high stone edifice that served as the monks' storehouse and safe haven. The hard brown earth, strewn with a carpet of dry, amber-colored pine needles, reminds me of the day camp I attended as a girl, catapulting my memories, in Proustian fashion, to simpler times, when my biggest worry was the outbreak of a pimple or getting picked last for volleyball, and my biggest fears were that a moth might fly down my shirt or a daddy long-legs would creep up the side of the toilet while I was in the camp's out-house.

Meandering alongside the Upper Lake and then the Lower, we walk in silence, human silence, I mean, because all around us Nature is singing her song, borne on the soft breeze that ruffles Jamie's light brown hair and ripples the surface of the loch. Just a few feet away the rush of a waterfall captures my attention, and I stand before it for several minutes, as if the clear rushing water replenishes my arid, aching soul. I don't feel like talking and Jamie surely senses that, in his Deanna Troi-like way.

I don't even know if we're walking *to* something, a destination, but it really doesn't matter. Although I am fascinated by the old stone buildings, the still-living remnants of history, I'm not here on a pilgrimage to honor them, or to see the stone that some call St. Kevin's bed. But there is magic in this place, in Glendalough, and I'm here for something; *that* much I recognize, even if it's that I journeyed all the way to a rural corner of Ireland and found a place that looks like upstate New York. Maybe that's it. Maybe that's why, even with my new friend beside me, I think I'm now ready to go home.

Fifteen

We cross back to the ruins via a little bridge.
A circle in a square called the Deer Stone carries its own mythic symbolism, as does a nearby tree to which, legend has it, a visitor must tie something of value to ensure that he will one day return to Glendalough. Who knows if I'll even want to return, but the alternative feels like a kind of jinx, so with an *ouch* I yank out a couple of strands of hair. Well, at least it's organic. Rhetorically, I ask Jamie if he notes the irony in such pagan superstitions abiding in comfortable harmony with this holy seat of early Christianity.

"That's Ireland, gorl!"

"Oh, look! I wonder who he belongs to."

"Make a wish," Jamie counsels me, as we watch the white horse blithely grazing just a few yards from the Round Tower. "Always make a wish whenever you see a white horse."

I *tch-tch* and the horse looks up. He looks so clean and cared for; no flies buzz around his face, and he doesn't smell. "I wish I had a carrot or an apple or something to feed him."

"Leprechauns are the only ones who can grant wishes," Jamie teases, handing me an apple from his backpack.

Tentatively, I hold out my hand, *tch-tch* again, and the horse ambles over; he's got all the time in the world. "Do I get two more wishes now?" Jamie slips his arm about my waist while our new equine friend enjoys his serendipitous snack. Tilting my head away from Jamie, the better to regard his face, I tell him, "I wish I knew where I was going from now on. Had a clearer idea. I know where I'm *not* going, but it's not the same thing. And I wish that, when I find it, I'm a huge success at it!"

"You want road signs posted on the rainbow and a guarantee there's a pot of gold waiting for you at its end."

I laugh. "Something like that. I suppose that's why they call it 'wishful thinking.'"

As we toodle back through the Wicklow Mountains through boggy glens and past balding hillsides, once again Jamie stops the car at the side of the road and convinces me to get out and walk across a precarious (or so it seems, once I'm on it) footbridge made of old railroad ties. Suspended far above the valley, I feel like I'm floating, while below me a narrow river snakes through it as far as the eye can see. The buffeting wind is fierce, but I could swear I hear it speaking to me. Challenging, if not *daring*, me to stand up straight and tall against its might, to be strong as an oak yet resilient as a willow, even as it tries to knock me off balance. It's a long, long way down, should I fall. My task isn't merely not to buckle; it's to fight back. To . . . well, to stand up for myself.

"I get your point, Jamie!" I shout into the wind. "Can I get back in the car now?"

He nods and beckons me, and I now traverse the bridge with far less trepidation.

Pulling up alongside my hotel Jamie says, "I'd invite you to dinner tonight, but I'm taking over for Niall behind the bar. He's got his first hot date in decades. But if you don't stop by Blackpools I'll be disappointed. But . . . say . . . would you come with me to dinner tomorrow night at my parents' home?" He fixes his gaze on the steering wheel, delivering his question to the inanimate object incapable of rejecting him.

"You want me to meet your parents? Tomorrow's my last night in Dublin, you know."

"Is that a yes or a no?" Jamie glances anxiously at me.

I lean over and gently kiss his cheek. "It's a yes. Sure, I'll go with you tomorrow night."

He breaks into a smile, the dark cloud scudding past, revealing his usual sunny countenance. "Thanks." And suddenly he adds, "You're not nervous about it, are you?"

"Do I have a reason to be?"

August 14, 8:00 A.M.—my last full day in Dublin

I'm glad I went to Blackpools last night, to see Jamie in action behind the bar. The place was absolutely jumping. "It's so crowded in here, you can't even find the jacks!" remarked the man on the next stool. I can see why Jamie loves this. Playing the convivial host comes to him naturally, and the live traditional music feeds his energy and the vibe of the pub in general. I admire the way he kept things humming, kept everyone's spirits up and spirits poured, and handled those who got out of hand with the

*psychological skill of a diplomat and the physical prowess
of a professional wrestler. I confess I found it sexy. I told
him that now I wanted to watch him fish, but he denied
me. Said I'd be bored, possibly seasick, and might be put off
fish forever when it came time for him to gut and filet their
carcasses. Okay, point taken, but I like being on the water.
Maybe more than Jamie does. At least he did promise to
pick me up later and show me where he goes to fish, as well
as where he lives. So that's how I'll spend my last day.*

*And without the what-to-do-about-whether-to-keep-
working-for-David decision hanging over my head anymore I'll arrive in New York prepared to update my résumé
and set off afresh, with a conscience clear and clean,
scrubbed with the salt sea air from the cliffs at Howth and
infused with Glendalough's pine-scented spirituality.*

Coffee. I need coffee. Lots of it. Off to breakfast . . .

Clontarf is a suburb of Dublin boasting green spaces, a castle
(okay, so it's now a hotel), and an enviable coastline. A bit like
a small town in Connecticut, actually, but for the number of
pubs and a greater amount of lace-curtained windows. It's here
that Jamie spends the wee small hours of the day, spreading his
nets from his thirty-foot trawler, the weather-beaten *Annabel
Lee.* She's not a particularly comfortable vessel, and Jamie was
right that though a "she" herself, *Annabel Lee*'s not terribly
chick-friendly. For one thing, she smells of fish.

"I used to live out here," Jamie tells me, driving along a non-
descript residential road. "Bein' close to the water and all made
sense, but there's no nightlife to speak of, except for a trip
down to yer local. I call it 'Yawn-tarf.' Not for me a town where
they roll up the sidewalks at ten P.M. Oh aye, it's lovely for
families and OAPs, but I haven't got me a family and I've got a

couple of decades to go before I become a pensioner. Pretty enough though, isn't it?"

"I wouldn't mind living by the sea."

"Well, Tess, if I'd met you twenty years or so ago, you might have made me change my mind. I'm more of a city mouse. Oh, I don't like the noise and the fumes, and Dublin costs an arm and a leg to live in these days—we members of the working middle classes have been sorely clawed by the Celtic Tiger— but give me the hustle and bustle. I love meeting people from different countries, different walks of life; that's what Dublin's like these days. A bit of a melting pot. The only place you'll find emerald green clothing and shamrocks all over everything is in the souvenir shops."

"And I came to Ireland for the four-leaf clovers and the lep-rechauns," I sigh.

"And ya didn't find 'em in Dublin." Jamie looks regretful. "But tell me what ya did find, Tessa Goldsmith Craig."

"Stop using my full name," I plea lightheartedly. "I found *you*. And something I'd mislaid for a lot of years: a little piece of me as well."

We grab lunch from a tiny takeaway chips place by the seafront promenade and clamber over the rocks on the Bull Wall to enjoy it. Scenic, but hard on the tush, and the wind whisks away the paper napkins and the empty vinegar packets. And after a midafternoon cocktail at Clontarf Castle, we drive back to Dublin. I want to revisit the Long Room at Trinity College Library, and maybe potter about their bookstore for a bit. Flopping down on the manicured Green, I fall asleep with my head on Jamie's thigh.

Having insisted on some time alone before the family dinner, I enjoy a luxurious bath and then a cappuccino from room service at the little table by my window as I scribble a line or two in my journal: *I think I spy Liam Doyle's hansom cab clop-clopping under my window and wonder if he'll be joining us this evening. Children's laughter wafts over from St. Stephen's Green and penetrates the edges of my gauzy curtains. A breeze rustles through hundreds of tree branches and riffles the viridian leaves. A nanny scolds. A car honks. For the first time in years—maybe ever—I'm not living up to someone's expectations of who I am, what I should be, or how I should behave in any given situation. I find myself smiling. I'm happy.*

"Now don't expect much from Crumlin," Jamie cautions me when he picks me up at Boynton's. He admires my tunic and fitted black slacks. "You're looking quite fetching, by the way. Buckle up."

"Thanks. What's a Crumlin?"

"A boring little suburb a bit south of here. But me parents are happy there; Ma can walk from the house to her volunteering job at Our Lady's Hospital for Sick Children, her old hairdresser just relocated to the neighborhood, and her garden is blooming, so she's happy as a pig in shite. And Da has the spanking new track at the local high school to keep him happy—they open it to residents in the off hours and he's an amateur marathoner. Does the Bloomsday run every year, and some other long distance events I never can remember the names of."

Residential Crumlin seems to consist of street after street of semi-detached homes with postage-stamp front yards, only slightly quainter than its counterparts in Queens, lower Westchester, or a middle-income development on Long Island. Jamie brakes his mini in front of the last building on a strip of terraced row houses. A setter roots around a hedge, as if it's looking for something that got away. I regard the pebbled façade of royal blue stucco. "Is this it?"

"Home sweet home. This is where I grew up." And as if he's reading my mind, Jamie adds, "Bleak, isn't it? The inside isn't much better, I'm afraid."

He raps the brass door knocker and a taut face peeps through the tiny window above it before flinging open the door. My nostrils are immediately assailed by kitchen aromas: corned beef, roast chicken, cabbage, baked goods. All the staples I expected somehow. "Jamie boy!" A gray-haired skinny man about Jamie's height throws his ropy arms about his son and clasps him to his bosom as though they hadn't met in decades. "And this," the man says, stepping back to appraise my appearance, "must be your new lady friend."

New lady friend? Well, that's a bit . . . extreme.

"Tessa Goldsmith Craig, I'd like you to meet my da, Eamon Doyle. Used to be the best taxi driver in New York—"

"They shoulda made the movie about *me*," Eamon jokes. I suppose he doesn't remember the plot too well.

"And the best—until he retired—hack man in Dublin as well. Hardest working man on four wheels."

Eamon greets me with a remarkably strong grip. "Woodworking," he says, noticing me noticing the firmness of his handshake. "Mo! Company! Maureen!" He looks back to the kitchen, but Maureen fails to appear on cue. "Herself has been in the kitchen all day." He leans toward us, adding conspiratorially, "So I'll advise yiz to compliment her cooking at every torn. Come, come inside! What're yiz doing standin' on the step like a pair of Jehovah's Witnesses?"

Eamon leads us along a rather dark hallway; much of the faded floral wallpaper is covered with family photos, mostly semi-candids that appear to chronologize the lengthy history

of Doyle family seaside vacations. The dog has followed us indoors, and working its way between our moving legs, begins to
sniff at my crotch before I can even begin to pet it.

"Down, Molly! Down gorl!"

"Da, I think Molly Bloom's a lesbian."

"What're ya talkin', Jamie? Dogs can't be lesbians."

We have entered the living room, small, also rather dark, except for the pristine lace curtains, and stuffed to the gills with
furniture and bric-a-brac. Maureen must spend a lifetime dust-
ing all the figurines because there's not a speck of dust to be
seen. I get the feeling that the tiniest mote would suffer instant
excommunication. Everything is immaculate in this human nest,
from the Beleek heirloom tea set in the mahogany china cabinet
to the portrait-style photos on the walls of family members and
the snapshots on the mantelpiece to the dried floral arrange-
ments displayed on the antique doilies resting along the top of
the spinet. Exploding my preconception, there is not a portrait
of JFK or the Pope anywhere in sight. The only sign of anything
remotely approaching disorder is a half-finished jigsaw puzzle of
Bangkok, cordoned off on a bridge table tucked into a corner of
the room.

"Well, make yourselves cozy," Eamon invites us. "Can I get
yiz a whiskey?"

"Absolutely," says Jamie, patting the gold velveteen, and I
ensconce myself beside him on the sofa.

I nod my head. *Make mine a double*, I think.

Eamon hands us our drinks, and after pouring himself a generous glass of Diet Coke, nestles into a cushy armchair upholstered in a riotous floral of brown and gold.

Finally, Maureen Doyle, a thickset woman with freshly
coiffed auburn hair, enters the room, wearing a gravy-stained
"Kiss the Cook" apron and a pair of oven mitts. "Forgive my

appearance," she says, wiping her brow with the back of her gloved hand. "I got the apron at a charity do."

Jamie rises and I do the same. "Ma, this is Tessa Goldsmith Craig. The American gorl I mentioned."

"Welcome to my home," says Maureen, extending an oven-mitted hand. "Oh, don't worry, it's not hot," she says when I tentatively reach to shake it. "I was takin' the bread out of the oven. It's Jamie's favorite. Comfort food, he cawls it. Jamie could nevuh marry a woman whose soda bread isn't as good as his ma's. I suppose that's why he's still a bachelor at forty. Isn't that right, Jamie?" She gives her mortified second son a wet kiss on the cheek. "I thought yaw . . . lady friend—it's yaw first time in Ireland, isn't it, Tessa—would like to have a traditional dinner, since all those fancy restaurants in Dublin see no value in our solid, classic fare, as they like to call it." I recall now that Jamie had told me his mother was American-born and raised. I notice now that her accent is more distinctly Irish, having been here for decades, I suppose, though sometimes a New Yawkism creeps in, like dropping some of her r's.

"Did you meet my babies?" She gestures toward a crib tucked into a corner of the living room, and I wonder why Jamie hadn't bothered to introduce me to the littlest Doyles. Grandchildren, perhaps? They're awfully quiet for infants.

Steering me by the elbow Maureen proudly shows me what she's talking about. At first I think the three figures are slumbering babies—two girls and a boy—and then I realize that they're dolls. "Oh, my God, they look so real," I breathe.

Maureen beams. "Thank you. I'm a good artist, aren't I, Jamie?"

As though she's handling a real newborn she lifts one of the girl dolls out of the crib and places it in my arms. "God, it even feels like a real baby!" The head and body are weighted just

right, the skin texture and tone, the eyes, hair, even the finger-
nails, look utterly naturalistic.

"This is Lorna," Maureen tells me, placing a kiss on the doll's
forehead. "Isn't she sweet? Makes you want one of yawr own,
doesn't it?"

"Well . . ."

"Ma!" Jamie's admonishment has little effect on his mother.

"Do ya have children, Tessa?"

"No. No, I don't, Mrs. Doyle."

"Aw, cawl me Maureen. How old are ya, Tess, if you don't
mind my asking?"

"She does mind, Ma."

"Well, if you're the same age as our Jamie, or thereabouts,
yawr gettin' a bit lawng in the tooth for it. So I wouldn't wait
too much lawnger. Maybe you should take Lorna with you. My
gift. Oh, don't look so concerned; she's one of dozens of reborn
babies I've got all over the house. I'll give ya a tour after dinner
and show you my little factory. It's in Brigid and Mary Margaret's old room. Jamie, don't look at me as though I violated a
sacred space. The U2 posters are still where the girls left them
when they moved out."

Eamon refills his Diet Coke glass. "Mo's got herself a thriving eBay business sellin' these reborn dolls. Hers are very
sought-after, ya know. Gets more than two hundred euro for
some of them. Plus shipping. Her business is even incorporated.
'Mo Cushla Babies.' "

"You have to admit it's cute," Jamie says out of the side of his
mouth.

"*You* have to admit it's *creepy*," I reply in equal fashion.

"Speaking of sacred spaces, Ma, is Brigid joining us this
evening?"

Maureen nods. "I sprung her from the community house.

But Sister Genesius wants her back there by eleven. I told Sister it was an important family dinner and promised her I'd
send Brigid back with one of my cawffee rings. That sealed the
deal." Turning to me, Maureen says, "Jamie tells me ya come
from my old hometown, Tessa. So what church do ya go to?"

"None—I'm Jewish."

Maureen fails at turning her wince into a smile. "Then, do
you attend a synagogue reguluh?"

"I'm . . . pretty much a secular Jew," I say, feeling the spiritual welts rising on my back from the grilling.

A key jangles in the front door, and a few moments later a
pretty young woman looking a bit like a refugee from the Eisenhower era in a knee-length brown skirt, pale blue sweater, and
white blouse enters the living room, dropping an enormous canvas backpack just inside the doorway. She has the most sparkling
eyes I've ever seen. Catching her mother's glare, she says, "All
right, I'll put it in the closet. Just don't let me forget it when I
leave." She disappears long enough to deposit what passes for her
purse, then joins us with a cheery "So I hear Jamie's got himself
a lady friend! Cool!"

Maureen kisses her daughter, and in a move that American
football fans would characterize as an "audible," mutters, "You
won't think it's so cool in a second." Raising her voice to a con-
versational level, she gestures toward me and says to Brigid,
"Meet Tessa Craig. She has no faith."

Sixteen

I am stunned by this spiritual body blow, and after a terribly long and awkward silence, am rescued by Jamie, who proposes that we all head into the kitchen to help his mother put the finishing touches on the meal. Both warm (literally) and cozy, the kitchen is covered almost wall-to-wall with maple veneers, from the cabinets and drawers to the refrigerator and the traditional dinette set with its lathe-turned legs. Above the little breakfast nook is a print of The Last Supper, and a crucifix hangs on the wall by the fridge, the first cross I've noticed on display in the Doyle home, though I did see a couple of plaster saints standing beside the Hummels and Lladros in the living room.

"It's just us this evening," Maureen tells Jamie. "Niall's behind the bar, we needed the twins to stay and wait tables, Liam is working until ten—and besides I don't like him coming to the table smellin' like a hawse, Mary Margaret's got her own family to feed, and Seamus is doin' something with his mates from school. At least it means there'll be less washing up!"

Eamon opens a bottle of wine to drink with the meal, but a lifetime teetotaler, he doesn't have a glass himself. "Besides," he says, "I'm a man of sport and my body is a temple." Maureen eyes me intently while her husband says grace. At least her cooking is outstanding—and I eat far too much. I'm relieved from being dragged any more deeply into discussing my personal life by Brigid, who peppers me with questions about life in New York.

"Is it really like *Sex and the City*?" she wants to know. "I was a big fan until my discernment began. I haven't seen the show since, I'm afraid. Sister Genesius isn't big on any telly that comes from your HBO. Since discernment is all about listening to what God is saying through prayer and in the events of our daily lives, it stands to reason, I suppose, that the Almighty wants us to think about more important things than shoe sales."

Making a mental note to pass along this observation to my cousin Imogen, I explain that much of the show is fantasy; freelance journalists in New York, unless they're moonlighting in a more lucrative field, could rarely afford a $600 pair of shoes.

"But ya have to admit the shoes are wonderful! It's my secret guilty pleasure. Ya know, I admit it's a wee bit shallow of me, but I do wish nuns could wear nicer shoes. If God doesn't care what you wear on your feet so long as you walk in His way, then what's so bad about Jimmy Choo?"

"It probably has something to do with the eschewing of worldly goods and all that," Jamie tells her with a wink. "Vow of poverty, remember?"

"It sucks," she whispers to me under her breath.

"Then why are you becoming a nun?" I whisper back.

"I'm looking for direction. And the path to Heaven seemed more clearly marked than most of the others. And for what it's worth—I disagree with Ma, and probably the Pope. I don't think you 'don't have any faith' just because you're Jewish and you're not religious. We're all God's creatures. If you want to know the truth, for the longest time I wasn't sure what I believed in either and how much I believed in it. I'm taking the veil because I think it'll give me the answers. I've still got a lot of years of study and training, though, before I take my final vows. Another year of candidacy and then two more years as a novitiate before I make my First Commitment. That's when I take the vows of chastity, poverty, and obedience for a period of three to six years, a time of further confirmation of my calling. Then, assuming we—the Vocational Director, the Spiritual Counselor, and I—still feel I'm a good fit for the Church and all, I'll make my Final Commitment."

"Sounds like it takes even longer than med school!"

"So, when do you go back to New Yawk?" Maureen asks me solicitously.

"Tomorrow evening."

She beams beatifically. "I bet you'll be happy to get back home."

"Can I invite yiz back to my place for a nightcap?" Jamie asks me, once we've made our farewells. "Ya look like ya need it."

"Your father's very pleasant," I sigh. "Your ma . . . well, she's . . . something else. And I don't know about her born-again dolls; I've never been much of a doll person. I like Brigid a lot. She was helping me understand the nun thing. I kind of envy her in a way for knowing what she believes in. Spiritually, I mean. Or at least thinking she does."

"She's young."

"What's that supposed to mean?"

"What I said."

"I'll take that nightcap now. What're you pouring?"

Jamie lives in a brick-faced freehold house not far from the center of Dublin; its façade, including the fire-engine red door, is one I can imagine Joyce's Leopold Bloom strolling by during his 1904 progress through the city. Perhaps it's an inside joke that Jamie uses a bronzed copy of *Ulysses* as a doorstop. "I moved here from Clontarf back in 1988," he tells me. "Before the Celtic Tiger bared its claws and prices shot through the roof. It's worth a feckin' fortune today if I had a mind to sell it. I'm doing all right, though. Each of us Doyles gets a piece of Blackpools's profit. And the place is hoppin' like a Mexican jumping bean most nights, so none of us is hortin' for money—providing we keep an eye on our own expenses."

His apartment is nicer than I expected it to be. Better maintained. Although the living room's mandarin orange walls make an already cozy space seem smaller, it's kind of an interesting (unexpected, certainly) contrast against the white marble fireplace.

"It has a homely feel, doesn't it?" Jamie says, grabbing a pile of dirty clothes and dashing up his cast-iron spiral staircase with the laundry stashed under his arm. I have to smile. What are the odds that both of us would reside in picturesque duplexes?

"You know that word doesn't mean the same thing in America," I call after him.

A few moments later, he bounds back down the stairs. "Sorry about that. Why, what's wrong with *homely*? You don't find my flat pretty?"

"Where I come from, the word means 'ugly.' We say *homey* to mean your 'homely.'"

Amused, he shakes his head. "You're confusing me, gorl. I thought in America 'homey' was a black guy." Jamie cops a hip-hop attitude, splaying his fingers; on him it looks laughable. "You know, a home boy." He arranges the scattered newspapers on his coffee table into a presentable pile, revealing an empty beer bottle. "Whoops. I should have hired me a housekeeper before inviting a lady over." He grins at me.

I think about how immaculate his mother keeps her home and consider that the apple fell so far from her tree that it landed in another county. I chuckle. "Unable to clean house yourself?"

"Ach. I hate it. They've been makin' self-cleaning ovens for years now. When're they going to make self-cleaning flats? So, do yiz like the color down here? Me decorator did it. A man named *Benjamin Moore*. It's me favorite color."

"Did I know that when I met you?" I tease.

"Aw, don't wince, Tess. Seriously, I love orange. Used to get me beat up every St. Paddy's Day." He shoves up his sleeve to show me a slightly wonky elbow. "Got the battle scars to prove it, too."

"You *brawled* over a *color*."

"I *brawled* over an *aesthetic ideology*. Let me give yiz the grand tour."

The living room and the bachelor-sized kitchen (though the amenities are all very modern) comprise the lower floor. Up the spiral staircase are the bedroom and bathroom—which I find not to be as clean as I'd hoped, though it's not as bad as it could be—and why is it that when guys use up the paper, they leave the new roll on the edge of the sink instead of re-placing it?

Curiously, the bedroom walls are a dull shade of taupe, al-most the same depressing hue as his parents' front hallway. But there's an even more striking feature: "Why does a fisherman who hates fishing sleep on a waterbed?" I ask Jamie.

"I used to get seasick until I bought it. Just kidding yiz. Ever try one?" He plops onto the mattress and smoothes out the Indian cotton bedspread. "Care to join me?"

As soon as I perch on it, I'm sort of sucked into it. Frankly, it takes a bit of getting used to. "So, where's your lava lamp?"

Jamie opens his bedstead cabinet and reaches into it. *My God, he really owns one!* He plugs the lamp into the wall and the goop inside it begins to migrate. "Wait here." He heads downstairs, returning a couple of minutes later with a bottle of champagne, two flutes, and an ice bucket. "Didn't give yiz enough time to go snooping in me drawers, did I?" he winks. "Here, hold these." He encourages me to lean back against the headboard and hands me the glasses while he pops the cork.

"Before ya go back to the land of stress and skyscrapers—which isn't entirely a bad thing—the skyscrapers, I mean, not yer retorning home—I want to make a toast . . . and to tell yiz something . . . something important. Something I can't keep carrying in my heart and not sharing with yiz. Forst," he continues, raising his glass, "I want to make a toast to the wonderful lady who has made the past week one of the best of my life."

I'm very touched. "That's so sweet of you."

"Don't sip yet; I'm not finished." He regards his glass. "All right, I'll make it quick before the bubbles fizz out. Tessa Goldsmith Craig, I'm in love with you. I know that a week ago we hadn't even met, but that doesn't change anything. It didn't even take me this long to figure it out. Oh, now yiz can drink."

Sure, we flirted. We kissed, made out a bit, laughed together, and I cried on his shoulder. I'm aware that there's a mutual attraction, and a certain affection as well. But *love?* I don't know what to say to this totally unexpected declaration.

Jamie tries to mask his anxiety. "Say something, Tess."

I take a sip of champagne, look into my glass, look away, take another sip . . . I'm not sure how to express what I'm thinking and feeling . . . how to be empathetic, yet candid. "I've had a wonderful week, too. Meeting you . . . getting to know you . . . the occasional odd . . . incident . . . notwithstanding."

"You looked great in the almost-buff. In this humble man's opinion. You're quite a fine-looking woman, y'know."

"Thanks," I blush, averting my gaze again by focusing on my champagne. "You know . . . I think you're quite a guy, Jamie. You make me *feel good*, and a woman couldn't ask for much more. But . . . I don't see where this can go in the long term. I'm getting on a plane tomorrow, planning to hit the ground running as soon as I arrive home. Since my nest egg is about the size of a Jordan almond, I've got to start looking for a new job right away. Whether you enjoy it or not, you're going to go back to your fishing. And we'll e-mail each other, I'm sure . . . but beyond deepening our friendship—which I'm not saying is a bad thing—where will it lead? It wouldn't be fair to either of us, Jamie. *Romantically*, without time to get past my three years with David, no matter who I become involved with, the next guy will be Rebound Man. I can't do that to you, even long distance. It wouldn't be just un- fair of me; it would be shitty. It wasn't lost on me that your fam- ily kept referring to me as your lady friend. So either you said something to them to make them think we're . . . you know . . . or else they jumped to their own collective conclusions.

"I want to be able to say 'I love you too, Jamie,' but I'm not there yet. Something like 'you know I've become terribly fond of you this past week' is so tepid it's insulting. You become fond of a *dog*, not a man."

Poor Jamie. He looks so glum. "I suppose that about says it all. Thank you for being honest." He grows very quiet. Withdrawn. As if all his natural gregariousness had been sucked out of his lungs. By me, really. I feel dreadful. And now his mother's cooking is beginning to sit in my stomach like a crock pot filled with lead.

"Maybe I should leave now. I'll try to catch a cab back to the hotel."

Jamie downs the rest of his champagne without looking at me. "No, please don't. Not yet. I was a fool to tell you everything I was feeling. I've only got myself to blame." He won't let me get a word in edgewise to counter this argument. "Stay for another little while longer. Keep me company. I don't want this conversation to be our last before we say good-bye."

I reach out for his hand. "What can I do that would make you feel better right now?"

He chuckles. Wanting me to say the words that in three years of dating, David lacked the courage to say to *me*. "In the cabinet below the telly there are a bunch of videotapes. Hand me the second one from the left in the front row."

The only thing in Jamie Doyle's flat that is organized and pristine and essentially not an unholy mess, is his video collection—and most specifically, his *Star Trek* tapes. I hand him the cassette, its cardboard sleeve a bit worn—from frequent viewing over the years, I suppose.

Checking first to be sure I've brought him the video he wanted, Jamie fires up his VCR and side by side, champagne glasses still in hand, we watch a 1967 episode titled "Metamorphosis." As far as I can follow it amid the pseudo-sci-fi mumbo-jumbo, the plot opens with the rescue by the crew of the *Enterprise* of a humanoid named Nancy Hedford, but centers on a space pioneer named Zefram Cochrane, originally from

Alpha Centauri, who has been marooned on another planet. Apparently he's been kept alive and eternally young for something like 150 years through the good offices of an alien he calls the "Companion." Spock, who discovers that the Companion is partly an electrical something-or-other, plans to short-circuit it, which doesn't entirely please Cochrane (I guess because he'd likely die if the Companion gets fritzed).

Mumbo-jumbo, mumbo-jumbo, and more mumbo-jumbo, lots of polyester and intensely serious exclamations, and we eventually learn that the Companion is a female who's in love with Cochrane. The idea that some alien has the hots for him repulses Cochrane, which causes our girl Nancy (who's been suffering from some sort of fever) to remark that she finds it strange that Cochrane runs from love while she herself has never had the chance to be loved. *Okay, Jamie, I get it.*

So the Companion inhabits (and thereby cures) Nancy's body so she can be with her beloved Cochrane, but she can't leave her own planet without dying, and in the end, he opts to stay there with her.

"Well?" Jamie says, switching off the TV.

I lean over and kiss him softly on the lips. "It hasn't made me a *Star Trek* convert. I'm afraid I'm missing the gene."

He holds me and kisses me deeply. I don't object.

"I'm sorry I still don't 'get' the allure, although I'd like to be able to for your sake. Don't you know that there are certain subjects best avoided in the interest of polite conversation: politics, religion, sex, and *Star Trek*?"

"And here I've been thinking it was the sex topic that always got me in trouble," he murmurs teasingly. I start to get up, but he tugs at my tunic. "Do you have to go, now, Tess? Stay a little longer, will yiz? Just for a bit. I want to feel ya fall asleep in my arms."

August 15—in the airport

*They make you get to the gate so early for these interna-
tional flights. Good thing I bought a lot of Irish whiskey
fudge at the duty-free shop. Stuffing my face with candy is
a pleasurable way to kill time, but so much for the idea of
saving the fudge for a nosh on the flight.*

*Jamie saw me safely back to Boynton's around one or
two in the morning. We shared more silence than conversation, but we didn't make love; just held each other for a
while. Making love would have opened up the biggest can
of worms at the worst possible time to do so. After admit-
ting that I wasn't able to fully reciprocate his feelings, how
could I possibly give myself to him, and then leave the
country a few hours later? That's pretty rude. And I long
ago outgrew the "If it feels good, do it" philosophy of my
late teens and early twenties.*

Whoops—they're announcing boarding . . .

As I shove my journal into my carry-on I hear the P.A. system announce "Will Mr. James Francis Doyle please report to
gate nine. James Francis Doyle, report to gate nine. Your flight
is boarding."

I hunt for my documents and shoulder my purse, then get on
line with the rest of the passengers bound for JFK. This flight
isn't as crowded as my outbound one; fewer families with children. Hopeful signs for catching some sleep, though I'll arrive
in New York shortly before bedtime in that time zone.

"James Francis Doyle, please report to—"

"I'm here! Hold yer horses, I'm here! I've got a full fifteen
minutes before ya shut the doors."

And I freeze upon hearing the familiar voice, immobilized

until a breathless Jamie, backpack slung over one shoulder, and wheeling a wobbly duffel, reaches my side. He turns to the man standing behind me. "Mind if I cut in? I'm with her."

"Jamie! What the hell are you doing here?"

"Hoping to be able to stay with yiz for a few days before I can find a place of me own. It's crazy sudden, I know, but I'm in love with ya, Tess, and I don't want to spend the rest of my life not doin' anything about it."

I must look totally sandbagged; and as the line snakes through the jetway, he's explaining to me that I won't be living with an alien. By virtue of his birth in New York, he's technically an American citizen although he carries an Irish passport. He's got his birth certificate in his backpack; he's even got a Social Security card. "As soon as her daughter married a man who was Irish born, me ma's ma was a fanatic about making sure her future grandkids would still be Americans. So Niall and I got Social Security numbers when we were still in nappies." Legally able to work, therefore, he assures me, "I won't be a borden atall."

A weeklong, whirlwind fairy tale has swiftly become a stark reality. Sure I could say, "No, you can't stay with me," but that feels cruel. I can relegate him to my living room couch. But *ohh*, what a lot to deal with all of a sudden. On every front. Jamie's appearance leaves me with no breathing room to get over my relationship with David on my own turf, with all the old memories and ghosts of our time together haunting me almost everywhere I go.

Be careful what you wish for, I ruminate dolefully. *In front of witnesses—Imogen and Venus—you said you wanted a chivalrous man to do anything in the world for you, to declare his love for you and swear that he can't live without you. Well, you got him. Now what are you going to do about it?*

Seventeen

 August 23

Jamie has been here a week, with scant progress toward finding his own place to live. Sure he circled the ads in the Village Voice and let his fingers do the walking on the Internet, even checked out a few of the listings, but in this market the early bird gets the worm, and Jamie's apartment hunting efforts could only be described as distinctly lackluster.

Boy, were Venus and Imogen surprised when they asked if I brought back any souvenirs and I introduced them to my temporary roommate. Venus is convinced he'll never move out because "deep down, 'the Empath' knows you don't really want him to do it." Imogen is certain that no man who is so wildly in love (or at least completely infatuated) with a woman that he ditches everything to follow her across the Atlantic just to be with her, is really such a

slob. She thinks it's an act—one he'll clean up in a twin-
kling once I accept his sloppiness as part and parcel of the
otherwise wonderful guy that is Jamie Doyle. "It's like
Beauty needing to tell the Beast she loves him before he can
become the handsome Prince again. Do I know relation-
ships, or do I know relationships?" She also asked me if he
knows anyone who can put together an authentic Irish
band for the bar and bat mitzvahs. If so, she might be able
to convince the twins to agree on a <u>Riverdance</u> theme.

And I'm looking at starting all over again on two fronts.
I've never been in this position before. I haven't a clue
what the current rules of engagement are regarding dating.
Is that what Jamie and I are planning to do? Hard to
"date" the man you're living with, even if you barely know
him. I have no idea how to do that. Not only that, al-
though I'm not sure I'd say I'm still <u>in love</u> with David, I'm
still not over him. It hasn't even been a month, and al-
though meeting Jamie in Dublin provided a highly enjoy-
able distraction, it sort of sucked up my healing time. Now
I'm feeling like I need to set the clock back to where I was
before we met so I can heal alone. That's also hard to do
when there seem to be errant sox everywhere: under the
couch, on the bathroom floor, next to the TV—and I found
one in the toaster oven yesterday. Don't know what that
was about! Not to mention the occasional empty beer bot-
tle, the dishes that found their way to the sink but not into
the dishwasher, take-out cartons on the coffee table, and—
most egregious, of course—the toilet seat left up.

And how am I supposed to focus on front #2—my em-
ployment situation—with all of this clutter around me? I
refuse to clean up his messes. I'm not his maid. And every
time I ask him to pick up after himself, he gets terribly

apologetic, but nothing really changes. I can't deal with it;
it's driving me nuts. I suppose I should be thankful that he
doesn't smoke. I have to begin a job search at forty years
old; I'm as out of the interview loop as I am from the dat-
ing loop. This morning I went downstairs to my home of-
fice to send out another résumé but first had to remove a
slice of cold pizza from atop my printer, where Jamie had
balanced the box.

He's living out of two duffel bags, one of which is the size
of Staten Island, and the only thing he's unpacked is his
collection of Star Trek *videos.*

This past week, every time I've gotten up the gumption
to really confront this Irish Oscar Madison, he'd surprise
me and melt my pissed-off heart by doing something sweet,
like bringing me flowers, or offering to cook dinner.

He has a job interview himself today. Or maybe that
should really read "Himself has a job interview today." I
hope he packed some Irish luck in one of those duffels.

"You are looking at a gainfully employed man!" Jamie announces, as he enters my apartment.

I slide my chair away from the computer and rush over to
give him a hug. "Why do you smell like *horse?*"

"It's better than *fish,* don't you think? I'll be drivin' a carriage through Central Park, just as Liam does in Dublin. Not a
bad way to make a living atall. Work outdoors, meet new people every torty minutes or so—at least that's what I've been
telling meself since none of the pubs I applied to need a bartender at the moment. And apparently I'll need to take some
sort of official test to become licensed to get people drunk before anyone'll offer me the job."

I love his accent. Jamie Doyle could say just about anything to me and it would sound like music. And I love the way his "TH's" disappear sometimes (like "trew" for "through") and his "I's" and "U's" become "O's"—like "torty" or "gorl" instead of "thirty" and "girl" or "torn" instead of "turn."

"Ya think I'm adorable, don't yiz?" he says, reading my mind as he kisses me.

"I do. A pig—but adorable."

He grins. "It's me corse." Taking my hands in his, he asks, "So, how was your day, dear?"

"Well, I have one job offer on the table, though of course I'm expected to perform it pro bono, since it's for family. Imogen asked me to help plan her kids' bar and bat mitzvahs. 'Since you're not doing anything with yourself these days,' she said to me. I'd say, 'Can you believe her nerve?' but if you know Imogen, it's not hard to believe at all. As far as a job I might actually *accept* goes, I'm speaking with some people on Thursday about doing some speechwriting—which may go hand in hand with a bit of image consulting—for New York's junior senator. Soften her image a bit without another Betty Crocker volte-face. Go for that earnest note, instead of the more strident pitch."

"Good luck."

"So much of politics is image. Public perception. Voters need to cast a politician in a role so that they can better understand the package, and the trick is to beat them to it. Cast yourself as a nurturer, for example—a mom, so that when you speak out loudly about an issue, or criticize governmental or institutional failures and those whose presence represents them, or raise a call to action, you're a mother bear protecting her cubs, not a harpie."

"What would you be if you were running for office yourself?"

"What?"

"Oh, I'm sure you've thought about it, Tessa Goldsmith Craig. I, for one, don't think you're a harpie. Nor are you the mother bear. So who are you?" He goes to the fridge for a beer. "Want one? I think we should celebrate my new job." He pours a Guinness into a glass, muttering, "This is a completely different animal from the real thing, ya know. Just for your information. Drinking this in New York instead of a pulled pint in Dublin is like getting a turkey borger when you ordered a porterhouse. You didn't answer my question, Tess."

"I've been thinking about it." I take a sip of his beer and make an icky-face. "Tastes like sweat socks. There's a bottle of crème de cassis in the liquor cabinet: right-hand door, top shelf. This could use a shot."

"My question."

"You can be pushy sometimes, you know? Okay, I'm a *nanny*. That's the role I'd cast myself in. For argument's sake let's accept the model that the government is the parent and the people are its children, each responsible to the other in certain ways—we pay our fair share of taxes—or should—and in return the government takes care of certain things: roads, schools, defense, et cetera. I'm not a mom in real life, so I'm not comfortable shoehorning myself into that parallel. As a servant of the people and as a member of our government, I'm not the mama bear and maybe that wasn't the best analogy for me to have used a minute ago when I was talking about the senator. Being the metaphorical stand-in for a mother or father may give a government representative *too much* authority in certain respects, especially when you start tackling privacy issues. No one wants their mom to have the right to read their diary or for their dad to be able to beat the shit out of them for finding copies of *Playboy* under the bed—especially when the father himself reads the magazine. But as a *nanny*, I'm in loco parentis of the children who are on my watch. I'm the nurturer when it's appropriate and the disciplinarian when it's necessary. And I go home every night after helping to tuck them into bed, safe and warm. Okay, I'm hopping off my soapbox. Let's go out and celebrate your new job. Though in your case, Mister Ed, I think a shower might be in order first."

"Right you are, Mary Poppins!"

Ten minutes later, torso still glistening, hair dripping on my parquet, Jamie pads into the living room, a brown towel tied about his waist. "Didja just call me a talking horse?" he demands.

"It was a joke. I was going for the horse-man thing. Bad analogy. Sorry. Heartily."

"Do I smell any better now?"

" 'Manly, yes, but I like it too.' " I was so embarrassed when he first got here; for an Irishman to discover the brand of soap I happen to use was such a cliché. Actually, Jamie smells like . . . like someone I want to make love with right this minute; clean, yes; but his own scent subtly insinuates itself, delivering a potent dose of sensuality.

And I allow my body, though clothed, to dry his with my heat, pressing myself against him, letting my hands explore his soft, thick hair, his neck and shoulder blades, his strong back, arriving finally on the globes of his ass. "You've got a great butt for a forty-year-old," I murmur, drawing him closer to me, close enough so that I know he's enjoying himself immensely, or immensely enough to inform me that Jamie did not inherit the "Irish curse."

"You do, too," he replies, cupping my tush through my jeans.

"Pilates. Where'd you get yours?"

"Soccer."

"*Ahh*. You know, the point of that game was completely lost on me when the players started wearing longer shorts."

"Now I just lorned something about yiz, Tessa Goldsmith Craig. You're a wolf."

"In chic clothing," I add, confessing my sin. "But what sets female wolves apart from their male counterparts in the pack is that we're turned on by more than the individual elements of a good body. For us, the whole is greater than the sum of its parts."

"You think men who appreciate the finer attributes of a woman's body don't care about her mind, her thoughts and opinions, her wit and wisdom, whether she's going to grab her porse and her house keys so we can head over to our local?"

Chuckling, I shake my head in mock amusement. "Clown."

The Pot o'Gold is a bit down at heel, but it's managed to stay in business for something like sixty years, steadfastly, even stubbornly, holding its ground while all around it, the last couple of decades of gentrification have transformed Amsterdam Avenue from a dicey strip riddled with drug dealers on the local side streets to a homey neighborhood where you can still find the occasional bodega nestled among the restaurants serving buffalo burgers and artisanal jams. Its fans cite its no-frills ambience as proof of authenticity, at least as an Irish-American watering hole. Its detractors call it a dump.

Both camps have a point. The Pot o'Gold is unapologetically unatmospheric, a faded map of Ireland commanding pride of place on a wall the color of tobacco-stained fingers, a relic of the original paint job (probably once a clean and bright shade of cream) performed during the Eisenhower administration, or perhaps even farther back, to the post WWII days of Bill

O'Dwyer's mayoral administration. It's steadily been losing customers, though. The place was hopping, even when I moved into the neighborhood several years ago. But now the clientele seems to consist of the regulars, some of whom start their drinking when the bar opens at 10 A.M., and those who have stumbled in, more or less accidentally, looking for something quaint, or a culturally appropriate place to spend St. Patrick's Day. Lately the owner has tried to prop up business by offering a free-delivery take-out version of their menu. But take-out fish and chips, as I'd reminded David a few weeks ago, just doesn't hold up.

As far as I can tell, Jamie likes this place, having discovered it the day after he arrived—well, on my recommendation, actually. He can sit and enjoy a pint in a pub that hasn't been yuppified to death or turned into a Disney version of an Irish pub. It's not immune from his criticism, though. According to Jamie, the bartender is putting too much of a head on the Guinness and is taking too little time to fill the glass. The fish and chips are pathetically lacking in taste ("These are freeze-dried from some tord-party supplier, not made fresh from scratch; no offense to who's back there, but you've got to have a countryman in the kitchen"). The tartar sauce obviously comes from a jar, the corned beef has been on a steam table all day and is as dry as a mother superior's blankety-blank, and where's the music? Why, he wants to know, does the dusty juke box seem to have been filled by someone who thinks the Pot o'Gold is an Italian restaurant?

Apparently, the bar's critics have more to gripe about than the décor.

"I've got to get me a bartender's certification," Jamie says emphatically, frowning into his beer. "I can't wait a minute longer. Excuse me a moment, my darlin'." I think he's headed to the loo,

but he steps up to the bar, and after a brief exchange punctuated by a hand gesture or two, walks behind it and gives the
hapless bartender (who no doubt considered himself an expert
at his job until now) a lesson in how to pull a proper pint.

He returns to the table measurably satisfied. "That's Will
Fogarty," he says, gesturing with his thumb toward the freckled
bartender. "He's just an actor. No wonder. Nice guy, though.
Pulling pints while he's waiting for his Big Break on Broadway.
He said he'd give my name to his boss, in case he got cast in
something and took a leave of absence. Wanted to know if I
knew an Irish band. Funny, I asked him the same thing. Thinkin'
this place could use some good music. I told him, 'Give me a
few weeks. I'll find one.' "

"You're going on a quest now?"

"Nah. One'll fall into my lap like a blessing from above.
These things just tend to happen to me."

"Cocky!"

"*Honest.*"

A week later, following a number of meetings and the submis-
sion of a handful of character references, I get the call from the
senator's office to board her ship of state.

I debate whether the first order of business should be to es-
cort the woman I plan to restyle as a mama bear on a listening
tour of the zoo.

Eighteen

 September 9

The last three weeks of summer are Manhattan's finest in the year. The air is crisp, the sun as mellow as a Golden Delicious. For me, it's always been a season of renewal and reaffirmation; is it any wonder that it heralds the start of a new year, according to the Jewish calendar? Although Rosh Hashanah doesn't begin for another four days, starting the season early I introduce Jamie to challah with honey, a hallmark of the annual celebration, and he kisses me with sticky lips.

Venus has been right so far. He hasn't even lifted a finger to continue to look for his own place to live, after his initial, and largely feeble, searches. And she was right about my not really wanting him to go, on one level. I had been so eager to live with David, with or without marriage, so my issues about jealously guarding my own space where Jamie was concerned didn't really hold too much water. After the first couple of weeks, he began working every day from dawn past dusk, at which point, if he smelled okay enough not to stop back home to shower and change clothes, he'd phone me from his mobile and ask if I wanted to join him over at the Pot o'Gold—where he'd occasionally volunteer to step in for Will when the actor had an audition to prepare for. Poring over his script, Will would occupy a barstool and "supervise," while Jamie would assume the mixology duties. My own role in this equation is undefined. On the nights I sit at the bar and watch Jamie work, I feel like a groupie of sorts—not a great role for an independent adult woman, especially one who was given the opportunity, by happenstance of an unhappy breakup, to regain her sense of self. For that reason alone, it's probably healthier in every way for me to stay home and work, since there's always something to write or research for the senator. But when I sit home alone with only a bunch of electronics for company I find myself missing Jamie and looking forward to hearing his keys in the door.

That said (or written), I've been thinking about my ex lately. Poor David is <u>still</u> being hammered by the tabloid press, while Bob Dobson has been running an endless stream of commercials with the tag line "If David Weyburn won't even tell us whether he's a straight arrow, what <u>else</u> isn't he telling us?" I'm sure RNC hit-man Len Avariss is the architect of this ugly strategy to keep the story before the voters. Bob Dobson lacks sufficient political experience and connections to pull off a smear campaign of this duration. Only the most powerful machine in the country can fan such a tiny flame into a seemingly endless *and devastating conflagration. By comparison, the Swift Boat debacle was slow-footed. A silly non-incident that at the very least should have stayed local, has become the focus of late night jokes: WaterGayte they're calling it now. Leno and Letterman are using David for cannon fodder. Even Jon Stewart has gotten into the act.*

I've thought about calling David, just to offer my moral support, if nothing else; several times I've had the phone in my hand, only to replace it in the cradle. And there's this, too: shouldn't I mourn a little more before I move on? Is Jamie Rebound Guy despite my best intentions to avoid dubbing him with that dubious honor? Is my passion masquerading as love because I passionately want it to?

I decide to go to the Pot o'Gold as often as I can, and probably more often than I should. In the several evenings I've spent sitting at the bar watching Jamie in action I notice that he has the tremendous capacity to make friends easily. His gregarious nature and loquaciousness, not to mention his charm, are a magnet for men and women alike. And one night in particular, I find myself feeling very jealous when an exceptionally pretty young American woman and her equally gorgeous friend from Ireland spend the entire night talking to him. I hadn't felt this way about him—yet, anyway—so this was something of a revelation delivered uncomfortably, in the form of a psychic sucker punch.

"I wasn't florting with them, ya know," he announces, hours later, on our walk back to my apartment.

"Did I say anything?"

"Your mouth didn't need to. Your eyes did the talking for it."

"I know you weren't flirting. Not on purpose, anyway. You were just being you. And people of all stamps and stripes respond to it on their own individual levels. I'm sure those two young women—like a lot of people you've met there—will stop in to the Pot o'Gold nearly every night from now on, looking for you."

"And if I owned the place, think how much better shape it would be in for that! Do ya know how many people patronize the same pub time after time because they like the bartender? Maybe he's cute. Maybe he listens to their stories, no matter how pathetic or boring. Maybe he pours longer ones than his competitors. The bottom line is that it's all good, as you Americans like to say. All good for the bottom line. Why are we talking about hypothetical financials, Tess?"

"Because it takes us off the uncomfortable topic of my twinges of jealousy. And my dawning acceptance of—" We've been holding hands, and I bring us to a halt under the suffused illumination of a street lamp, a goosenecked metal giraffe. Looking into his eyes I admit, "My dawning acceptance of the idea that I'm falling in love with you. But you're still way ahead of me on this one, so . . . I'm expecting you to catch me when I finally do."

Jamie folds me into his arms and our mouths meet as I press my body into his. It isn't until a passerby, full of twenty-something swagger, shouts "Get a room!" at us, that I realize we've overstayed our welcome in this particular neck of the asphalt jungle.

"Race you home!" I cry, sprinting down Amsterdam. He catches up with me and grabs me about the waist just as I round the corner of Seventy-eighth Street. Breathless, we arrive at my brownstone, laughing as we sink onto the stoop together. Jamie stretches out on the cool steps, extending his arms like a martyr. I lie back against his arm; winning a free neck massage from the pulsing of his heartbeat through his bicep, while at the edge of the curb the leaves of a young tree whisper to its neighbors on the breeze.

"It's gossiping about us," I pant, pointing at the tree.

Jamie's chest rapidly rises and falls. "Have you ever done this before?"

"Have fun in my own city?" I ponder the question, sifting through decades of assorted memories. "Not lately."

"Ahh. It's all a grand adventure, gorl. People tend to forget that. They're too busy trying to *become*, instead of just *being*. If you're tryin' so hard to become something—or someone—you forget what life is all about in the very pursuit of it." He smiles into the sky. "I told you the Irish are born philosophizers. Ever see stars in this part of Manhattan?"

"You mean—?"

"I mean Lyra and Orion, not Regis and Kelly."

I'm ashamed to confess my answer. "I haven't had time?" I say meekly, offering my response as if I wanted him to vet it for validity.

He gives a derisive snort. "Well, there's a couple of them up there pokin' their faces through the pollution, so you should give them some respect and attention for their efforts."

"Did you make a wish?" He nods, still stargazing, and I recite the nursery rhyme in my head before making my own. "Hey there," I say, turning my head until I can see his profile. "Wanna go inside?"

In my living room the air is practically electrostatic. Jamie, perfectly attuned to the slightest nuance, is following my lead. To his credit, though I would have kicked him out on his butt if he'd pushed things, he never has.

I slide onto the couch beside him as he removes his Wallabies. He's the only man I've known since the 1970s who still wears them. It's somehow endearing. This *must* be love. Or something not too far off.

And yet it's hard for me to look him directly in the eye. *My*

God, am I fearing rejection? Instead I tilt my head in the direction of the staircase. "Can I invite you up for a nightcap?"

Rising from the couch, he looks like he wants to carry me up to my bedroom à la Rhett Butler, but the logistics (the steps spiral) preclude such a grand expression of conquest. Instead, Jamie's hands never leave my body as we ascend; grabbing my ass, caressing a thigh . . . and the classic romantic preliminaries (lighting candles, locating CDs to provide just the right level of musical underscoring) fall by the wayside. We don't need props to set the mood; not tonight anyway. We're already on sensory overload just with the knowing that the pleasurable process of learning each other's flesh, scent, taste, the texture of touch-me-there skin, is about to begin, the entry into and exploration of heretofore foreign territory a passionate journey that requires no passport.

There'll be time for taking our time at other times. We both recognize that without the need to mention it.

Tonight isn't about later; it's about now. The lidded pot that has been on the simmer for a few weeks, proximity increasing the temperature of its contents, has come to a boil. Shoes are shucked, jeans are shed and pitched into a corner, tops divested of in short shrift, underwear lands who-knows-where, ablutions are discreetly made, throw pillows tossed, coverlets swept back, lights doused; arms embrace, lips meet each other, hands find hair, teeth shoulders, hungry tongues taste nipples, nibble bellies, brush thighs, tease ecstatic secrets from our deepest recesses, bodies mesh and melt together creating a rhythm both unique and timeless as the room grows more redolent of scent and sensation; sweat gathers into tangy pearls that are drunk or kissed away by cushiony lips engorged with euphoria, heavy-lidded murmurs morph into open-eyed cries, involuntary tears, and breathless smiles.

Mutual satiation is no surprise. And when Jamie finally leaves the landscape of my body and rolls back onto the damp sheets, I turn into his embrace, the rapid rise and fall of my chest expressing the happy dance of my heart.

And suddenly we both start laughing; and if we know why, or whether it's even for the same reason, who can say because neither of us will tell. And Jamie props himself up on one elbow and gazes intently into my eyes.

"I have a question for yiz, Tessa Goldsmith Craig," he says in a tone both earnest and seductive, and I think *uh-oh* because he couldn't possibly be asking me . . .

When he pops it, his grin could illuminate the room. "Are you hungry?"

Nineteen

The following afternoon, still in the rosy throes of afterglow, I'm sitting at my computer in the midst of working on a speech for the senator, when I receive a call from David.

"Tessa, it's me; can you talk now?"

In David's verbal shorthand, this question means (a) are you alone; (b) are you in the middle of something you can't put aside; and (c) I need to speak with you in person. "Are you calling about Dobson's media blitz?" Even Jamie, who suffers from male-pattern remote control issues can't land on a channel without hitting a Dobson commercial. "The 'What would you call an environmental advocate who can't come clean himself?' is a particularly egregious swipe. Where are you? . . . All right . . . I'll see you in half an hour," I say, and end the call. "That was David," I tell Jamie. "He needs to talk to me about something. From the tone of his voice, it sounded pretty important."

Jamie visibly tenses. "And you're goin' to go runnin' off to him?"

"It's not like that, Jamie. This is professional. Purely professional. I was the one who decided not to work for him anymore, remember?"

"Well, it looks like it didn't take much for you to change your mind."

"He's in trouble."

"His timing is shite. Funny how exes are fitted with radar to know when *their* exes have just been rollin' around the sheets for the first time with a new lover."

"Don't do this to me now, Jamie. Please. It wasn't my idea for you to follow me across the Atlantic Ocean." I realize this was the totally wrong thing to say. David's campaign crisis has nothing to do with Jamie's head-over-heels love for me. Jamie is hurting too; I'm caught between two men who, right at this moment, are scared and vulnerable.

"Are ya throwing that in me face, now?"

"I'm sorry I said that. I didn't mean it." I release an exasperated sigh. I'm in over my head right now. And beginning to get tetchy myself. "Jamie, I am going down to David's campaign headquarters, not to his bed. I give you my solemn word on that. For God's sakes, David was the one who dumped *me*— remember? Whatever it is he needs to speak to me about today, I'm sure it's got nothing to do with my body. I'll see you later!"

Within the hour, David and I are sitting behind closed doors at his re-election headquarters.

David is more agitated than I've seen him in some time. "Even with my war chest Dobson's outspending me three to one. And every one of them an attack ad, since he has neither an original idea nor a record of his own to run on."

"I know. It began with him introducing himself to the voters to the rate of two million dollars' worth of TV time a week, but he's certainly progressed past his bio as a former college wide receiver and a bootstraps-tugging CEO."

"It's ugly. Very ugly. Have you seen the polls, Tess?"

"I thought our official position has always been 'We don't pay attention to polls; the only polls that count are the numbers on election night.'"

"Yeah, but our unofficial position is that we dissect the poll numbers like crazy and strategize on how to address them. Tess, I'm only going to say this to *you*. For the first time in my political career, I'm scared I might not win this one. And . . . by the way, you said 'we.'"

"I what?"

"You said 'we.' And 'our'—as in 'our official position' and 'we don't pay attention to polls.' Tess, I'm asking you—for the third time, I guess—to take your old job back. I'm appealing to you not just for my sake, but for the district and the country's future well-being."

A silence settles between us.

"Tess . . . ? What do you say? Third time's a charm, as the saying goes."

"And if I deny you a third time, does that make me a Judas?" I fiddle with the rim of my paper coffee cup. "David, I'll give you advice and counsel—friend-to-friend—but I still don't think it's a good idea for us to work together again. Not now. It's too soon. Besides, I just started a new job. And to be honest with you, I'm not comfortable about jumping her ship to re-board yours."

David releases a horribly deflated sigh. "I understand . . . even though I was hoping you'd see things differently. But I need your consent on something—something it goes against every pore in my body to do." His jaw twitches slightly, one of his physical cues that he's uncomfortable. "Though it violates my privacy and my better judgment, I'm going to call a press conference and cut the albatross loose. Put a stop to 'Watergayte.' I'm going to announce that I'm not gay, and that until recently I had a steady girlfriend."

"Are you asking me if you can divulge my name?"

"It's none of their fucking business."

"But if they push you?"

"I will tell them I had a long-term relationship with a former staffer. Why are you laughing?"

"This isn't a laugh; it's a chuckle. I'm thinking that if you tell them that, you'll never get another moment's sleep until you start dating someone else. Don't you realize that admission will make you America's most eligible bachelor?"

"It's a devil's bargain, I know. And it's killing me that I'm even considering making it. But it may be the ugly price I have to pay to put this all behind me and get on to the business of getting re-elected and saving the world from the Bob Dobsons who like to pretend that the separation of church and state is just a quaintly antiquated suggestion. And there are in fact people in my district who think that prayer in the public schools isn't such a bad thing. After all, in this county the Pledge of Allegiance still contains the words 'under God.' But it's the thin end of the wedge." He leans across the conference table anxiously. "Tess, right now you're the only one I've shared this with."

"You haven't even floated this balloon with Gus?"

"Not yet. I wanted your blessing to 'out' you, if it came to that."

I rest my forehead in my hands. "David . . . *ohh*, David . . . if you recall, I was the one who made that suggestion to you in the first place. Way back in your apartment on the night you . . . chose to put an end to our personal relationship. My God, if it means the media can stop chewing on this months-old bone, then do it! Hold the press conference, and end it by saying that it's time to put this b.s. behind us and stop distracting the voters. Time to put the focus *entirely* on the issues. But you know all that already. While you're at it, challenge Dobson to a series of debates. I'll look forward to watching you mop the TV studio floor with him."

"When I set up a date for the press conference, I'll let you know."

I leave David still sitting in the campaign headquarters conference room, his handsome face a picture of determination and despair.

A couple of days later I meet Cousin Imogen for a cocktail in TriBeCa. She'd driven into Manhattan for an Afternoon Delight with Roger the party planner. "A polo match," she tells me, heaving an enormous sigh. "I'm so relieved the kids finally agreed on something. I swear to God I thought I was going to slit my wrists over this. So the reception after the service is going to be held at the Bridgehampton Polo Club. Let me tell you, Roger had to pull a lot of strings to put all this together at the last minute. I had to make a sizeable donation to their upkeep fund—I mean how much could oats and a handful of horse blankets cost?—pay *triple* to have Tiffany's print the invitations with a one-week turnaround, and we'll have to FedEx all three hundred of them in order to give people enough of a heads-up."

"You're saddling up a passel of thirteen year olds on polo

ponies and sending them out on the field or whatever they call it, with long sticks in their hands?"

"*Mallets.* And yes! Isn't it so Ralph Lauren?!"

I admit that well, yes, I suppose it is, and she insists that I bring Jamie to the bar and bat mitzvah, though I warn her it may come as a bit of a culture shock to him. On the other hand, this wildly over-the-top brand of celebration is alien to *most* normal people, even other Jews.

"Imogen, isn't there any self-awareness in a culture that prides itself on the concept of *tzedakah*—giving charitably to the less fortunate—when you spend as much money on a four-hour party for a group of teenagers as it would cost to send thousands of African children to school, or provide their families with clean drinking water?"

"Save the speeches for your shiksa senator." She shakes her head. "You don't get it, Tess."

"What's not to get?"

"It's . . . this is what our set *does.* You can't *not* do it."

"Well, *I* could. But then again, I'm not in your 'set.' Remember the classic example our parents used to use? If Johnny jumped off the Brooklyn Bridge, would you do it?"

"Well, in our case, we've got a yacht waiting for us in the East River with a giant air mattress on the bow."

Venus arrives, fresh from Jeffrey's, having determined that a coveted pair of thousand-dollar boots will disintegrate on the streets of Manhattan if one wears them often enough to amortize the purchase into affordable bites, and despite the fact that she had planned to perform in them during the Dance for Cancer fund-raiser at Pink Elephant.

She gives me a hug and a kiss before sitting and stowing her purse on the floor between her ankles. Imogen immediately leans over to her and whispers something. They both glance at me, and Venus cups her hand to Imogen's ear and whispers her reply. Then they sit back in their chairs and regard me, grinning like a pair of Cheshire Cats.

"We can tell," Imogen says. "Do I know relationships, or do I know relationships? My radar is impeccable, but I was waiting until Venus got here for confirmation."

"Confirmation of what?" I ask her.

Venus rests her chin in her hands. "You finally did it, didn't you? You must have; your whole face looks different—your complexion, your color. Your posture is even different: you're sitting up straighter. There's the distinct look of the contented about you, T."

"My sex life is not open for discussion, ladies."

"Aha!" exclaims Imogen.

"Since when?" demands Venus. "Clearly I don't need to ask how it was."

"I wouldn't tell you. Not in chapter and verse, anyway. Contrary to outward appearance at this particular moment in time, my life is not an HBO episode."

"Okay, then, share this: do you love Jamie?"

The infusion of carnality into the mix is so new. I can't dissect things and don't want to. Putting our relationship under a microscope . . . right now I don't want to go there with my girlfriends. I analyze enough in my journal, where I confessed to feeling a little guilty about being so happy and satisfied so soon after my breakup with David.

"I haven't told him I do yet." This will have to suffice as an answer.

"Has he said it again to you?" Venus wants to know, after ordering a Cobb salad without dressing. Her willpower perpetually astounds me, arousing my envy as well. I'm such a bacon-cheddar-burger kind of woman that it's a dietary sacrifice to ask the waiter to hold the bacon.

I chuckle. "He tells me he loves me every day. Right before he heads off to feed and water his horse. Did I ever tell you that his carriage horse is a mare named Diesel?"

"And you haven't said it back. *Hmm*," muses Imogen.

"Shades of David," adds Venus. "Maybe *you two* were the perfect couple after all."

I ask her if she's deliberately playing devil's advocate and receive a Mona Lisa smile.

"You do know that despite his daily affirmations, and no matter how much he says he loves you, he won't marry you until his mother dies," she reminds me, disposing of her croutons onto my plate.

" 'A lady's imagination is very rapid: it jumps from admiration to love. From love to matrimony. In a moment,' " I tease.

"Thank you, Miss Austen."

"Only it's *your* imagination doing the leaping here, not mine, V."

"Oh, don't tell me you haven't thought about it," Imogen counters.

"I've already been married."

Imogen looks at Venus. "She's being evasive."

"I definitely have strong feelings for Jamie, but I'm not ready to think about being married to him. Not yet. It's been enough of an adjustment to live with him! And FYI, Imogen, he *didn't* become any less of a slob because we started sleeping together."

"You told her he'd do that?!" Venus is dismayed. She's never been able to stomach Imogen's willingness to be dishonest, even if my cousin lies with good intentions.

"I thought it would help," Imogen says defensively. "Speed things up a little in the romance department. I didn't expect her to believe me. Tessa isn't ordinarily so naïve."

"Then she *must* be in love," Venus concludes.

On my way home I stop to pick up a copy of the late city edition of the *New York Post*. Jamie insists they have the best sports section. Splashed on the front page in 72-point type is the headline: SECOND HEART BREAK FOR WEYBURN.

Switching my cell phone off "vibrate," I discover a plethora of messages from the press requesting a comment from me as his former head speechwriter. Bottom feeders. I return none of their calls.

Panicked, I phone Jamie's mobile first, catching him in the middle of taking a golden anniversary couple from Wisconsin around the lower reaches of Central Park. "Did you read the papers? David had a second heart attack! Did anyone call our apartment before you left for work? Do you know where they took him?"

"Mo cushla, I haven't got the answer to your questions. I do feel guilty as shite though because I got so upset with you for runnin' down to his campaign headquarters like that. Men can get jealous too, y'know? But I was off-base, and I'm sorry about your old . . . boss. Now take three deep breaths and call your friend Gus."

"Right. Of course." I guess I called Jamie first because you always tend to phone your closest loved one in a crisis. I guess that makes him . . .

I speed-dial David's campaign manager. "Gus! Where is he?" I bark into the phone.

"His home-away-from-home, darlin'. St. Luke's. I'm on my way over there now, though I don't know if they'll let us in to see him. I don't know how bad things are. Like the man said, 'All I know is what I read in the papers.' "

"Don't go all Will Rogers on me now, Gus. I'll see you over there."

I run into Gus Trumbo in the depressing CCU waiting room. David is already listed as being in "stable" condition, though he remains confined to the Cardiac Care Unit.

Dr. Gupta doesn't keep us waiting long. "Has Congressman Weyburn been under any additional stress recently?" she asks us.

"Beyond the usual it takes to run for re-election?" Gus snorts.

I place my hand on his arm. "The congressman came to a major decision a couple of days ago. A very difficult one, because it flew in the face of his principles."

"He did?" Gus looks amazed that he hadn't been informed.

"I'm guessing, since you didn't know about it, that David—Congressman Weyburn—was still agonizing over whether or not to go through with it." I tell Gus and the cardiologist about David's press conference plans.

"The newspapers didn't report the whole story," Dr. Gupta tells us. "Because they didn't know it. We had to perform by-pass surgery."

I can actually feel the blood draining from my face. Gus and I exchange anxious glances. His lower lip is trembling.

"I spoke with the congressman before he went into surgery," says the doctor. "I explained to him that his age can make for an even better recovery . . . but that *recovery* is a ways off. These things take time. When we . . . I am speaking about the medical community . . . see such a relatively young man with such a condition, it presents a red flag, so to speak. The congressman will have to take it easy for several months in order for a full recovery to take place."

"What are you really saying here?" I ask Dr. Gupta.

"I am saying, as Congressman Weyburn's doctor, that it is not in the best interests of his health to continue to pursue this re-election campaign."

"It'll kill him to withdraw," Gus replies angrily.

"I think what Dr. Gupta is trying to tell us is that it could kill David if he *doesn't*."

"Our best hope for the future health of the country brought down by a crock of bullshit," Gus says, crushing his baseball cap between his hands.

"It's a damn national tragedy is what it is," I lament. Referring to Len Avariss and his cronies, I add, "Those bastards are evil. I wonder how they sleep at night." I sink onto one of the leatherette couches and let the tears flow.

"They don't, sugar. They prowl about the country by moonlight in search of *genuine* red-blooded Americans to feed upon, for only by sucking out another's life force can they sustain themselves; and even then it's merely a temporary victory. They must continually replenish their conscience in order to appear by day to have a shred of humanity."

Hours later, we gather around David's bedside while Dr. Gupta delivers her verdict. David is crushed. In fact, he looks very much like he wants to cry. But there he is, once again hooked up to beeping, blinking monitors and stuffed with tubes.

"You fought the good fight, big guy," Gus murmurs. "But I think the doc makes a good point. And fuck-it-all, I think you've got to go along with it."

"Do it, Gus," David says evenly. "Release a statement. You know the drill."

I feel like I'm attending a funeral for the living. There's a long silence between us. My heart is breaking: for David, for his constituents, for the country. "What will you do now?" I ask him.

"Except for the facts that I need to heal and that Congress is in session, I'd love to disappear for a while. Drop off the planet and go someplace where no one will find me. Tasmania. Mars. My mother's condo in Boca." He asks for a moment or two alone with me. "Call me when you want to, Tess. I've missed hearing your voice."

I was miserable over his condition, but now I feel even worse. Wiping away a tear I whisper, "I still love you, pal," into his ear.

On the way home I start to ponder whether it's the same kind of love as I'm beginning to feel for Jamie, or whether it's another variety altogether, the kind where nostalgia and an abiding affection create a special chamber in the heart for someone. And although you may never actually visit that place, you've accorded them a permanent rent-controlled lease. In New York real estate terms, it means they're never going to move out.

"I'm sorry about David," Jamie says, leaning down to give me a kiss as he attempts to catch a head of lettuce before it rolls off the kitchen counter. "He seemed like a politician with some integrity for a change."

"I'm glad to hear you approve of my taste in men!"

"What would it say about me if I didn't?" When he's not working late Jamie's taken to making dinner. Getting me to eat more greens and cooking a lot of fish. The man certainly knows his fish, even when it's not beer-battered and deep fried. As he's apparently never met a pan or a pot or a dish he likes to wash, by default this task has fallen to me in the equitable distribution of labor. How arduous is it to put something into the dishwasher? Of course, *I* never liked doing dishes either.

The nightly local newscasts all lead with the story of David's departure from the campaign, his bid to win a third term tanked by his second heart attack and subsequent bypass surgery. Reporters then trot out the specter of "WaterGayte" and David's subsequent inability to make the rumors disappear in a steadfast decision to stick to the real issues as another determining factor in his decision to withdraw from the race.

"At this point, we have no idea who the Democrats will tap to replace this favorite son of New York," Suki Glassman smirks. "But they don't have much time. With the November election only six weeks away, they'll have to scramble to find someone who can capture the voters' hearts, especially in the district that boasts the highest number of dog runs in the city, with a Republican challenger who is a household name in the pet care industry and has limitless financial resources and the backing of the entire party machine behind him. Mr. Dobson has also floated his 'faith-based balloon' as he terms it, calling for the more active participation in the community of churches and synagogues as a way of steering young people at risk onto a straighter moral path, as well as alleviating the already strained government coffers from bearing the lion's share of the financial burden.

"But there are other issues at hand," reports Suki. "Dobson promises to pressure the Mayor to rescind the Pooper Scooper laws and lift the restrictions on city parks that limit the areas open to the free expression of our animal friends. Bob Dobson's PAW—Pets Are Worth it—proposals would seek to roll back what he calls 'the burdensome restraints placed on the personal freedoms of pet lovers that compel them to always travel with a purse full of plastic bags, and be forced to choose which outdoor spaces to frequent for their recreation.' "

They go to some footage of a recent Dobson press conference. "The current laws infringe on Constitutional liberties, and as soon as I find out exactly which those are, I'll be . . . I'll be holding another press conference."

Enough. Enough to give me a raging headache. I might as well have steam coming out of my ears. Outraged by the circumstances, both pervasive and specific, that drove David back to the operating table and forced him to withdraw his reelection bid, I feel a rant coming on. "You're a bastard, Bob Dobson! A natural disaster in human form. You, Len Avariss, and your rich, tin-eared cronies who live to destroy things instead of build them—unless it's your own corporations getting the no-bid contracts! How can Americans have any faith in their leaders when they've so betrayed our trust? And the media ought to be ashamed of themselves. TV, newspapers—the Fourth Estate is riddled with termites. What would Edward R. Murrow have to say if he saw the short shrift given to journalistic integrity in this day and age! TV news directors want to grab ratings; newspaper editors try to compete with them for everyone's precious time. No one has time for substance. That's considered stodgy. Old hat. What does it say about our society when the most honest news reporting is presented on a comedy show? You cite facts, you're at best a wonk and at worst a bore."

Jamie grins broadly. "Well, well, Tessa Goldsmith Craig. You've got an Irish temper after all!"

"I hope the Dems can come up with someone viable pretty soon. Someone's got to make sure this moron doesn't get a ticket to Capitol Hill." I switch off the TV and head into the bathroom to down a couple of aspirin. Although I feel like my head is going to explode, it also feels good to let it all out. My parents, many of my friends (Venus excepted), and just about all of my former beaux (including David), were always embarrassed every time I raised my voice, expressed an angry thought in a sudden outburst, or became "too passionate" about something. It made them palpably uncomfortable, so I learned to modify my behavior and put a cork in it as soon as my naturally outspoken nature began to bubble back to the surface. Whether he's amused or impressed by my outburst, I'm unsure; but Jamie's acceptance of who I am, even when I'm not putting a very good face on it, or being my best self, goes a long way.

And then . . . I have an epiphany.

I hunt down my address book (finding it on my desk, obscured by a back issue of *Rugby World*) and flip the pages. Not finding the number I want, I dial information and request the number for the Midtown Manhattan Reform Democratic Club.

"Is that the downstairs buzzer? I'm on the phone," I call out to Jamie. "Can you get it?"

"Shite!" I hear something clatter in the kitchen. "Hold yer horses a minute!" he shouts at the intrusion.

I bring the phone into the bathroom for a bit of peace and quiet. Jamie is shouting into the intercom. "Who is it? Who? What??! All I can hear is static through this feckin' thing."

"Hello? Joe Williams, please. It's Tessa Craig." I wait until Joe picks up on his end. "Joe. Tessa. I'm your woman. . . . What? . . . You know exactly what I mean. Don't throw your support anywhere else until we've talked. . . . I'll meet you and your people tomorrow morning and we'll discuss it. . . . Nine A.M. . . . *I'll* bring the coffee. Hey Jamie!" I shout, covering the receiver with the palm of my hand. "I'm going to run for David's congressional seat. Not only that, I'm going to crush the bastards who sent him back to the hospital!"

I expect to see his face light up, but Jamie's stricken look doesn't alter. "What? What's up?"

He points accusingly at the intercom. "Me mother is on her way upstairs."

My stomach does a free fall. Stunned, I return to my phone call. "Joe? Lemme call you back in a few. Something's just come up. Literally."

Twenty

As my apartment comprises the top two floors of a narrow brownstone, it will take Maureen Doyle another minute or so to ascend the three flights to my landing. "Did you know she was coming to New York?" I ask Jamie, who, by his expression, clearly didn't. No wonder he'd never bothered to mention it.

She knocks emphatically, failing to locate the doorbell, I suppose. After taking a deep breath Jamie opens the door, and there's his mother trying not to appear winded. Hanging back by the staircase is a striking young brunette, her prettiness obscured by her dowdy denim skirt and oversized Trinity sweatshirt. I realize it's his kid sister Brigid. Each of them has a suitcase of powder blue molded plastic, circa 1973.

"Well. Aren't ya going to invite me in?"

"Of course. I'm sorry," I apologize, disoriented by her surprise appearance, particularly as my brain is still focused on my phone call to Joe Williams at the Democratic Club.

Maureen motions to Brigid, who follows her like an obedient duckling into the apartment.

"I got your e-mails," Maureen tells her son. "Lemme look atcha. Brigid, does Jamie look happy to you?"

Brigid regards her brother. "He does, Ma."

"That's what I was worried about."

Brigid gives Jamie a hug, saying, "I told her we shouldn't come."

"Why'd she spring you from the community house?"

"The application of additional guilt. She's had me saying novenas and Hail Marys ever since you left, but then she figured that bringing a nunlet along with her was as close as she would get to convincing you that God is on her side." Brigid gives me a hug. "I'm so sorry about all this. It wasn't my idea y'know." She lowers her voice to a whisper. "Will you show me all the places from *Sex and the City?* I watched it like a fiend back when I was in college. Just once in my life I want to try on a pair of Manolos. Then, God forgive me, I can die happy."

"That doesn't sound very spiritual to me."

"I told you that night at dinner, I'm on a journey. I'm not even so sure I want to arrive at the original destination. And I'm only twenty-three, so I don't want to make a terrible mistake I'll regret for the rest of me life. But don't tell Ma or she'll have a heart attack."

"Where are you staying then?" Jamie asks his mother and sister. They exchange glances. "Didn't book a hotel, did yiz?" He shakes his head in disbelief and looks to me in consternation.

"I have another bedroom, but I use it as an office. The living room sofa's a convertible, though. You're both welcome to share it. How long are you planning on staying?" I ask Maureen, an echo of her double-edged question to me back in Dublin.

"Until they find a hotel room, right Ma?" Jamie says. "Forst thing tomorrow we'll make some phone calls."

My experience thus far of Doyles who make sudden travel plans is that "until they find a place of their own" soon becomes relatively permanent. And the timing couldn't be worse for a pair of unexpected (and somewhat unwelcome) houseguests. Having my new lover's disapproving mother and Sister-in-training sister under the same roof will quite obviously cramp our blossoming romance—plus I placed a phone call not five minutes ago that could change my life as of tomorrow morning.

"I suppose you just assumed you could take advantage of Tessa's good nature," Jamie says to his mother, as Brigid volunteers to help me make a pot of coffee. Not that I need help, but she's keen to disassociate herself from her mother's venture. "It's called freeloading, Ma."

"You're one to know about taking advantage," she argues. "I'll tell you all the upheaval your little holiday has caused this family. Niall's taken up your fishing, Liam's behind the bar, and your father—a man who worked all his life to put food on the table and clothes on his children's backs, and who had finally begun to enjoy the fruits of retirement, is driving Liam's carriage. He don't even like horses, but at least he knows the hack business like the back of his hand, and ya can't expect a teetotaler to tend bar, standing on his feet for hours on end as though he's a man of forty-two. To answer your question, Tessa, we're not planning to stay long; we're here to fetch my second son and bring him back home before his family business goes to ruin. Jamie, your father and I agreed that we'd buy your return ticket. I hate to put something on credit, but—"

"Desperate times call for desperate measures?" Jamie retorts.

Jamie's an adult; I'm going to stay out of it and let him fight his own battles. Somewhere along the line I learned the life lesson that a woman should never come between a man and his mother, because if she interferes it'll come back to bite her in the butt one day. If you want to keep him, keep your own counsel when it comes to the woman who labored to bring him into the world, no matter how much *he* may disparage her on any given day.

I serve the coffee with a tray of store-bought cookies, about which Maureen works hard not to express her negative opinion. "If I knew you were coming, I'd have baked a cake," I tell her, my words coated with placid sweetness. She may be a formidable opponent, having guilt and DNA on her side, but she's not a terribly clever adversary, having shown her hand immediately. However, my mother used to say, "You catch more flies with honey than you do with vinegar," and it doesn't serve anyone for me to be nasty. Funny how a few weeks ago I was sure that I didn't want Jamie to enter my life and intrude upon my space; and now, minute by minute in fact, I'm becoming surer that I don't want him to leave.

"The last meal you two probably ate was airline food I'll bet. Why don't we all go out and get something more substantive to eat?"

Maureen checks her watch. "Ten-thirty is getting late for me. Especially as my body clock is on Irish time. Thank you for asking, but I think I'd like to get unpacked and get some sleep."

"I'll go!" volunteers Brigid. "I'm starved." This has the immediate effect of changing her mother's mind, as Maureen is not about to permit a "nunlet" to spend any time alone with her wayward son and his faith-less (in her view) lady friend.

Naturally, we bring Brigid and Maureen to the Pot o'Gold, where everybody knows our names and Jamie's greeted as if he were a rock star. As if to prove his point that a pub, and not a fishing trawler, is his natural habitat, he takes a turn behind the bar after we finish our meal and the tips come pouring in amid the spirited banter. I'm incredibly grateful that this evening the bar is devoid of overly flirtatious women bellying up to the bar in their belly tees.

I notice that Brigid, nursing a whiskey, is clearly impressed with her big brother's popularity. With her short, tousled jet black hair and porcelain complexion, she could easily be taken for any one of the secular twenty-somethings here tonight. Watching Maureen take it all in I wonder if she's thinking back to her own New York City youth. The Pot o'Gold could just as well be any Irish bar in Inwood during the 1950s and '60s.

After I meet with Joe Williams at the Midtown Manhattan Democratic Club first thing in the morning, my life may suddenly become incredibly busy, but I think it's the better part of valor to extend every possible courtesy to Jamie's mother, not from any raging desire to get on her good side (understanding this may never be possible), but because I very much want to be a good hostess. "Is there anything you'd like to see while you're in New York City? Any place you're keen on visiting? I'll be happy to show you what we've done with the place in your absence."

"Oh, God, yes!" exclaims Brigid. "First I want to see St. Patrick's Cathedral. Then I want to go to Au Bar and Jeffrey's. I'll love yiz forever if you show me where Sarah Jessica Parker drinks and shops in real life."

Maureen shoots her daughter a dirty look. "You shouldn't be caring about such things."

"*Ohh*, Ma. I take my discernment very seriously, but it's not like I'm a *Francisan*. How can I know what it is I'll be givin' up if I don't know what it is I'll be givin' up?!"

Now, this kid would make a great politician!

"And I'll never have another chance like this again!" Brigid insists.

"To tell ya the truth, I wouldn't mind hopping the subway to the old neighborhood," Maureen says. "But then again, I hear it's changed a lot. I'd probably be disappointed. All my old haunts have probably become bodegas or Starbucks. 'You can never go home again,' they say."

What a downer.

"I brought you a present, Tessa," Maureen tells me, unsnapping her suitcase and removing a parcel carefully swathed in tissue paper and bubble wrap. She unspools the layers herself, revealing one of her born-again dolls, a sandy-haired little boy with sleepy eyes, his tiny thumb shoved into his rosebud of a mouth. Placing the doll in my arms she tells me, "His name's Sean, but-cha can change it if you want."

"Thank you, Maureen. This is very . . . generous."

"Hold him for a while," she suggests. "Makes you realize what's really important in life."

No doubt about it, her craftsmanship is astonishing, but I'm not entirely sure what message she's trying to deliver. A shot of adrenaline to my maternal instincts? A tacit offer to trade one boy for another?

"There's something I don't get," I murmur, as Jamie and I snuggle that night. "Here we are, two forty-year-olds who are too freaked out to have sex while his mother is on the premises, even if she's sleeping one floor below us and we're behind a closed door. This is a situation we have both determined cannot be permitted to last indefinitely. Of course there's also a virgin under the roof—at least as far as I surmise—and not only that, she's a nun-in-training. Between the two of them, Maureen and Brigid, we've got built-in birth control.

"What don't you get?" whispers Jamie.

"Your mother's obvious disapproval of me despite her own personal romantic history. Here she is, an American who married an Irishman herself. Is it because I'm Jewish? Or because I'm nonpracticing, so not attending religious services regularly is even worse than being another religion entirely?"

"Ya know, you Americans have a way of torning everything around so that it's always all about *you*. It's one of your national corses which has become individual habit. The reason my mother disapproves of our relationship has everything to do with *me*. Not you."

"Care to elaborate?"

"No, I *don't* care to," he replies, hugging me tighter. "Because you won't believe me. So I want you to ask her yourself. You'll see I'm right. Bet you a milkshake."

"Why a milkshake?" I giggle. "Oh, please don't tickle me, Jamie; I'm one of those people who can't stand it."

"Why a milkshake? Because you've had a craving for a chocolate milkshake for a week now, but like all you American women you're always watching your weight so you don't dare splurge, even if it's for a little nothing that will make yiz happy. So *I'm* buyin' you that chocolate shake. By winning our bet. And ya know something else? I'll think you're just as sexy even when you've ingested another five hundred calories. I might even be tempted to fancy you just as much with another *thousand* in your belly."

"What might persuade you to arrive at that conclusion?" I tease, allowing my fingers to play across the planes of his chest.

He places his hand on mine and slides it in a southerly direction. "Touch me there," he murmurs. "A lot."

Twenty-one

"Obviously, we're racing against time here. We need to collect enough petition signatures to get someone on the ballot in November. So are you in or out? Are you ready to support my candidacy?"

Feeling a bit like Joan of Arc, this is what I tell Joe and a handful of the other local kingmakers over cups of diner coffee and a plate of Stella d'Oro cookies in the back room of a theatre district storefront.

"I've always believed passionately in making the world a better, safer place, and standing up and fighting for genuine educational and economic opportunities. Come to think of it, who would say they *didn't* feel the same way? But I've always helped achieve those visions from behind the scenes. I'll level with you guys. Until David had his second heart attack, I've never actually pictured myself doing it front and center. But now I feel I can't *not* pick up the banner." Pointing to myself, I say, "You're looking at his legacy in terms of his ideology, but without the baggage. Look," I add, reaching for a cookie, "Dobson is already trying to hone in on David's key constituency. Have you seen his POOP commercial? He's standing down at Pier 90 talking about how when he gets elected he'll sponsor a bill he calls the Port Operations Oversight Procedure. I'm certain he intends for the voters to confuse it with David's CACA—Cruise Ship Accountability and Culpability Act— legislation and think it's the same thing. It's a typical Republican ploy to name bills after exactly what they're *not*—like their Clear Skies bill actually allows for continued pollution. His Port Operations Oversight Procedure calls for no oversight whatsoever! It's a continued free pass for the cruise line industry. But voters will never learn that, unless they phone his headquarters or log on to his web site to request a copy of the white paper. POOP stinks!"

Wilfredo Figueroa scrutinizes me with a gimlet eye. "Tessa, there are two factors involved in our decision-making process. One: we need somebody who's *keyed up* about running for Congress. We need someone with ambition. With a fire in their belly. Obviously, you fill those criteria."

"All of which is fine, but which brings us to factor number two," adds Tamika Roberts. "We need someone who can win."

They cover all the bases in my résumé—Ivy League degree, former mayoral staffer, blue ribbon panelist on the city's Committee on Diversity, speechwriter; and they thoroughly grill me about my positions on everything from abortion to zero-tolerance policies. We word-test several scenarios, to see how a Tessa Craig candidacy might be perceived by the voters:

- I've never run for office, which makes me an outsider (then again so is Bob Dobson, and that's the main plank of his political platform); yet I've been a political insider for decades, which could lead to the charge of being a hack.

- I've been one of the policy architects of David Weyburn's platform and he's beloved in this district—or was, before the voters were deliberately distracted. Will my ties to David help or hurt a Tessa Craig campaign and how do we counterpunch if it's the latter?

The interview process gets my political juices revved up even more. "By the way, I'll disclose that you came highly recommended," Joe Williams tells me, plundering the two remaining cookies as our meeting winds down. "About a half hour after our conversation last night, I received a phone call from your former boss. He was calling from his hospital bed. Congressman Weyburn said yours was the first name that sprang to mind when it came to tapping a replacement to run for his seat. And I have to say that he didn't sound surprised when I told him we'd already spoken. I'm probably not talking out of school to say that he spoke very highly of you, not just as someone who really knows the drill on Capitol Hill, but as a person. He had a lot of good things to say about your commitment to public service, your compassion for others, your intelligence and diligence, and what he mentioned as most important to him, your integrity. Of course you don't see enough of that nowadays. Especially among politicians."

I feel a lump rise in my throat when I tell them that for me these qualities feel as natural as breathing. "It's not hard to stand up for what's right when you've been inspired by the best hope for a better day that this country has seen in years. And, now, if you'll excuse me, I have to go to church."

Joe gives me a very strange look. "Isn't today *Rosh Hashanah?*"
Whoops.

Well, if there is a Judeo-Christian God who is allegedly omnipresent, He/She/It is just as likely to be in St. Pat's as anywhere else.

I meet Maureen and Brigid on the steps of St. Patrick's Cathedral. At this time of day, there aren't too many people visiting this vast neo-Gothic monument to Catholicism. In the low light the handfuls of tourists move in pairs and clusters amid the faint aroma of frankincense, speaking in hushed tones in a half dozen languages. The Germans, Japanese, French, and Russians, and the occasional midtown office worker on her lunch hour stop to light a candle or simply to slide into one of the long wooden pews and gaze upon the majesty of the apse as they meditate, cogitate, even pray in its most recognizable form: knees bent, head bowed, hands clasped.

Maureen and Brigid had dipped their fingers in the font and blessed themselves as soon as they set foot inside the cathedral. Facing the altar, they genuflect and cross themselves again before the three of us take a pew about two-thirds of the way up the nave, where the light is more golden, the enormity of the edifice a bit more manageable to a supplicant so dwarfed by the height of the sanctuary. As they begin to pray, I sit quietly, respectfully, but taking silent bets on what Maureen Doyle just asked for from her Lord.

"According to Merriam-Webster's, the word *catholic*, when used as an adjective, means 'comprehensive, universal, broad in sympathies, tastes, or interests.' Why did you *really* come all the way to New York?" I whisper to her, anxious to learn whether the root of her displeasure is the disapproval of the Jewish-American lady friend, or whether Jamie was right last

night when he assured me it had almost everything to do with
him.

"Jamie has a very big heart, Tessa, as I'm certain you've realized by now. Big enough to always have room for his family.
The Doyles are very big on family and we have ways of doing
things that have endured for generations. The way we see it,
Jamie's disturbed the natural order of things by jilting his responsibilities and jumping on a plane. When Jamie sent us an
e-mail to say how happy he was in New York, with no word
about when he was planning to return, we held a family meeting and determined that I should come over and fetch him before Blackpools goes to hell in a handbasket."

She tilts her head to cast me a sideways glance. "I know what
you're about to say—I can read it in your face. 'Jamie's an adult,
a middle-aged man even, if you will, he has free will to make
his own decisions and I'm an ogre for acting like you're taking
him away from his family.' Which you are, Tessa. Your life is
here and my son followed you home. And I'm sure you're about
to insist that you didn't make him do anything he didn't want
to do. He thinks the sun rises and sets in you, ya know? I
haven't seen enough of you yet to know why."

As I suppress a smile, Maureen adds, "Which still doesn't
change the fact that he up and bolted on the family business
like a spoiled child and left us scrambling to rearrange all the
pieces. When you're a Doyle, no matter how old you are, family
comes first."

It's a bad idea to get into a debate, so I hold my tongue, and
remembering my grandmother's advice, leave it to Jamie to
have it out with his ma.

"Don't look at *me*," Brigid says, clasping my arm as we leave
St. Pat's. "I was just trilled to get a free trip to New York! Do
you think we could go to a Sephora store now?"

Maureen clucks her disapproval. "Nuns don't need lipstick and mascara."

"But I'm not a nun yet. I won't be for years," she argues. "Besides, where in the Bible does it say you can't wear cosmetics?"

This kid cracks me up. "You might have a future as a constitutional scholar if you change your mind about taking the veil, Brigid." Come to think if it, if she put her mind to studying Talmud, she'd give some of those old rabbis a real run for their money.

"I'll make yiz a deal," Brigid says to her mother. "I'll go to church every day we're here if we can go to Sephora. Is there one near where you live, Tessa? A Catholic church, I mean?"

I tell her that the Holy Trinity Catholic Church is on West Eighty-second Street, just three blocks as the crow flies from another New York City landmark: Zabar's. You gotta love the multiculturalism of the Upper West Side. David Weyburn's constituents. Could be my constituents. Oh, God. That's huge. I wonder if it would be okay for a non-religious Jewish woman to dash back into St. Patrick's on Rosh Hashanah and ask God for a bit of guidance.

Returning to my apartment after a very long afternoon of sightseeing (having learned from the Visitors' Center in Times Square that there's a *Sex and the City* locations bus tour), I find a thick envelope addressed to Jamie from a company in Dublin called Glavelock. I stash it in my purse in case his mother is trying to read anything over my shoulder. He's at my computer, a pile of paper that wasn't there this morning, resting by his elbow.

"Welcome back!" He rises and greets me with a soft kiss. "How did yiz enjoy Manhattan then?" he asks his family. Before they have the chance to reply, he demands to know how my meeting went with the politicos, as he calls them.

"I have mixed feelings," I sigh. "On the one hand, I hate to be the candidate of a political machine—I mean we literally met in the back room! On the other hand, I need them. Which is why I wanted to approach them before they had the chance to reach out to anyone else. If I'm going to run for David's seat I need the manpower that the Democratic Club members are in a position to muster, in order to get on the ballot and fight the good fight against Bob Dobson."

Jamie appears to be surfing the net while I'm talking, typing and scanning the screen, so I shut up until he assures me he's still listening. "You said 'fight the good fight against Bob Dobson.'"

"In 1928, presidential candidate Herbert Hoover promised a chicken in every pot and a car in every garage. He won. Then came the depression and his empty rhetoric was no more effective than spitting into the ocean. What can Bob Dobson promise that he's capable of delivering? A hound in every household and free kitty litter for all? I love dogs too, but c'mon! Someone's got to uphold David's political legacy and then some. Tackle the issues he hadn't yet fully addressed. Otherwise, we've got . . . well, we've got Dobson. The man who believes in liberty and justice for those who agree with his agenda, and to hell with the rest of us."

The printer begins to whirr and hum. "Well, I hope they gave you their backing and their blessing because the clock is ticking here."

"What are you talking about?"

Jamie grabs the sheet of paper shooting out of the printer and dramatically gives his arms a quick shake as though he's shrugging up his shirtsleeves to get down to work on something. He picks up a pen. "If you're running for Congress, I've only got a couple of weeks left to file this registration form."

"At the risk of sounding like a broken record, what are you talking about?"

"What do ya think I'm talking about, m'darling? In seventy-two more hours, I'll have been living here for thirty days. I'll be eligible to vote!"

His mother blanches as I suppress a smile. I suppose that means he's got no immediate plans to go home after all.

"You got some mail today," I tell him during our first chance to be alone all day. I take the fat envelope out of my purse and hand it to him. "Who or what is Glavelock?"

Jamie opens the envelope with all the eagerness of a kid on Christmas morning. "A realtor." He thumbs through the documents. "I contacted them to put my flat on the market."

"You . . . ?"

"Oh, brilliant!" he exclaims. "Torns out Niall can represent me at the closing with a Power of Attorney. All I do is sign the form they sent me. Do ya know a notary public?"

"*You* do!" I smile.

"You're a notary?"

"Yes—you're selling your apartment?"

"Yes!"

"This is a *huge* decision, Jamie. I mean . . . have you really thought this through?"

He nods and grins, slipping his arm around my shoulder. "So I'd be grateful—and make it very much worth your while—if you'd look over these papers and notarize my signature. I'll overnight it back to them tomorrow."

"Are you doing this for me? Because such a big step—"

"There ya go again, my American darling. Always thinking it's got to be about *you*." Jamie laughs. "I think I'm old enough to

make my own life-decisions, Tess. I may be a huge fan of spontaneity, but I don't do things quite as lightly as you might imagine. Like selling my home, even if I've received an offer for well
over half a million euro."

"You've—!?"

"If you're goin' to be this articulate during your debates, Bob
Dobson might actually win, ya know." I try to digest this information and all its implications. "You think I'm moving too fast,
don't yiz?" I'm sure he sees me blush and knows he's right
again, the Empath! "Don't worry, I'm not asking you to marry
me yet."

Yet. Hmm.

"But I will ask ya to do me a favor. Keep this under yer hat. I
don't want me Ma, or even Brigid, lorning about this just yet."
He shoves the papers back into the envelope and covetously
slides it under his pillow. "There'll be time enough for that. I
want to get all me ducks in a row forst."

The next day, after notarizing Jamie's signature on the Power
of Attorney, I meet with Gus Trumbo. What does he think of
the idea of my running for the seat?

"A no-brainer, sweetheart."

And how to go on the offensive with Dobson's crowd?

"Don't worry about the double-edged sword with the Washington insider/outsider thing. We can play that card to win. You
know enough about the game to be able to get something done
down there. But Len Avariss and the Dobson campaign can't
touch you on the fact that you lack experience by virtue of
never having held political office, because Dobson may have
more money than God, but he pitches kitty litter for a living.
Tessa Craig will be a fresh face, if that's what voters are looking

for, but it's a face that lawmakers—well, close to half of them, anyway—already recognize and respect."

And the willingness of David's devoted and hardworking reelection campaign staff to work for me?

"Number one, they know you and like you; number two, don't give it a second thought because all they know about your personal life was that you were David's head speechwriter; and number three, as of two days ago they all need a job, even the volunteers. Especially the volunteers. Look at Mrs. Schnipkin. A woman who used to be a union organizer and now lives in an assisted living home. She'd waste away from loneliness if she had no place to go. You'll be giving an old lady—and all her friends—their best reason to get up in the morning. These women need to be needed. They're eager to work. And they love you; you're like a granddaughter to them. They'd do anything for you. Even try to fix you up with their grandsons. Listen, between you and me and the lamppost they all wondered when that wonderful Mr. Weyburn was at least going to ask you out for a drink. They thought you'd be the perfect couple."

"Yeah, so did *I* at one point. At one point that lasted three years. So does this mean you'll manage my campaign?"

"I'm so *on board*, woman, I'm already wearing my deck shoes." We shake hands and then Gus gives me a huge bear hug. "I suggest you go to bed early tonight because it's the last sleep you'll get until after Election Day."

Note to self: try very hard not to mention to Mrs. Schnipkin and her friends that I am currently involved with an Irish Catholic until after the first week in November.

Twenty-two

 September 15

Gus Trumbo's a true Georgia peach; he's already mapped out a strategy, given my campaign staff their marching orders, and mobilized the volunteers, who will hit the streets first thing Monday morning with the sea-green nominating petitions. They'll stake out key locations from subway stations to cinemas, scoping out registered Democrats in the district who have nothing against my being on the November ballot. There are a handful of fringe party candidates running as well, but the real horserace is between Bob Dobson and me. Gus felt that we shouldn't hire a separate press secretary or spokesperson; he thought it made better sense to handle those duties himself. Fewer links in the chain of command. Positioning me (like David) as a Progressive Pragmatist (the most fitting descriptive for a social liberal who is a fiscal realist), we hammered *out our talking points on the key issues facing my future constituents:*

- *Because Manhattan unfortunately remains a terrorist's bull's-eye, we must make sure that there are security measures in place to protect our ports and our mass transit and ensure that they are state-of-the-art and financed through a common-sense system of funding;*

- *Civil rights and right-to-privacy protections (keeping a sanctimonious government out of our bedrooms and our sickrooms), insisting that the Constitutionally mandated separation of church and state be vigilantly and rigorously maintained; and*

- *Education. Even with a lot of kids in private school in the well-heeled neighborhoods of this district, there are also tens of thousands of public schoolchildren in over-crowded facilities—kids who don't have nearly enough school supplies, textbooks, or an outdoor space for recess and gym classes, let alone enough truly qualified and passionate teachers.*

Did I mention that I turned down Venus's offer to host a fund-raiser for me? She was ready to call in her markers with a few former colleagues, and her name, even after years of retirement, is still legendary in her corner of the world; but after "WaterGayte," the last thing I need is for the press to jump on Tessa Craig's fund-raising party at a strip club. I told Venus about Maureen Doyle's surprise visit and what an expert she seems to be at laying guilt trips. As busy as I've been, I've made a point of reaching out to Maureen, trying very hard not to see her as the enemy. Poor confused Brigid seems to be embarrassed by her mother. I have to say, I can't see this young woman as a nun. She seems so secular. She has a curiosity and an energy not unlike Jamie's, which makes me conclude, though admittedly I scarcely know her, that Brigid in a convent would be like Jamie in the army, places where joie de vivre and spontaneity are anathema to the system.

Venus reminded me to just be myself, echoing Jamie's comment that Maureen's behavior has everything to do with her son and next to nothing to do with me. That said, I realize that "myself" loves to play host in my hometown, even if taking time to do it is the last thing I need. I'm very house-proud. And in this case, since Jamie showed me in and around Dublin for a week, the least I can do is reciprocate for his family.

But when are they going to leave?

Jamie will be accompanying me—at Imogen's command, more or less—to Emily and Jacob's bat/bar mitzvahs tomorrow, but I feel terrible at the thought of leaving Maureen and Brigid home like two housecats while Jamie and I dance the Electric Slide after sipping Pimms Cups at a teenage polo match. Yet it's not right to drag the distaff Doyles with us. For one thing I doubt they'd enjoy it, and for another, we're talking about a $200-a-plate event. Although money seems to be no object for the Becksteins, I can't expect them to foot the bill for another pair. And it would also put Brigid and Maureen in the position of having to give a gift to two kids they've never met and will undoubtedly never see again. Still, Imogen is pushing for their presence, and my cousin is nothing if not persuasive.

Maureen utterly mortified me yesterday. I awoke to find her on her knees scrubbing the parquet in my dining gallery with Murphy's Oil Soap. Evidently, my apartment is not clean enough for her. The housekeeper only comes every other week, and it's all she can do to keep up with Jamie, because I refuse to pick up after him. I won't be his cleaning lady and I'm not his mother—something which is even more obvious when you put the both of us under the same roof. But still . . . I guess what I want to say in defense of my home (and my new lover) is that it may be messy, even cluttered—and I never had clutter until Jamie arrived; I hate clutter—but it's definitely not dirty. Maureen Doyle evidently disagrees. I suppose that while I'm incredibly insulted, I shouldn't be surprised. Her own home was absolutely spotless. You could have eaten off the toilet seat.

We're all mired in an unspoken stalemate, a family filibuster. Maureen and Brigid aren't leaving unless they take Jamie with them. Jamie shows no inclination to return to Ireland, and in fact, his recent behavior—bidding farewell to his tangerine dream of a living room by putting his flat up for sale, and registering to vote here the minute he became eligible—demonstrates his increased entrenchment in Manhattan and in my life. I still haven't digested the magnitude of the former deed, but the latter was a very romantic gesture. Better than flowers or chocolate. Lots of boyfriends will buy you a bouquet or a box of bonbons. But how many of them register to vote for you? Literally for you. Of course you actually have to be running for something . . . so I guess the number's pretty low.

*　　*　　*

There might as well be a red carpet unfurled in the parking lot of the synagogue, but that's a Great Neck bar mitzvah for you. Double the ostentation when the soon-to-be-man (and woman) of the hour are twins. Amid the air kisses and the exclamations of Mazel tov! Shabbat shalom! and Happy New Year, the Reform Jewish equivalents of desperate housewives ask one another in a mixture of curiosity and envy, "Who are you wearing?"

The Doyles, none of whom have ever set foot inside a synagogue, are very surprised at the starkness, even asceticism, of the sanctuary, especially when they compare the exotic plumage of the female guests to Temple Beth Shalom's mostly unadorned, blindingly white stuccoed walls.

"They're pretty spare on adornment," Maureen remarks.

You can see where the congregation's money has been spent if you know where to look. The lobby walls are adorned with original Ben Shahns and inside the sanctuary the bimah is flanked by a pair of Chagalls, the only color in the room apart from the violet carpet. I can see how someone unused to architectural expressions of modern Jewish sensibilities might think the place resembles an art galley, rather than their notion of a traditional house of worship. Of course there are no statues, and nothing is carved, embellished, or in any way ornate. Even the organ is unprepossessing.

"Without all the bells and whistles, how do people know God is here?" Brigid whispers to me as we take our seats. Dr. Beckstein, Jacob and Emily's father, hands out programs to everyone, greeting well over two hundred people by name and thanking them for attending this momentous event.

The service gets under way, when Rabbi Shulman, a short and portly man of middling age greets the congregation and their guests. I place a bet with Jamie as to when the rabbi will lose his rectangular, rimless spectacles, as the eyeglasses, precariously hovering well south of the bridge of his nose, are poised to take a dive at any moment.

"We celebrate the bar mitzvah of Jacob Beckstein and the bat mitzvah of Emily Beckstein in interesting times," the rabbi intones in the archetypal drone that has always left me with a cold distrust of his ilk as true men of God. "I say they are interesting times because today—the Saturday that falls between the New Year celebration of Rosh Hashanah and Yom Kippur, the Day of Atonement, is called Shabbat Shuva—the Sabbath of Repentance. This Sabbath, unlike every other Shabbat, we are asked by God specifically to look within ourselves and repent our wickedness, atone for our sins, and return to Hashem with a renewed commitment in our faith, for only then can we be assured that He will inscribe us in his Book of Life for the coming year."

"Is that true?" Jamie asks me.

"I have no idea," I whisper back. "I know all about atoning for your sins on Yom Kippur, which falls in a few days, but I've never heard of Shabbat Shuva. I do know this: since your mother thinks I have no faith, it's unlikely that this boring rabbi is going to get me to perform a religious one-eighty, which puts me at risk, according to him, of getting blue-penciled out of next year's edition of the Book of Life. So maybe we should say our good-byes *now*."

He smiles. "Take your tongue out of your cheek, gorl, and listen to what the man has to say for himself."

"Now, whyyy," whines Rabbi Shulman, "should we put a damper on the biggest day of Jacob's and Emily's lives since the one that brought them into this world, after their mother travailed for thirty-six hours in labor?" Imogen, in a cream-colored Christian Dior suit, simpers and blushes.

"It was thirty-*seven* hours!" Dr. Beckstein calls out.

The congregation titters.

"But to answer the question . . . the entire history of the Jewish people is one that is full of sorrow and pain—of suffering—in equal measure with joy and celebration. In the world of theology, the Jews are 'the little engine that could.' It was faith in his ability to triumph that took the little engine that could to the end of his journey, despite the doubters and detractors. Our story is much the same. Our faith in Hashem has enabled us to survive the worst odds over the millennia. Shabbat Shuva calls upon us to return to our faith in God—or else.

"Or else *what*, you ask. The parsha that Jacob and Emily will share today, which coincidentally mentions the biblical Jacob, so the Becksteinal Jacob will chant that portion, is Chapter 52 of the Book of Deuteronomy. In it—for those of you who don't speak Hebrew, God castigates the children of Israel for their failure to keep their faith with Him. He is terribly vengeful and angry, vowing to hide Himself from their decadent and irreligious lives so that, absent His intervention to protect them, all nonbelievers will end up destroyed in a way that these days would resemble a Jerry Bruckheimer movie. He promises lots of explosions, cataclysmic eruptions, brutal tortures, and vicious murders."

"Brutal tortures and vicious murders are more along Quentin Tarantino's line, I think. See, this is why I'm not religious—or ever could be," I whisper to Jamie. "What kind of a God is this? At least your people believe that 'God is Love.' "

"Oh, our God's a guilt-inducing SOB sometimes, too."

"In Chapter 52," the rabbi continues, "God calls these children of Israel 'a very froward generation in whom there is no faith.' "

I catch Maureen glancing at me. "I'm beginning to take this personally," I mutter, and Jamie slips his hand into mine.

"What does *froward* mean?" he murmurs.

"*Disobedient*," Brigid whispers back.

"And what is the punishment that Hashem has in store for Moses?" asks Rabbi Shulman rhetorically. "This is a God who doesn't want to know 'what have you done for me *lately*, but what are you doing for me *now*?' Leading his people through the desert for forty years might as well be ancient history in Chapter 52 of Deuteronomy. Because Moses trespassed against Hashem in the wilderness of Zin, he will be shown the *vista* of Canaan— the Promised Land—from the mountaintop, but he will never be allowed to enter it himself. Although his flock will be permitted to go forth, Moses will die without ever setting foot in the Promised Land because he abandoned his faith in God.

"Now what does that have to do with us today, sitting here in comfort and contentment, about to usher Jacob into manhood and Emily into womanhood? Despite their new distinction, they will still have responsibilities: responsibilities to their parents—even if it's just getting good grades and not running up cell phone charges—and responsibilities to Hashem to 'keep the faith' as they used to say when I was a seminary student in the 1960s. This is the time of year to repent the occasions when our lack of faith in God kept us from walking in His way, and to atone for the sins we committed in the past year."

"You guys ask forgiveness for your sins only once a year?" Brigid is amazed.

"Yeah, we stockpile them until the High Holy days. Yom Kippur, specifically. And when we do atone in temple, we do it collectively, reciting the words in that book you're holding, unless we're exhorted to engage in silent prayer."

"No confession?"

I nod my head. "We don't tell a rabbi what we've done the way you confess your sins to a priest every week."

"I wonder why the Church has never tried that."

"Hmph. This rabbi's speech is almost *Baptist*; tonally, anyway." I nudge Jamie. "Did you read this?" I point to the English translation of the Deuteronomy parsha. "It's full of fire and brimstone!"

The woman sitting behind me raps me on the shoulder with her program. "*Shhh!*"

"This is also the time of year for remembrance and reflection, as well as for repentance," Rabbi Shulman intones in his soporific singsong. "Have we been all that we could be to our families, our coworkers, and our friends? Have we been good neighbors this past year? Have we balked at giving generously to charity, claiming that money is tight, and yet that same month we somehow find the cash to buy a six-hundred-dollar pair of shoes?"

I glance around the room to see if anyone is squirming, but they all have poker tushes, their body language giving nothing away.

The Beckstein twins are charming, perhaps Emily a bit more so, as she seems to be enjoying herself more and sounds less tone deaf on the parsha. Funny how musical instincts aren't always democratically passed down through the DNA. Proving there's no justice in genealogy, both kids, unfortunately, have inherited their mother's overbite.

Following the service, we gather in the lobby "for a little nosh," as Imogen bills it. This so-called snack consists of seemingly limitless bounty from the appetizing department, from dozens of bagels to pounds of whitefish salad to slabs of sliced Nova Scotia to platters overflowing with honey cake and rugelach.

"Eat up!" exhorts Dr. Beckstein, "for in twenty minutes we

travel to Bridgehampton for the reception—and I refuse to let anyone leave on an empty stomach!"

I notice several old ladies, dressed to the teeth, but obviously from the old school that never passes up an opportunity to take anything ostensibly free, or at the very least, deeply discounted. They're carefully wrapping paper napkins around their bagels with cream cheese and nova and stuffing the booty into their purses. No wonder they were schlepping such oversized bags with their Jaeger suits.

Dr. Beckstein rushes around making sure that those with cars have the directions to the reception, and those without have directions to those with cars. I've rented a vehicle for the day. Since I rarely have the need for one, I don't own a car. Where I live it costs almost as much to insure and garage one as it does to rent an apartment.

The periodontist brandishes a white handkerchief and waves us off, as one by one our autos leave the parking lot. Having behaved during the nosh like a Catskills tummler, he suddenly switches gears from Yiddish to British. "Pip-pip, cheerio, folks! We'll see you at the polo match!"

Twenty-three

During the hour-and-a-half drive to Bridge-hampton, small talk reveals that none of the four of us has ever seen a polo match. "I doubt we'll see anything approaching the genuine article today, either," I surmise.

But I should not have underestimated Imogen—and Roger, whom I have yet to meet. Upon our arrival at the polo club I keep staring at every guy who looks official or industrious, wondering if he's my cousin's younger man. My imagination has cast him as the heterosexual version of a Chelsea Boy, but every one of those I spot appears to be a cater-waiter or one of the professional Argentinean polo players hired by the Beck-steins for the afternoon to teach the kids the game.

"All right, who wants to play polo?" shouts Dr. Beckstein. He has changed out of his three-piece suit and into an ensemble entirely out of a Ralph Lauren ad. On him it looks like a costume. His salt-and-pepper brush moustache, male pattern baldness, and somewhat zaftig physique give the lie to his desire to create the impression that he is to the manner (or even manor) born.

Fortuitously, enough of the teens chicken out of saddling up to leave a number perfectly divisible by eight, as there are four players to a side, and of course there are two sides to everything. But as the Becksteins are hosting a reception for three hundred people, more than a quarter of which are Jacob and Emily's friends, acquaintances, and classmates with whom they participate (or against whom they compete) in myriad afterschool and weekend activities, this polo match could go on till dawn. With six chukkers in a polo match, the Argentine coaches and umpires decide that each group of eight kids will play two seven-minute chukkers, and there will be two full matches, with the official five-minute halftime in between.

"At least it'll keep them from getting into the scotch," Jamie quips.

The kids have been equipped with protective gear, including special rounded spurs and a whip, and have been outfitted in team jerseys (numbered 1 through 4, to denote the player's position). The young teens will be playing for either Jacob's Ladder or Emily's List—Imogen's idea. I get the feeling that if the twins themselves had chosen the team names they would have been something like Jacob's Demons and Emily's Hellions.

A waiter strolls by with dishes of strawberries and cream while another offers us a choice between a glass of champagne or a Pimms Cup. The three Doyles and I accept the latter, and make ourselves comfortable on one of the checkered picnic blankets which Imogen has been distributing to various clusters of guests. "Tally ho!" she says in the worst English accent I've ever heard in my life.

Jamie raises his glass in a toast. "Up yours."

I crook my finger at my cousin and she bends down to speak

to me. Like her husband, she is on to ensemble number two: a tight pair of breeches, tall boots, and the type of bright red (officially called "pink") jacket worn by the men who fox hunt and call "Riders up!" during the triple crown. "So, which one is Roger? I've been dying to know since I got here."

"I can't point," she replies, her jaw clenched into a frozen smile, as though she's pretending that she isn't actually speaking or received a shot of Botox not two minutes ago. "It's impolite."

"Then gesture with your riding crop."

"He's over by the grownups' beverage table, talking to the bartender. Wait—don't let anyone know you're looking," she hisses desperately.

"What difference does it make if someone sees me turn my head toward the bar? Maybe I'm looking to see if they put out any Grey Goose. Maybe I'm even looking to see what Roger looks like because I might want to plan an event of my own. After all, now that I'm running for Congress, I'll need to host a lot of fund-raisers in the next few weeks."

"Ohmi*god*, how's that going? Mazel tov on that, by the way."

I cup my hand to my ear. "Sorry, I can't hear you over the thundering of hooves." I can't believe how fast this game is. I'm impressed that no one has fallen off their horse yet, and some of those kids are incredibly brutal. If they're still this ruthless when they grow up, I despair for our future. There are a lot of anger issues out on that field.

Imogen raises her voice, at which point she could probably be heard by people playing polo in Poughkeepsie. "I said congratulations, Tess! And how's it going so far?"

"I'm getting my bearings, building a war chest. I'm going to need a big one, even with the matching donations from the campaign finance board, if I have a chance of getting my message out there . . ." Okay, now I see who she's talking about. If the guy I'm looking at is Roger, he's tall, dark haired, slender . . . seems quite promising. He's the physical inverse of Imogen's husband. My focus is broken when the man turns around. I nearly gasp. To me, Roger looks like a young Jeff Goldblum. I try not to look too stunned. "Sorry . . . lost my train of thought for a minute. Your . . . friend looks very . . . tall."

"You don't think he's a hunk?" Imogen is devastated by the thought that I might not share her taste in men.

"If he makes you wild with euphoria, then that makes me happy too. Though at some point you might want to seriously rethink your marriage. So where was I?"

"You were talking about needing money."

"Right. So Dobson's got more money than a Saudi prince— well, maybe not quite that much—but he's prepared to spend whatever it takes to win. If he could go door to door and hand each registered voter a check for a grand if they'd vote for him, I'm sure he'd do it. Meanwhile, I've got an ad agency writing commercials for me and we shoot the first one next week. I just hope we can pay for it. It'll be an uphill battle to introduce me to the voters on a relative shoestring."

"Good luck. I'm waiting, you know."

"For what?"

Imogen takes a sip of my drink. The smacking noise she makes with her lips appears to be a sign of approval. "I showed you mine, now you show me yours."

"My what?"

"For a Harvard graduate you can be so dense sometimes. Your *man*."

"Oh, God, of course. Forgive me." I introduce Imogen to Jamie and then to his mother and sister, and Imogen gushes over how pretty Brigid is and how all the young men (she means the ones over thirteen and under thirty) will go wild over her. This remark makes me suddenly realize I never told Imogen that Jamie's sister is on her way to becoming one. Then she pulls me to my feet and drags me off toward the edge of the tent.

"You didn't tell me he was so adorable! He's no Roger, of course, but I've never gone in for *shaigetses*. Except for David, you always seem to go for the non-Jewish ones. So tell me, does he . . . is he . . . ?"

"You're blushing. Yes, he is. He was born here, not in Ireland and in our generation they did it in the hospital to every boy, regardless of religion, unless you told them you wanted to wait eight days and have a bris."

"Just checking," she giggles. "I was watching you two at the nosh after the service. You looked very happy together."

"We are," I sigh. "We'd be even happier if his mother went home."

A P.A. announcement interrupts our little tête-a-tête. "*Señors y señoras y señoritas*, it is halftime now . . . and you know what that means . . ."

Dr. Beckstein grabs the mic from the Argentinean. "All right folks, everybody up on your feet! It's time for a little divot stomping!"

Amilcar Bauttista, the professional polo player, explains what all this means—in effect, any willing spectators get out onto the field and tamp down the overturned turf with their tootsies. With this crowd, it's more amusing than it sounds, as women are urged to dig in their Choos (which probably does the ground more harm than good) and the men are encouraged to get out there in their Ballys and Maglis and (in Dr. Beckstein's word) partaaaayyy!

"This much I know," Jamie murmurs to me as we stomp away, "*women* aren't supposed to wear the pink coat." He chuckles, but can't contain his laughter. "What's your cousin dressed for? Halloween? I think she thinks polo is the same as a fox hunt."

"I think she thinks red is her color," I say.

With the halftime over, the adults return to their blankets, to be greeted by setups for a proper afternoon tea: tiered stands displaying finger sandwiches, scones, and little tea cakes. The condiments—ramekins of clotted cream, lemon curd, and jam, along with a plate of lemon wedges, a cream pitcher, and a sugar pot are delivered upon our arrival, and then the tuxedoed cater-waiters go from blanket to blanket with pots of tea. It's all terribly civilized here in the shade. On the field, however, some of the kids still look like they want to brain each other with their polo mallets.

To my delight, finesse triumphs over brute strength, when by the end of the afternoon, Emily's List emerges the winner of most of the chukkers. Although several of the rungs of Jacob's Ladder demonstrated a remarkable propensity for violence, which is apparently par for a polo course—the sport is not as genteel as I'd imagined—many of Emily's friends take riding lessons, and thus are better equestrians than their male counterparts. The girls are over the moon when they each receive a kiss on the cheek from swarthy Amilcar and his Argentinean buddies.

As if they worry that we'll stop having fun if we stop eating, after the matches the Becksteins urge everyone to step inside and freshen up for round three—the cocktail reception. Followed, naturally, by a multicourse dinner.

The invitations had suggested that a change of clothes might be in order (the better to have more to shop for and show up in), but only the Becksteins dressed up for the polo matches. The rest of us adults who wore tasteful silk suits and subtle brocaded jackets suitable for a synagogue at 9 A.M. had the option of either remaining so clad until the dinner winds down sometime around midnight, or to bring along something flashy for the night shift. Of course Maureen and Brigid weren't prepared for this. I've loaned Jamie's sister a short-sleeved black cocktail dress which sets off her ivory complexion like a dream, but I own nothing that would have fit Maureen and didn't think it was right for her to have to go to the trouble of purchasing something for the occasion. We ended up finding a lovely designer label suit at the local thrift shop. It was in superb condition and a bargain at any price, so I made her a gift of it, and she's elected to wear it all day. Most of the men will be changing into tuxes this evening, but Jamie's wardrobe lacks such formality. He wore a tweed sport coat and dark slacks to the temple this morning, yet feeling the need to do me proud in front of my family, surprised me by going out and renting a tux for the occasion.

Evidently the Becksteins didn't think about the fact that there would be several dozen women and girls vying for a place at the mirror in the club's ladies' rooms. There's as much elbow jabbing as primping, and a great deal of space hogging.

"Now aren'tcha glad you're goin' to be a nun?" Maureen asks her daughter. "None of this silliness."

"Ah, I *knew* that was the reason I decided to marry Christ!"

"Don't they teach you in that community house not to sass your own mother?" Maureen replies huffily. "Tessa, that bronzey-brown suits you," she adds, complimenting my cocktail dress. Well, maybe a kindly disposed heart does beat under that sturdy brassiere after all.

Inside the reception hall itself (no need for a sign; our noses guide us), cooking stations line the perimeter, serving up what Jamie dubs the Foods of All Nations. There are, in fact, flags to aid the guests in locating the tapas, sushi, pasta and antipasti, dolmades and spanikopita, blini with sour cream and caviar, mini quiches, egg rolls and dumplings, sticks of sate, and for the Ashkenazi Jews who can't skip a meal that doesn't include our own brand of "comfort food," there are knishes, and a carving station offering slices of corned beef and pastrami, with plenty of mustard and seeded rye to match.

Watching Jamie's mother load up on the corned beef, I feel compelled to remark, "See, Maureen, we have something else in common besides loving your son and being born in New York."

The cocktail reception is a gourmand's wet dream, and I have no doubt we'll all be exhorted, if not commanded, to dance it all off in another couple of hours. Needless to say, there is an open bar, and trays of champagne and red and white wine are making the rounds for those who prefer the grape to the grain or are too lazy or impatient to suffer the crush at the liquor tables.

Dinner is just as lavish and just as international in flavor (though everything is short on taste—in both meanings of the word): choice of gazpacho or vichyssoise; Chilean sea bass with Peruvian purple potatoes or steak au poivre with pommes frite; and for dessert, tiramisu, baklava, or crêpes suzettes—however, for someone who may find the portions too small, the traditional Viennese table groaning with gooey pastries and petit fours is open for business. Clearly no one was concerned about having a kosher menu unless the dairy items are faux-milchig.

"What do you think they do with all the leftovers?" Brigid wonders. "I hope they donate them to a soup kitchen. You could feed half the poor people in Dublin with what's not being eaten tonight." I can see she's not comfortable with the wretched excess. Then again, what normal person would be? Maureen was nonplussed by the contents of the goody bags that had been placed on each guest's seat prior to their arrival in the banquet hall. Included with the Toblerone bars, and bottles of Ralph Lauren's Polo fragrances, is a tooth-whitening kit and a coupon good for a 20 percent discount off one of Dr. Beckstein's periodontal procedures.

Yet all of this is staid and stodgy compared to the pièce de résistance—the entertainment. Suddenly the room goes dark and a DJ pumps up the volume. Jamie estimates it's 10 percent melody and 90 percent percussion. My chair starts to wobble and dance on its own from the vibrations.

"Let's hear it for the Beckstein twins!" the motivator booms into a microphone, as behind him a wall of screens is illuminated and flashes with quick cuts of Emily and Jacob, a video photo album from birth to thirteen, accompanied by a pounding beat that would give a deaf person a migraine.

"Are you ready to party hearty?" the motivator shouts, then turns the mic on the guests. "Gimme a YES!" he encourages.

"Yes," the guests reply in unison.

"A little louder. Gimme a YES!"

"Yes."

"I can't hear you!"

"YESSS"

The motivator then shouts, "And now let's give it up for the people who made it all possible—*Mom and Dad*: Dr. Sid Beckstein and his lovely wife, Imogen!"

And, to the accompaniment of tumultuous applause, on come Sidney and Imogen, dancing all the way, waving their hands in the air as though they're at a rave. The two of them are on to outfit number three, Sidney in his tux and my cousin wearing a sparkly blue gown straight from the Pamela Anderson collection for mothers of the bar mitzvah. It plunges everywhere and Imogen doesn't have the hard body necessary to carry it off. They join hands and kiss cute in front of the screens, which now display a montage of snapshots from their marriage.

"Now give it up for Big Sister!" the motivator commands, and Shauna, looking sheepish and out of place in a black pantsuit, joins the rest of her family.

"And put your hands together for the man and woman of the hour—Jacob and Emily Becksteiiiiiiiiiiiin!"

I can't help myself; I begin to laugh because this intro makes the twins sound like they've just tied the knot, not broken their ties to childhood. Several of the guests stomp and clap. Jacob and Emily enter—each riding a pony—from opposite sides of the screen. Behind the DJ a burst of fireworks threatens to burn it down. I can't believe the polo club let the Becksteins do this with their animals—someone must have neglected to disclose the plans for simultaneous pyrotechnics and a throbbing bass line. The terrified horses are then led "offstage" by staff members after the twins dismount.

"Speech! Speech," demand a number of guests. Imogen and Sidney oblige, acting as mock-shocked as an Oscar winner who pretends not to know they had a one in five chance of taking home the statuette.

"They say that planning a bar mitzvah costs an arm and a leg," Sid begins, "so when you've got twins, I suppose you're left with nothing but a torso. I guess that makes this my *stump* speech." No one laughs. "Anyway—my wife is the funny one in the family—anyway, I'm glad you're all here tonight, and some of you have been with us since this morning, to share in another Beckstein milestone. So eat, drink, dance, and be merry because when the American Express bill comes, I want to know I got my money's worth."

I'm mortified by his crassness. It plays into all the awful

stereotypes. The Doyles look somewhat stunned. Imogen then delivers a staggeringly maudlin speech recounting in rich detail her long hours of labor, each one of the twins' personal milestones until now (kind of hard to play This Is Your Life when a kid is barely thirteen), and ends by thanking her precious babies who she knows will always make her proud, and the two men without whom this event would not have been possible: Roger Scheinbaum the party planner, and her adoring and adorable husband Sidney.

I scan the room for Roger and find him leaning by the door, an inscrutable expression on his face.

Jacob then pulls a damp piece of paper from his pocket. Clearly not a natural at this, he stiffly reads his prepared text as though it's unfamiliar, thanking "my mom, Imogen Beckstein, and my dad, Sidney Beckstein, and my twin sister Emily Beckstein" (as if we don't know who these people are) "for making my life possible." He's followed by Emily who speaks off the cuff, and keeps it short and sweet: "Thank you Mommy and Daddy. I love you both very much."

Suddenly, the music breaks into a samba and a half dozen muscular African-American guys dressed in gauchos and sombreros, their chests bare and oiled, begin to dance, encouraging the guests to get up and join them. Maureen looks as if she's gone into shock. When the samba segues into a pulsating hip-hop beat, the gauchos are un-velcroed and the sombreros tossed aside. I take a stab at how the dancers might have gotten the gold lamé yarmulkes to stay on their totally bald heads: double-stick tape.

Maureen now wonders, not without acerbity, what bare-chested black men in yarmulkes have to do with religion, or for that matter, what any of this riotous cacophony has to do with

Jewish ritual. Jamie reminds her that Irish wakes tend to be real rip-snorters, too, though he admits that he's yet to see any half-naked hip-hoppers at one.

"It could have been worse," I say, trying to be heard above the music. "Imogen invited Venus to come and lead a pole-dancing clinic for the girls. She wisely declined. Can you imagine those thirteen-year-olds encouraged to dress and act even sluttier than they already do? If I'd gone to a party looking like that at their age, my father would have grounded me for life."

And then a klezmer band is introduced, solely, it seems, to perform the Hebrew hit parade, starting with "Hava Nagila." You've never really danced the hora until you've done it to the accompaniment of manic percussion that nearly obscures the melody. Three hundred people are encouraged to get up from their seats and do the grapevine. The tune, such as it is, morphs into "Siman Tov U Mazeltov," which means "may good luck come to us," during which the circle dancing grows more frenetic. Dr. Beckstein beckons to a handful of his friends who plop Emily and Jacob onto a pair of chairs and then hoist the furniture over their heads, dancing and bobbing. Emily, a bit nervous about this little ride screams to her dad, "Don't drop me!" while Jacob appears to be negotiating with Dr. Beckstein's dental partners to jog him over to the bar. The men oblige and Jacob is handed a huge glass of scotch.

When the twins have been returned to earth, the klezmer band slows the tempo a bit and strikes up a third tune. Grabbing my hand, Brigid pulls me onto the dance floor. "I know this one!" I look at her in disbelief. "It's a mazinka. Jewish people dance it when the youngest child in a family gets married. I lorned it in the international folk dance class they made us take in secondary school." Brigid bursts out laughing. "Oh, Tessa, I wish you could see yer face. You look absolutely gobsmacked! C'mon, I'll teach it to you!"

Brigid is less confident, however, when it comes to other kinds of dancing. Men seem to be drawn to her. Maybe they're attracted to the nun aura; they just don't have a clue what it is. But her looks, and the energy she gives off just sitting still have gained her several offers to dance. She turned down the first guy because she didn't think she should be shaking it in that context. By the fifth request, she was just feeling too shy to dance with a man. By the tenth, she found herself reluctantly acquiescing, but she was so confused by her own decision that she must have seemed quite a cool customer. Oh, if only they knew why!

The motivator announces a five-minute breather, to give people enough time to enjoy a cup of coffee and shovel a pastry or two in their mouths. Meanwhile, thanks to the open bars and the bottles of wine and champagne on every table, the circle dances spin a lot faster—or maybe it's the room that seems to be revolving at such velocity.

"Okay people, fun's over! It's time to shake yaw bootaayyy!" screams the motivator. The lights are doused completely, and the six dancers reappear wearing neon necklaces and bracelets, and twirling neon hula hoops. In the eerie light, they pull a half dozen Long Island matrons to their feet, and toss the hula hoops around them, so that the women find themselves gyrating crotch to crotch with a topless hunky black guy. They seem to be having a great deal of fun, actually.

There is only one slow dance all night. "This one's for the old folks!" shouts the motivator. "So all you members of the Geritol generation, let's see you up on your feet!"

"I think they're playing our song," Jamie says, extending his hand to me. "May I have this dance, Tessa Goldsmith Craig?"

Under a disco ball the size of Pluto, we sway to the strains of "The Time of My Life," the theme song from *Dirty Dancing*. I wonder if *Jamie* was subjected to dance classes in secondary school, because he's barely moving, but right now it doesn't much matter, because it feels so good to be in his arms. Exhausted, and suffering from a raging headache (what a surprise!), I rest against his shoulder, enjoying the feel of his hand pressed against my back, telegraphing through the energy radiating from his palm that he's here for me. Another five minutes of this and I'll be fast asleep and therefore in no shape to drive. I hope he knows how to find the way home.

By the time the dancing winds down, at least two hours later, the stilettos have been stashed under the tables, ties have been loosened, jackets removed, Jacob has been caught in the empty cloakroom making out with Emily's best friend, and Emily has thrown up all over the ladies' room. But as long as there's still food to be served, the beat goes on. The chocolate fountain would probably have been a bigger hit, had it been unveiled earlier in the evening. Here, at last, is something the old ladies will have a hard time stuffing into their purses.

Our drive home is mercifully silent. Brigid and Maureen have fallen asleep in the backseat. Jamie the Empath knows how uncomfortable I am with the day's ostentation. *What you saw today isn't . . .* is what I'd like to tell him—his mother and sister too—but I feel that if I were to apologize for it, in some way it would make me feel like I was apologizing for Judaism. I may not be a religious Jew but I am a proud one.

"Thank you for coming with me today," I murmur. "It was an

insanely long day, emphasis on the *insane*, and you were a real brick throughout the whole thing."

He smiles and squeezes my hand. "Ach, I just chalked it up to a study in cultural anthropology."

"Nevertheless. You're a prince for doing it and I love you."

His grin is bright enough to light all eight lanes of the Long Island Expressway. "Now you tell me? When I'm wearin' a seat belt and can't do a thing about it?"

Twenty-four

 September 20

*It might be my imagination, but those three little words—
three big words, actually—have magically manifested themselves in a number of wonderful ways. First, I feel fabulous.
Having told Jamie I love him, even if it didn't exactly happen during a Hallmark moment, I feel lighter and unbur-
dened. Sex was good before, but in the past few days we've
reached a different, and very pleasurable, plateau. As far
as Jamie's charm quotient goes, there's more swag to his
swagger (dare I say more cock to his cockiness?), and mir-
acle of miracles, his unholy messiness is almost a thing of
the past. Almost. At least now I can find some of my own
things amid the clutter. This new development has Maureen more anxious than any increase in affection between
her son and me. Picking up after himself—that one's got
her nervous. Besides, she's taken to scrubbing my apartment*

daily, as if to disinfect it, and now it looks as if she might someday be out of a job.

Jamie says that his mum thinks she'll wear him down with her presence. The poor man could be a frequent flyer to perdition for all the guilt trips she's laid on him since her arrival. But she won't confront me with her Irish-American temper because she's saving a fortune by not staying in a hotel. Nor, despite her chilly treatment, have I demanded that she leave and leave us alone. I still haven't found a way to connect to her, even though the paradigm is the same: American woman from New York/Irish man. But, as Jamie would immediately remind me, Maureen's mission has precious little to do with me. He's shirked his re- sponsibilities to his family, and the fact that he's happier than he's been in years irks her just as much, if not more.

Meanwhile I've got plenty else on my plate. I'm gearing up for a speech on Education, and we're shooting the first of a fistful of campaign commercials tomorrow. Many of David's usual contributors came through with sizeable donations to my war chest so that I can begin to get my message out to the voters. I'm up against an opponent with limitless funds who has opted out of the Campaign Fi- nance Program so that he can spend whatever he wants. Trotting out the gimmicks, his sidewalk volunteers are handing out dog treats to voters with the phrase "Bob Dob- son: Gnawt pawlitics as usual." Oy. But voters eat them up; or at least their pets do.

Although at present I'm polling nine points below my opponent—which makes me very nervous—Gus Trumbo assures me that I shouldn't worry. Dobson was able to get a leg up on the name recognition front while David was still in the race by flooding the airwaves with commercials. Voters may not yet be buying into Dobson's positions, but they sure as hell know who he is. Gus is trying to bolster my spirits by telling me that the women in the district will go heavily for me. I've got a lot to say about education, safety and security, and protection of our resources, and that plays well with mothers and grandmothers who want their kids to have safe streets and subways, clean air and water, and an equal opportunity for economic advancement, not to mention the guarantee that I'll fight like hell to make sure Sesame Street *stays on the air. It's the male demographic he's more concerned about winning over. Female candidates are often perceived as either not knowing as much as their male counterparts, or not being as tough as guys believe a man would be on a number of issues— crime for instance—or, the converse of that perception— that a woman's a shrew for demanding accountability and responsibility from corporations, trade unions, and individuals, whereas a man fighting the same fights would be viewed as a strong and capable leader.*

In fact, Dobson has been appealing to men by putting himself over as a red meat-eating regular guy (as if I eat what instead? *Afalfa?) who knows how to take care of business, given his creds as a CEO who took a single yellow dog dish and parlayed it into an empire. However, my numbers jumped a few points when, unaware that his mic was still on, Dobson told a bunch of reporters that "the* little lady *never ran a thing in her life, except maybe a bake sale."*

Stephen Sondheim wrote "You gotta have a gimmick," and ours attracts more attention than throwing the people *a bone. So if it's an unfortunate truism that voters remember the candidates by their publicity stunts and not their ideas, the Craig campaign will not be outdone by Len Avariss and his team of spin doctors. We can't compete with Dobson's advertising budget, so we've got to go grassroots. Venus, with that drop-dead gorgeous body and all that hair, has been stationing herself outside key venues in the district, wearing a white baby tee that says "I want to talk to you." Few men can resist. Sad, but true, most of them have spent their entire adolescence and half their adult lives dreaming about a woman like Venus approaching them. And once the fly has entered the web, the Harvard alumna who is as articulate as she is stunning asks about the political and social issues that are important to them right now, and then explains how Tessa Craig will deal with their concerns, handing each guy a white paper on the key subject or subjects. Her method of quite literally attracting the voters has proven to be such a success that Venus has rounded up a number of her former colleagues, given them a crash course in local politics and its relevance on the national stage, and sent them out to hit the pavement. The women have been unkindly dubbed "Trumbo's Bimbos" by the <u>New York Post</u>, but I'll bet it's selling them a lot of papers; every day for the past week they've run a photo of at least one of Venus's sultry satellites. Actually, I stole that last phrase from the <u>Daily News</u>'s coverage of the phenomenon. In this dog-eat-dog campaign, Bob Dobson has suggested that we might have Venus's women mud wrestle his volunteers instead of he and I sitting down and debating the issues.*

Bob Dobson, who hails originally from Arkansas, must want to run for Congress in New York because he's got his eyes on a bigger prize. And even if New Yorkers see through carpetbaggers' rhetoric, we tend to vote for them anyway. Look at RFK and Hillary Clinton. Of course Dobson is neither of those. But I've been trying to locate his Achilles' heel so I can stick it to him there.

"Stick to <u>message</u>; you don't have time to go negative," Gus has advised me. "Dobson's capable of shooting himself in the foot, even with Avariss's eagle eye on his ass 24/7." I feel like David's legacy is slipping through my grasp though. We're fighting to preserve an ideology, here. If I lose, I lose a whole lot more than an election. Was I naïve enough to think it would be a sleigh ride all the way down to Capitol Hill?

"Hey, Tess, are you home? I brought yiz a present!" Jamie announces through the door. I hear a scratching, followed by a *"shhh!"* And then, "Can you open the door, please? I've got me hands full."

And there is Jamie Doyle standing on my threshold, cradling a rust-colored puppy, whose affection for his new dad is obvious.

I clap my hand to my heart and burst into tears. "You bought me a dog! Ohmigod, you bought me a dog. I've always wanted—"

"I know. Remember that time in Dublin when I mentioned that I just knew that about yiz?" He hands me the puppy, which immediately begins to explore my collarbone. "And it's an Irish setter," I sniffle. The dog doesn't quite know what to make of my tears.

"Of course it's an Irish setter! Whatja expect from an Irishman? A Cavalier King Charles spaniel?"

"What's his name?"

"Her. It's a bitch."

I give him a look. I know that's the proper term, but still . . . "Well, we should name her something Irish. What do you think of calling her Lady Gregory?"

Jamie shrugs. "A bit posh, but she's yer dog."

"I guess we should wait to see what kind of a personality she has before we consign her to something inappropriate for the rest of her life."

I place the dog on the living room floor, briefly wonder if she's been toilet trained or if that's *my* job, and throw my arms around Jamie. "You are wonderful. I . . . I really don't know how to properly thank you. No one's ever made one of my childhood dreams come true."

"I figured she'll come in handy for your commercial. I thought ya should have a dog like the other people in the dog run. Bob Dobson will be eatin' his own biscuits for lunch if you muscle in on the one territory he thinks he's got fenced in: the pet owners. Now you're one of them."

And so we did a bit of quick rewriting and shot a spot called Dog Run just beyond a public playground, where my little Maeve, named for a great Irish queen (with her long neck she looks kind of regal the way she sits), frolics with her peers, then snuggles beside me as I introduce myself to the voters and talk about "making sure we've got a safe place for all of us to play . . . whether we're with our kids or our best friends" . . . using the requisite buzz words and catch-phrases regarding the environment and counter-terrorism measures so the voters know I'm going to fight like hell to protect them from any kind of harm, whether it means being truly tough on corporate polluters and other corner-cutters that harm our environment, or fighting for every available resource to keep our skies, our harbors, and our mass transit systems safe.

By the time the commercial is aired, we're hoping all the die-hard dog lovers will become Craig supporters as well.

September 23

I've been stressing over my Education speech, wondering whether to include a section that may push a lot of buttons and cost me key voters, but it's one that I truly believe separates me as a Pragmatic Progressive from the garden variety liberal too often demonized by the right. I've written:

"As much as I admire the reason unions were formed in the first place—to stand up for safe conditions in the workplace, mandate an eight-hour workday, eliminate child labor—the unions have become a part of the problem when they should be a part of the solution instead. Too many educators who should never have been hired in the first place, or else put out to pasture years ago, are allowed to languish in ineptitude and mediocrity, rising according to the Peter Principle to their highest level of incompetence; and your children are suffering the consequences of their inadequacy and lack of creativity."

Of course my position on English-language immersion for non-native-speaking students might set off bells and whistles among the liberal base as well. I'm feeling like I'm chickening out if I don't include it in the final draft, and I risk a further drop in the polls if I do:

"Economic freedom begins with education. It begins with English-language immersion classes early on, when studies show that kids are most likely to learn a foreign language with greater rapidity than their older counterparts. Here's another area where I disagree with many of my colleagues. We are a glorious melting pot, which makes our stew so

richly flavored, but we're doing our kids a disservice by consigning them in grade school—their most formative years—to classes in their native tongues, when the language of the American economy, of technology, is English. When their English-language skills lag from the get-go, very often many of these kids never catch up; they end up left back or left out of the ability to obtain genuine economic freedom."

When I worked for David I had enough distance to allow me to gain some perspective. Now that I'm the candidate, I find myself questioning my instincts and second-guessing myself. I'll run it by Gus; I've got to trust his judgment on this.

A few nights later, while Maureen is bent over a 500-piece jigsaw puzzle of Oslo, and I'm at my desk redrafting the speech, Brigid anxiously asks if she can talk to me.

"Well, I'm kind of curious about how all that works," she says as she helps me set aside my research. "Like how do ya lorn all the things ya need to know to write something like this, but that's not what I've been wanting to ask yiz. Do ya mind if we close the door?"

"What's on your mind?"

"I'm all like topsy-torvy lately. I've been going to Holy Trinity every day since ya told me where it was, and I even tried atoning for my sins on your special day this week. Since I figured it was God's day to listen, He might lend me an ear as well. It's big, ya see."

I wonder aloud what monstrous deed Brigid could possibly need to atone for.

"So like I said, I've been goin' there every day about the same time; maybe noonish, and this being a residential area and all, you don't get too many people paying God a call on their lunch hours. Didja know there's a police station just up the block from the church?" I nod my head. "So . . . this is . . . you have to promise not to say anything to Mum . . ." Brigid runs her hand through her short hair and laughs. "Oh aye, I've got the social skills of St. Francis." She slides her butt onto the floor and leans against the sofa in my home office. "It's quiet as a tomb inside the church when I get there. I think I've only seen a priest wander through once or twice. Usually for the first half hour or so it's just me sitting there in the pew starin' at the crucifix, askin' questions in my prayers.

"But every day there's been a man come to pray and for the forst two days we pretended not to see each other, for he was cryin' when he prayed, and I think he was embarrassed that someone else was there to see him so. I mean he's no ba-by . . . broad back, gray-haired and all; and a very lived-in face, too. Though I pretended not to notice it. I would hear footsteps behind me and torn to see who was comin' in. And he would always take the very last pew on the right, where I would sit up front on the left. On the tord day he smiled at me, and I didn't know whether to smile back, bein' a friendly porson, but not wishin' to give him any ideas o'course, so I torned my head back to our Lord and tried to think pure thoughts. I think he thought I was a bit standoffish. The gray-haired man, I mean, not Jesus.

"Then yesterday he came up and asked if he could sit beside me. 'Want company?' he asked me, and I shrugged and moved over so's he could join me. 'I've been noticin' you,' he whispers and I see his eyes are sad. They're Irish eyes, too, I can tell—I have a way of knowing these things, don't ask me how—so I ask him his name, and as sure as I'm a candidate for the veil, he tells me his name is Anthony *O'Reilly*. Captain O'Reilly from the police station up the street.

"'Anto,' I say to him, looking deep into his eyes. Tessa, they're so black you can hardly see his pupils. 'Anto,' I say very softly, 'can ya tell me why you're so sad?' And then it all comes pouring out of him, like he's at confession almost, and he tells me he was a forst responder on 9/11."

I feel a chill creep up my spine as though I've walked over a grave. I don't know what's coming, but I know it's not going to be pretty.

"His partner never made it out of the rubble, and all Anto remembers of that morning was that he was running, running north. And he says, to this day he doesn't know if he was a coward or a hero for his memory's all gone blank of some of the things that happened. He can't even remember if he tried to save Mike—his partner—or even if he was in a position to . . . but every day he says he hates something deep inside himself for not being able to rescue him. Mike had just gotten married six months before; his wife Joan was expecting their forst . . . you know Anto's only thirty-eight years old, but he looks fifty.

"He told me he still can't seem to resolve his feelings of remorse and that he would do anything for contrition. He moonlights as an accordion-playing circus clown at pediatric wards and volunteers at the soup kitchen in the basement at Holy Trinity—that is, when the church isn't renting it out to a movie company as a holding space for their background actors. Do ya know there are homeless people right here in your neighborhood? Camping right on the doorsteps, I suppose, of the people who live in the brownstones and send their children to fancy schools. It's true the world over, I guess, but to me New York seems like the richest city in the world.

"'Well, a soup kitchen, that sounds like a good thing to do,' I said to him, since I couldn't think of anything else to say. You know nuns can't hear confession, and I think that's one of the bummers about the Church. And here's this man who looks like he wants to pour out his soul into my hands . . . it's almost as if he knows I'm a little bit . . . it sounds both immodest and daft to say 'closer to God,' but you know what I mean.

"I tried not to smile when he told me I seem different from other women he's met. Especially when he asked me if I wanted to go to the Starbucks with him. 'No, I'm afraid I'd better not,' I said to him. 'Why?' he asked me. 'I'm not at liberty to date,' I answered, so he asked me, suddenly norvous like a schoolboy, 'Oh, then you're *going* with someone?' 'In a manner of speaking,' I said."

"So you didn't tell him—?"

"I couldn't tell him I'm a nunlet! I couldn't say, 'I'm in the middle of discernment, Anto, so I won't be having that half-caf latte with yiz.' I know he'd become all weird, and there'd be no way we could even just be friends after that. At best he'd be asking me if I'd rap him on the knuckles with my ruler, and at worst he'd think I'd go all judgmental on him if he does so much as swear. He's a soul in torment, Anto is. I sat there in the church . . . just the two of us . . . and I wanted to be able to heal him." Brigid begins to fidget with the hem of her skirt. "But more than that, and this is the part that distorbs me . . . I wanted to offer Anto more than *words* of comfort, more than a sympathetic ear. I wanted to hold him." I watch a tear make its way down her right cheek. "And I don't know what God has to say about this, and maybe He'll find a way to punish me for my actions, somehow, for I know they were wrong—for someone on my vocational path—but they weren't wrong for a person; for a compassionate person I know it was normal. I put my arms around him anyway and held him close. And I didn't have to tell him it was all right to cry; he just knew somehow. And we sat there in the pew, me rockin' him almost like he was my baby. The Father walked through and looked at us, and I tried to avoid his gaze because I didn't want him to see right through me and say that what I was doing was a sin.

"It was nothing sexual, at least I didn't think it was, but it was so deeply personal. And it made me feel good to know that I was helping Anto in the way that he needed, truly needed, not through rote or empty directives to say novenas and recite Hail Marys. This—with Anto—this afternoon—this was the most spiritual I have ever felt in me life. Mum would have a cow if she knew. But I want to help people—help them person-ally, one at a time. Like I do on the teen crisis hotline in Dub-lin. Like I did with Anto today. So I'm going to join him and volunteer in the soup kitchen. And maybe one of these days I'll tell him the truth. I don't know how long I can stay out of the Starbucks with him. He says he was never a churchgoer until after 9/11. And even now, he's not sure he believes, but believ-ing that there's something out there, up there, that can comfort him and ease his pain, is better than believing that nothing and no one can, he says. 'I'm glad I've met a religious girl. I like the way you come in here every day, when you must have plenty of other places to be. My mother would be very impressed with that. She'd never kick *you* out of the house and call you a tart, like a couple of the women I've dated over the years.'" Brigid buries her face in her hands. "I know he was trying to make it into a light moment, but the poor man has no clue what a crisis of faith *I'm* having!"

I sit beside her on the floor, and when I slip my arm around her shoulder, she begins to weep. "I don't know what I want," she sobs. "I thought I did, but now it's all topsy-torvy. I thought I had a calling . . . but . . . but is it possible I was just bored? I don't even know the answer to that. I'm too old to be bored.

There are days when I don't even know why I wanted to go into the Church except that I've always known that I want to help people. Through the Sisters of St. Joseph, I'm learnin' how to counsel troubled youth, and it makes me so happy when I see that we can really make a difference in someone's life. But lately I've been thinkin' I don't need to spend my life in a convent to do that. Maybe the truth is I don't like responsibility, and if I become a nun every plan for my life is already set; I've no decisions. And maybe deep down, that's what I wanted. Not to have to think too hard. But being here in New York . . . well, let me ask ya, what kind of *nun* loves *Sex and the City*? I should be thinking it's an abomination—all that swearing and fornicating and inappropriately grand fixations on shoes—when to tell yiz the truth, I never minded swearing, I'm dead curious about sex, and I'd give anything just to *try on* a pair of six-hundred-dollar sandals and know what it feels like, just once! It doesn't mean I can't help a sixteen-year-old addict torn her life around and believe in the word of Jesus Christ." Brigid grows momentarily thoughtful, then suddenly clasps both my hands in hers. "You're a woman of the world; tell me—is it really everything it's cracked up to be? Sex, I mean."

"Well, it depends on a lot of factors, actually: whether you're in love with the person—which could make even tepid sex spectacular; whether you're in lust—in which case the act can be a bit of an anticlimax, so to speak, if it doesn't live up to the fantasy of it. Then there's technique . . . *yours, his* . . . there's experience . . ."

"Would it be worth leaving the calling for is what I'm askin'."

"Oh boy," I sigh. "I *really* don't want the responsibility of responding to that question. If you feel you've got a calling to be a nun, that's a rare and precious thing, and I would never want to throw a monkey wrench into it. You can't talk in generalities here; each situation is unique. And deeply personal. Look, I've got a recipe for brownies that some people tell me is better than sex, so who am I to judge their preferences?"

Brigid suddenly breaks out into laughter. "Oh, Jaysus, Mary, and Joseph, it's in the Doyle genes!"

Her laughter is infectious and without needing a reason, I catch the bug. "What is?"

"When did Jamie know he was in love with you?"

"I guess you'd have to ask *him* that. But he said the three little words within a week of knowing me. I think it was after only five days."

"It's a family corse," Brigid sighs. "We Doyles fall like boulders: hard and fast. Oh, Tessa, I think I'm in love with Anto. And I'm certain he feels almost the same. Why else would he ask me to Starbucks and say that I'm the kind of gorl he'd bring home to meet his mum? Tess, I need your help."

I hand her the box of tissues so she can dry her tears. "Anything you want."

"Tessa, how do I tell this poor unlucky son-of-a-gun that I'm plannin' to become a nun!"

Twenty-five

Before I deliver my Education speech, I decide
to road test the salient points at a breakfast meeting
in my living room. Gus Trumbo is there, of course, and I've
invited Imogen and Venus to join the Doyles and Brigid's new
pal from the police department, Anto O'Reilly. Maureen has
baked shortbread for the occasion.

Curious about the political process in America, Brigid asked
me if she could become involved in my campaign. In the past
couple of weeks, she's gone from feeling aimless and confused
to focused and forthright, having assumed the responsibility
of coordinating my volunteers, a task she accomplishes with
the zeal of a missionary. By now she knows each of their personal histories, and her natural warmth and compassion, im-
bued with a spirit that comprehends the meaning of true
devotion, makes her an inspiring and inspired leader: my very
own Joan of Arc.

"I, for one, want to know what qualifies you to discuss what's good for the children when you haven't had any yourself," Maureen challenges me.

"Ah. Good point. In the weeks you've been living here on the Upper West Side, how many women pushing strollers do you see when you go out for a walk?"

"When?"

"Anytime. Weekdays, weekends, mornings, afternoons."

"Sometimes I see even more prams than cell phones out there, to tell you the truth."

"Right. This district is chock-full of our country's future, Maureen. And every one of those little kids being rolled up and down the neighborhood deserves an equal chance at the American dream, wouldn't you agree?" Maureen nods her head. "While I don't have kids of my own, as a candidate I've earned the nickname 'The Nanny' because I'm looking out for *everybody's* kids with every ounce of diligence and concern for their welfare and well-being. And our public school systems often fall short, being guilty of neglect when it comes to educating all of our kids with our tax dollars. Kids look up to adults, expecting that grown-ups won't squander their trust in them. And for too many generations, our governments at every level have betrayed that fragile trust. And we *tsk-tsk* and shake our heads, and lament that it's a pity and a shame. Our public education system is very, very broken."

"So how're *you* gonna fix it?" Gus prompts. "Give me specifics. I want a reason to vote for you, not just vote *against* the other guy."

"For one thing, when I get to Washington I'm going to hold this administration's feet to the fire, getting them to put *our* money where their mouth is, making sure that the No Child Left Behind Act is properly and adequately funded so that it can make good on its initial promise. Public education tries to give the broadest coverage to the largest market, and when it fails, as it too often does, it's because it doesn't try to meet the individual needs of the students. By painting with the widest brush, half our kids are falling through the cracks of the system."

"Watch those mixed metaphors, sugar," Gus warns jovially.

"You know a good speechwriter?" I shoot back.

Imogen raises her hand. "Tessa, are you talking about public or private schoolkids?"

"I'm talking about public schoolchildren right now. And there's no reason why they should get shafted. If they start out on an unequal footing in terms of the quality of their education, that's more than likely where many of them will end up. An inadequate education dooms our kids—the future of America—to a permanent economic purgatory, keeping them in poverty in perpetuity unless we make some huge changes to the system."

"All right, then. I'm a cop. Do you have any *concrete* changes to propose, and how are you going to pay for them without, say, taking money away from the NYPD?"

"New York doesn't have to rob Peter to pay Paul, Captain O'Reilly. There's millions of dollars of pork in the Department of Education budget and I'm not talking about the mystery meat in school lunches. I'm going to demand that the DOE ruthlessly cut waste. Insist on oversight so that corrupt custodians can't embezzle the money that's earmarked for our kids' pencils, crayons, and textbooks. Do you know that New York City school custodians get *over forty million dollars* every year—placed into bank accounts under their own names—to purchase goods and services—they don't buy just mops and sponges—and *still* our kids don't have enough textbooks and school supplies?"

Venus shakes her head in disgust. "Why don't they just shop at Staples?"

"Good point. I think I'll include that in my speech." I make a margin note. "These guys have such a cushy contract that they're not obligated by their union to vacuum a rug, or to paint any section of wall over ten feet high; and they can put a few extra bucks in their pockets by hiring subcontractors to wash the windows. They're in charge of jobs like replacing door hinges, but aren't allowed to order the parts themselves, because—get this craziness—purchasing *hinges* falls within the purview of the Department of Education itself! It's Orwellian."

"Did any of yiz know that over the past couple of years at least two criminal rings of janitors on the take have been brought to trial here in New York City?" Brigid asks the group. "Now, what could be worse than stealing from innocent schoolchildren? And they're all good Cat-lick names, too. For shame! You can be sure that's not how they were raised in the Church."

Venus raises her hand. "I have to say that what pisses *me* off no end is that our public schools claim that in order to teach the basics, they've got to cut what they like to call the 'extras.' Music. Art. Shop classes. The very subjects so necessary for a well-rounded education, that help our kids grow into healthy and well-balanced adults, are the first to be removed from the curriculum because a bunch of bureaucrats think they're a waste of money."

"Another good point, V. And the fact is that there already *is* enough money in the budget to pay for all those so-called 'extras.' The problem doesn't need more money thrown at it; it can be solved by reallocating what's already in the mammoth budget." I then call on Brigid's new friend, who looks like he has something more to add.

"The shortbread are delicious, Maureen," he says.

"I'm an old-fashioned sort and I'd prefer it if you'd call me Mrs. Doyle. But thank you, Anto."

"That would be Captain O'Reilly, Mrs. Doyle."

"Do you have any idea what the annual budget is for the New York City Department of Education? Any inkling?" I ask.

Jamie raises his hand like an eager schoolboy. "A billion dollars?"

"Guess again. Fourteen billion dollars. Fourteen. *Billion*. Dollars. To educate 1.1 million kids in 1200 schools."

"I'm not even sure I know how much a billion is," Brigid confesses.

"If you placed a dollar bill on a table every second—one Mississippi . . . two Mississippi . . . three Mississippi—twenty-four hours a day, at the end of about eleven and a half days, you'd reach a *million* dollars. If you applied the same formula to count to a *billion*, it would take you *thirty-two years* to reach one billion dollars."

"Give me a minute. I'm still wrappin' my brain around that," says Brigid. "Wait—448 years of nonstop counting to reach fourteen billion."

"So, Shakespeare could have started during his lifetime and you'd still be counting the same fourteen billion," Venus muses.

"Except that they didn't have dollars then," Imogen adds.

"Look," I say, "we can still pay the teachers more; we can still make sure the kids have textbooks. We can still construct new schools so there aren't thirty-five kids shoehorned into a classroom where the teacher is forced to adjudicate instead of educate. There's *gobs* of money in the school budget, but we're permitting the new tenants of Tammany Hall, the vastly bloated Department of Education, to mis-distribute it like mad. Instead of cutting staff and trimming the fat, the bureaucracy has grown."

"Tessa, why do you care so much?"

Maureen's comment casts a pall on the room.

"How can someone *not* care?" I reply.

"My son upped and left his family and his job in Ireland to follow you all the way here to New York and stake his life with you. Now you want to run off and become a congresswoman. Living in Washington for most of the year. And where does that leave Jamie?"

"You talk about children, Maureen. You believe that children are the greatest gift a woman can have, yes? Well, go to the window and look down the street in both directions. Why should there be mothers out there whose kids will end up with so much less than other mothers' kids—when in the richest country in the world there's no good reason for it? I'm not going to stand by quietly while each year, right here in New York City, the greatest city in the world, 550,000 of our 1.1 million public schoolchildren are failing. We're got a fifty percent dropout rate. That's not okay! I have the opportunity to make a difference in the lives of tens of thousands of those mothers and kids. Not only can't I turn my back on that chance, I'm courting it. And where is it written that being a congresswoman means that I can't start a family of my own?"

"Unlike Brigid's candidacy, Tessa's doesn't mean she's a celibate, Ma. For two years—more if America's lucky—Tess will be only three hours away by train, less by airplane, and I've got some plans of me own that will keep me mightily occupied whilst she's out of town. I may not be home much meself."

Maureen scrutinizes her son darkly. "What are you going on about, Jamie?"

He glances at his watch. "My goodness, is that the time? Who's comin' with me to Tessa's speech?"

There's a nip in the air this morning. It's only the first week in October, but the kids on their way to school are wearing jackets for the first time this season. They look like mini Michelin men, trudging stiffly as they struggle with the heft of their backpacks and the fullness of their coats. The press is clustered on this lackluster patch of asphalt that passes for a playground at one of the local public grammar schools. A twelve-foot-high fence surrounds the space, which is punctuated only by a rusty basketball hoop. I've seen prison yards that are better equipped for recreation.

We're set to begin at 8:15. Gus scans the playground for reporters, recognizing representatives from the local TV stations and the city's major newspapers. "All the usual suspects in place, darlin'," he whispers in my ear. "By the way, I'm glad you didn't wear a suit today," he adds, giving my wardrobe the once-over. "Too tailored. The skirt and sweater work much better. Warm tones, soft fabrics, minimal jewelry, fit your image. This is working for you. You're shivering, Tess. Want my jacket?"

"Until we start, thanks," I say, appreciating the loan of his sportcoat. Don't want any ENs on camera, particularly since the media possesses the uncanny ability to require very little fodder before dishing up a smorgasbord of a scandal. The last thing I need is any visible nipplage through my sweater. I can just imagine the *Post*'s headline: TESSA MILKS IT ON THE PLAYGROUND. Briefly I wonder what it is about the political ego that makes people forgo coats and hats, even scarves, during outdoor public appearances. Is it an "I'm so strong I can withstand an arctic blast in my shirtsleeves," or an "Oh, God I don't want to look fat on camera" thing?

"T-minus two," Gus tells me, and I hand back his jacket. I usually speak from memory, with notes on index cards for flow. Since I write my own speeches, I'm so familiar with what I want to say and how I want to say it that most of the time I don't refer to my notes. This morning, they're tucked into my purse.

The crowd cheers and moves closer as I step up to the portable podium. A number of people carry placards saying CRAIG FOR CONGRESS and WEST SIDERS ARE TESS SIDERS in royal blue letters. Many of them are neighborhood moms with kids attending this school. Several have brought their dogs along.

"Greetings, everyone, and thanks for coming out on this chilly morning. My name is Tessa Goldsmith Craig and I am running for Congress."

When the applause dies down I say, "Now I may be a Democrat, but when 'business as usual' doesn't work for me—even if the programs are sponsored by colleagues on my side of the aisle—you can bet I'm going to have a lot to say about it. I intend to propose and support commonsense policies with tangible benefits in the real world. There are a number of issues on which I'm going to challenge the status quo. Someone's going to have to have a really good reason if they're going to say to me, 'Well, we've always done it this way,' and expect me to accept that and move on. I don't want to hear rhetoric; I want to see action!"

Following some applause, I add, "This morning I want to talk about education. It actually pains me to say that in every sense of the word, our schools are failing our children. Failing to educate them—and when the school fails to educate, the children fail their classes."

I hit the points we covered over Maureen's shortbread earlier this morning, and make an additional point about the custodians.

"As a society, we *say* we place a high value on education. Our teachers are our heroes, we say. But heck, why bother to bust your butt scrimping and saving to send Junior to college—in the hope that perhaps he will be inspired to return to the classroom as a teacher—when he can cut class, drop out or flunk out, and still make a damn good living as a school custodian? Because on average, the 838 school custodians—who clean 1200 schools, by the way, so you do the math and figure out just how filthy your kid's school is . . . those 838 custodians make more money than most of the teachers do."

And then I move to the subject of the teachers themselves. "We need to be encouraging passionate individuals, eager and hungry to share their knowledge and wisdom, to enter and remain in the teaching profession, not be giving a free pass to lousy, out-of-touch, uninspiring teachers just because they're tenured. We don't tolerate social promotion for the students; we shouldn't tolerate it for their teachers and principals. And *yes*, we need to be paying teachers a fair and competitive wage, commensurate with that of teachers in other large cities. Yet that doesn't mean we have to throw more money at the problem in order to fix it. Let's say you're at the local Laundromat: would you keep feeding quarters into a clothes dryer that doesn't seem to be doing the job, on the foolish expectation that more money will mean that the machine will suddenly get hot enough to dry your stuff?"

After I get into my how-much-is-a-billion perspective, I say, "It's time for a shake-up across the board when—not just in New York City but all over America—so many of our schoolchildren are denied the opportunity to compete fairly in the world market because they leave school ill-prepared to become viable, flourishing members of the workforce. While Singapore is exporting its remarkably successful HeyMath system that makes an often arcane subject more intellectually accessible, we continue to deny tens of millions of our own public schoolkids the ability to really participate in any meaningful way in the American Dream, condemning them to an American nightmare. An inadequate education fosters a permanent underclass and the institutional poverty that prevents most of these children from ever being able to climb out of the mire.

"In my view, when policies don't work, it's time to rethink them, not just throw more money at them. It's your money, folks. *Our* money. When a school system fails to educate, what are we paying for? Elected representatives serve the public on your hard-earned quarters. When I come before you and let you know where I stand on a given issue, it's a *job interview*. I'm ready to work overtime to be sure that New York City gets as much back as it contributes. For too many years we've been depositing more tax dollars into the giant 'one-armed bandit' of our federal government than many other Americans, and receiving far less than our fair share in return.

"*All of us* want a *more secure America* and a *better future* for our children. It's time to *demand* effective government where ethics, accountability, and mutual responsibility are not scoffed at, a government which is *authoritative, not* authoritarian. We *can* be a place where broad prosperity is a reality and not a pipe dream.

"If you hire me this November to be your advocate on Capitol Hill, you can bet that every day I'll be there with my giant metaphorical plastic bucket, demanding that we get our quarters back—to put toward our city's safety and security in a truly meaningful way, fighting for all the resources we need to make sure that *every* New Yorker, regardless of their socioeconomic bracket, has equal odds when it comes to achieving the American dream."

"Go Tess!" shouts Jamie, as I step away from the podium. A number of women gather to shake my hand.

Gus grabs the mic and announces my web address. "Tessa personally answers every e-mail she receives," he tells the crowd. "So let her know how you feel about something and she'll open up a dialogue with you."

As the last of the group disperses, Jamie slips his arm about my waist. "I'm proud of you, ya know," he says, giving me a squeeze. "Seein' you standing up there with your passion and your fire and your determination. I didn't know yiz when you were behind the scenes, but this is your element, gorl. You'll be a grand parliamentarian: a fist of oak in a velvet glove."

"Tell me," I tease, sliding my hands underneath his corduroy jacket. "will you be wearing this tee shirt to my swearing-in?"

"Oh aye, I've been planning on it," he winks. The brown shirt, which looks like it's seen many washings, bears a logo for the Dublin Hooligans rugby team, and beneath it the slogan "no brain, no pain."

"That's not a real team, is it?" I ask with furrowed brow.

"You can't be serious, gorl." The playground is now empty, except for Gus Trumbo and Jamie's relations, who are well out of earshot. "The house is sold now, ya know. My flat in Dublin. There was a shite-crazy bidding war, and I ended up with 925,000 euro for it. A feckin fortune." I realize that's over 1.1 million in U.S. dollars. "Venture capital," he adds, with a mile-wide grin. He kisses me full on the mouth. "Tessa Goldsmith Craig, I'm goin' to be realizing *my* American dream."

Twenty-six

 October 24

We're in the homestretch; less than two weeks until election day, but I needed to get away from it all for a while. On Gus's advice, I played it safe in my Education speech, steering clear of the potentially toxic topics, and it went over well, enabling me to cut Dobson's lead to only four points—with the usual "plus or minus three percentage points" caveat—leaving us (on the upside) in a statistical dead heat. Gus is convinced that it's still anybody's ball game. But Dobson is jamming the airwaves with attack ads, slamming me in two different commercials. In one spot he positions me as an inexperienced neophyte ("Just because Tessa Craig wrote for a congressman, it doesn't make her right for Congress"). In the other ad he paints me as a Washington insider, literally in bed with the denizens of Capitol Hill. "They say that politics makes strange bedfellows," Dobson drawls, then proudly pokes his chest with his thumb. "But this businessman will put an end to business as usual." In typical mudslinging fashion, neither ad makes any mention of what Dobson would actually do if he got to Congress, or why he deserves to be elected instead of me. I'm having to develop a rhino hide against his slings and arrows.

A burst of late, but still-glorious Indian summer has turned New York into a shimmering golden bowl and tugged at my soul to step outside and revel in it. A last hurrah before late autumn's breath blows chilly once again. Of course, for me this is a working nature break, because I've got a speech to tweak and numerous papers to review, and because I'm a compulsive multitasker I've also brought the sweater I'm secretly knitting for Jamie, but there's no reason I can't do any of it outdoors. Besides, there were just too many distractions at home for me to work on my speech there. Maureen, who by now has completed jigsaw puzzles of every European capital, has grown testier, fretting about being homesick and missing the rest of her family and her thriving reborn doll business, although she's not made a move to return to Ireland. It's strange to me that as a native New Yorker herself, though she's been here for weeks, she hasn't displayed even the slightest tinge of hometown nostalgia. She's not even mildly curious to visit the rest of the city to see how it's changed (or not) since her departure so many decades ago. When I took her and Brigid up to Washington Heights to visit the Cloisters, Maureen just sniffed and remarked, "We've got plenty of Catholic things back in Dublin. Whaddo I need this for?"

Sitting out here in Central Park, admiring the gold and russet glory of the trees that ring the Great Lawn my mind *tends to wander . . . two pleasant-looking shirtless guys and their gorgeous golden retriever are playing Frisbee. Frisky Maeve, restless by my side, is dead curious about their game. I love days like this. I'm lying here on a blanket, letting the sun warm my face. The sky is so blue and there's just the hint of a breeze, and suddenly I'm craving cider and a freshly made donut, warm and crisp on the outside and . . . okay, I should be working on the speech instead of writing in my journal. But I'm not . . . and I'm thinking about Brigid and what she'll do about her cop, and what she'll tell her mother if she decides to go out on a date with him. And this gets me thinking about whether les femmes Doyle ever plan to leave my apartment. Haven't they gotten the hint that Jamie is pretty well entrenched? He's now working full-time at the Pot o' Gold, having passed an accredited bartending and mixology course and received state certification permitting him to serve alcohol to the public. He told me he took the course in order to be conversant with local liquor laws, even though he thought the instructors were clueless on a couple of counts. "Their speed test is a feckin' joke. How are you expected to sorve up twenty drinks in six minutes when it takes three to pull a pint of Guinness!" He tendered his resignation as a hansom cabbie, and his goal appears to be a career where he never needs to wear anything more formal than a tee shirt.*

Maureen had a cow when Maeve used the born-again doll she gave me as a chew toy. She hadn't the heart to spank the dog, but she terrified the hell out of the poor puppy. Maeve began to howl and the neighbors called the cops, and who should show up at the door but Anthony O'Reilly and his current partner, who happens to be a very attractive policewoman—the first one I've seen wear-

ing lipstick and eyeliner who wasn't a TV character. And Brigid began acting horribly strange—well, horribly strange for a woman planning to become a bride of Christ, not for a young woman enmeshed in a conflicted attraction to a man who doesn't know her secret and spends most of his day in the company of a comely chica who knows how to use a 9-millimeter.

An entrepreneurial soul strolls across the lawn selling bottled water, so I buy one for myself and one for my buddy Maeve, pouring it into my empty tuna salad container. Her thirst quenched—but apparently, another craving left unsatisfied, she suddenly bounds off in pursuit of the golden retriever. Was she ever spayed? Why do I not know this!? Is she old enough to be in heat, or is she just curious? I've never had a dog before! Please, God, tell me this is a fool's errand on her part! Are they fighting, playing, or shtupping? I am so not ready to deal with doggy sex.

Whoops! Oh, shit!

I drop the journal onto my blanket and dash off in pursuit of my amorous puppy, fearful she'll end up the worse for this encounter, whatever kind it is. She's several yards from me and by the time I reach her, she and the retriever are entangled in what appears to be some highly energetic canine foreplay, which neither the retriever's masters nor I are able to break up without risking some bodily harm ourselves. In fact the two bare-chested Frisbee players seem terrified of entering the fray. I have no clue what to do—Maeve didn't come with a manual—and after shouting her name numerous times proves fruitless, I try to grab her leash. Unsuccessful, I steel myself to try to tackle her. Or maybe I have a better chance at grabbing hold of her new inamorata; he's bigger and is in an easier, well, position, for me to attempt an interruptus before we get past the point of no return. I've seen movies where garden hoses are turned on the dogs, but there's nothing like that handy in the middle of Central Park. This is what I get for giving my dog a name which in Gaelic means "the intoxicating one." *Make a decision, Tess!*

Here's hoping the barks are bigger than the—

I fling myself at the pair of dogs. Damn, the retriever is a lot heavier than I'd anticipated. *No, no, dog—down, dog—I am not a bitch, no matter what Bob Dobson says about me.* What seems like an eon later I emerge, clutching Maeve like a parcel. Understandably, she's both exhausted and sexually frustrated. At least that's what her "thanks a whole fucking lot, Mom" expression seems to say.

"You're both bleeding," one of the retriever's owners says. Maeve's got a really nasty cut just above her snout. "I'm sorry, I don't have anything—Jason, do you have any Band-Aids?" His companion dolefully shakes his head.

"It's okay, I have some water back at my blanket," I say, trying to catch my breath. I touch my hand to my face, where I realize there are a couple of stinging cuts. "And I'm sure I've got some tissues in my purse."

I was so anxious to break up the two dogs that I'd abandoned everything, including my bag, an unwise move in Manhattan. Miraculously, my purse is right where I left it, with my wallet still untouched. I find a few paper napkins, stuffed into my purse during one of many stops—the compulsory gustatory tour every candidate finds themselves making along the campaign trail: a bagel with a schmear here, a slice of pizza there, a taco or two, a stick of sate, a plate of Kung Pao, sushi, spanikopita—it's a wonder I haven't gained twenty pounds since I agreed to run for David's congressional seat. "You, young lady are oversexed!" I chide Maeve gently. And despite her wound, she looks at me as if to ask, "Shouldn't that be a *good* thing?" Dampening the napkins, I try to clean off Maeve's face, but it's not enough to really cleanse the wound. I gather up my journal and the yarn for the sleeve I was working on, and stuff them back into my bag. Then I wrap Maeve in the blanket and grab her leash, juggling everything as I race out of the park.

I haven't a clue where the closest animal hospital is, so in my panic I take her to the nearest place where people won't make a fuss if I take the time to try to clean her up, where I know there's a first-aid kit with some iodine in it, though of course I don't even know if you can use iodine on a dog's open cut. I bring her to the Pot o'Gold. Jamie's there now; he grew up with a dog. He'll know what to do.

I blow through the door in a complete panic.

"Jaysus, Mary, and Joseph, what happened to *you?*" Jamie exclaims.

"We got caught in a dog fight. Dog fuck, actually," I amend, lowering my voice.

"My poor, poor babies," he says, stepping out from behind the bar and folding me into his arms.

Breaking the sweet embrace I ask him, "Is her cut bad? Do we need to take her to the vet?" I practically shove the poor little puppy into his face. "Can you fix it?" I murmur plaintively.

He looks nervous. "Tess, the health department will have everyone's arse in a sling." There are only a few patrons in the bar. I don't recognize any familiar faces, but then again, I don't tend to frequent bars, even the Pot o'Gold, this early in the day. Jamie grabs the first aid kit and a couple of bar towels. "Meet you in the ladies' room," he mutters in my ear.

I drop the blanket and my big purse on one of the back tables. The bag is spilling over with stuff and sort of flops onto its side, but I'll deal with it later. Hurt dogs come first. I carry a fretting Maeve into the tiny restroom and a minute or so later Jamie steps inside, and hands me a shotglass.

"What's this for?"

"Anesthetic. No, not for *her*, silly! For *you*. I figured you might need it to calm your nerves. You haven't looked at your own scratches yet, have yiz?"

It's not cocktail hour by a long shot, but I toss back the whiskey.

While Jamie inspects the puppy's face, I check mine in the mirror. There are a *few* scratches, in fact; not pretty, but nothing too deep. Nonetheless, I hope they heal by the end of the week. Dobson and I are set to debate on Sunday evening at one of the local news studios, and of course I've got a number of personal appearances to make from now until November sixth.

"I think it looks worse than it is," he tells me, of Maeve. "You'd better hold her still while I clean the cut. That part isn't goin' to make her too happy."

The judicious application of soap and water seems to do the trick, though I can't tell which the puppy likes less: the pain or the washing. "You're my hero. You know that, right?" I say, bringing my lips to his.

"That I do. But I love it when you remind me."

"You're probably Maeve's hero, too." The puppy licks his face affectionately. "See?"

"That's because I'm one of the people who feeds her, walks her, and kept her from an emergency visit to the vet this afternoon."

"Nevertheless. We both love you for it. And I love you for a few more reasons than that. Just keep the Milk Duds away from my printer in the future, okay?"

He looks shocked. "I didn't—!"

"Jamie . . . ? They *roll.*"

We exit the ladies' room and I return to the back table to gather up all my stuff. "If this pub thing doesn't work out, you could always check out veterinary school," I tell Jamie. "See you back at Casa Craig." Another soft kiss on the lips from Jamie and I'm out of there.

It's not until I get home with Maeve and empty my purse, that I realize—with great horror—that my journal isn't in it.

I am paralyzed with panic.

"Is Jamie at the Pot o'Gold?" Brigid asks me. "Do ya want me to call him?"

"Yes—please. Ask him to scour the area near the back table where I'd left my bag."

"Are ya sure it's not folded up into the blanket instead?"

I shake out the blanket, just in case. "Never more positive."

"Maybe it fell out of your bag on the way home. Let's retrace your steps," she offers. "C'mon, Mum. We'll scour the neighborhood."

Leaving Maeve in the apartment, Maureen, Brigid, and I comb the streets of the Upper West Side in search of my journal, poking through trash cans, scouring curbsides, and finally reaching the spot on Great Lawn where I had parked my blanket before the dog fight incident, though I'm certain I shoved it back into my bag after rescuing Maeve. No trace of it—which is more or less what I'd expected, but Brigid thought we should cover all the bases, just in case. The Frisbee players with the golden retriever are gone. We ask the few remaining people in the area, those souls desperate to catch the last rays of Indian summer sunlight, whether they saw anything, but we come up empty-handed. My heart threatens to pound right out of my chest, even as I attempt to appear calm. After all, these folks are potentially my voters. Some picture of unruffled leadership I'd make, if I showed my panic at this moment!

Disheartened and demoralized, we leave the park. "I need a drink," Maureen sighs.

"Make mine a triple," I say. The previous shot of Jameson's hadn't even made a dent.

"I could use one too," adds Brigid. Her mother gives her a dirty glance. "What?" She looks a bit squirrelly, as if she's afraid Maureen can read her mind.

We head back to the Pot o'Gold. I bury my face into Jamie's shoulder for several moments and enjoy the security of his embrace. "We didn't find it," I whisper.

"Oh, mo cushla," he murmurs. Stroking my hair, he adds, "Go in there and have a nice cry, and I'll have some mollification all ready for you when you come out."

In the claustrophobic ladies' room at the Pot o'Gold, I burst into sobs. My life is in that book—every compromising detail, my deepest feelings and darkest thoughts. Mentally, I beat myself up over not taking everything into the ladies' room with me in the first place, even if there was no place to hang it up or put it down.

Everyone in the bar knows who I am; Tessa Craig can't have a nervous breakdown in front of them. Jamie pours my whiskey into a ceramic coffee cup and counsels me to sip it slowly. I know it's bass-ackwards, but I request a beer chaser. Sitting in a booth with Maureen and Brigid, I pray that this is a nightmare of horrific proportions from which I will soon awaken, with nothing worse than a cold and clammy sweat for my troubles.

Homesick for Irish cooking, Maureen orders a plate of fish and chips. In the past few weeks, since Jamie's been talking extensively with the pub's owner, the kitchen has vastly improved and now the dish much more closely resembles the one served at Blackpools.

Brigid tucks into a burger. She looks nervous. After a few bites, she starts drumming her fingers on the table. "Mum . . . I need to tell you something."

Maureen looks up from her fish, fork poised in midair. "Is something wrong, Bridge?"

"Wrong? I . . . I don't know that it's *wrong*, but it's . . . Mum, I've met someone. A man."

"And?" Maureen asks anxiously, shoveling the morsel of fish into her mouth before it falls off the fork.

"And . . . I'm not so sure I want to go ahead with becoming a sister. Poverty and obedience are tough enough to vow, but—" She glances anxiously at me. "I'm having second thoughts about the chastity . . . the . . . celibacy thing. Mum, I'm thinking of calling an end to my candidacy and leaving the community house. I'm no longer certain I can commit to the decision I made last year . . . and which I may regret for the rest of me life."

Maureen's face turns crimson. The poor woman, utterly blindsided by her daughter's confession, looks like a blowfish. She begins to cough and gasp for air—and all of sudden Brigid and I realize that she's choking.

"Jamie! Help! Does anyone here know the Heimlich maneuver?!" Poolside images of David Weyburn and Kelly Adonis flash before my eyes.

Jamie vaults the bar and in a split second he's at the booth, trying to help his mother. "What happened?!"

"I told her I was thinking of callin' a halt to my discernment and she torned all red and started choking," a highly flustered Brigid tells him. "Have I killed Mum? Oh, God, it's a sign. I never should have thought about sex."

I'm on the phone with 911 and they're summoning an ambulance. Jamie's Heimlich efforts are proving unsuccessful. I can hear the siren already, but his mother's color has gone from red to blue by the time the ambulance lurches up to the curb.

The EMS technicians part the bar's patrons like Moses and the Israelites fording the Red Sea. One of them, thumping on Maureen's chest, dislodges a fishbone from her throat, but she's not reviving. As Jamie races into the kitchen to eviscerate the cook, the paramedic administers mouth to mouth, but it becomes apparent that it's going to take more to get her heart started. The paddles come out and after five calls of "Clear!" they're once more getting signs of life, enough to get her into the ambulance. I've been holding my breath—and Brigid's hand—throughout this ordeal. Maureen and I have never quite gotten along, but of course I'd feel dreadful if she died. Especially in this way, after choking on a fishbone, for God's sake.

Jamie leaves the bartending duties to one of the waiters and we all pile into the ambulance. During the tense ride to the hospital, Maureen's heart stops again. Several terrifying moments later, the paramedic has jump-started her once more, but only after administering an injection. I can feel my nails digging into my palms from gripping Jamie and Brigid's hands so tightly.

For me it's "déjà vu all over again" as Maureen is wheeled into the E.R. and from there, having been stabilized, straight up to the cardiac care unit. And damned if Dr. Magali Gupta isn't the cardio on duty tonight.

"Miss Craig, I'm sorry to see you here again so soon," she says to me.

"Some people have heart attacks and other people seem to give them," I sigh gloomily. "I guess I'm a carrier." I introduce her to Jamie and Brigid, who provides Dr. Gupta with her mother's medical history.

"She's always been healthy as a horse. Until now. I gave her a bit of bad news back there in the pub and I was afraid it killed her."

"Well, it all began when she choked on a fishbone, really," Jamie adds. "Someone's getting sacked tomorrow morning."

"She did die, though," Brigid says. "Even if it was just for a few seconds."

Dr. Gupta reviews her notes. "Well, her heart did stop—"

Jamie and I exchange a look. Is it possible that we're thinking the same thing?

"So she *did* die, you're saying."

"Yes, Mr. Doyle. Technically speaking, your mother did die."

"But she'll be all right from now on?"

"I would like to be able to guarantee that. I can assure you we will do everything we can for her. She'll need to undergo some tests to determine whether she actually had a heart attack. We won't know anything for sure until some time tomorrow."

"And I'm supposed to go home and get a good night's sleep, I suppose," Jamie fumes. In his frustration and powerlessness he looks very much like he would like to put his fist through something.

Downstairs, Brigid flips open her mobile and places a call to Captain O'Reilly. "Hey, it's me, Brigid. I need to talk to yiz about something," I hear her say. "Can we do it tonight? I really want to see you."

She grabs a cab and heads off to meet her cop, and Jamie and I return to my apartment and undress for bed. "I don't want to go through another day like this ever again," I mutter.

"She's going to be all right," Jamie says, trying to sound strong. "Isn't she? I want to say I feel it in my bones, but I just can't tell." He chuckles. "I think New York City has affected my empathetic powers."

He snuggles me close. "Don't sell yourself short," I murmur. "You knew what *I* needed just now. Your Mum'll be okay, Jamie." I settle back against his chest, seeking his warmth. "Because that's what I want to believe."

"And you'll get your journal back," he whispers, nuzzling my neck. "Because that's what *I* want to believe."

And damned if he isn't right. When we go downstairs the next morning to check on Maureen at the hospital, sitting on the shelf by the mailboxes is a brown envelope addressed to me on a printed label. I eagerly tear open the wrapping to find the diary intact. There's no note attached.

I dash back up to the apartment to stash it in my bedside table for safekeeping. On my way back down, I catch the headline of the morning paper lying on the doormat in front of the second-floor flat. I freeze like a deer staring down the muzzle of an M80. My photo is splashed on the front page of the *Post* just below the headline: TESSA MESSA.

And the exclusive—all over pages 2 and 3, CONGRESSIONAL CANDIDATE'S JUICY BITS REVEALED. Not only was my journal found—it was delivered to the editors at the *New York Post*, which has taken gleeful liberty in publishing particularly personal entries, "outing" my long-term relationship with David, the racy details of my current love life, the musings over my campaign strategy, and my diatribes against Bob Dobson and the Republican machine.

I swipe the newspaper and, white as a sheet, meet Jamie in the vestibule. "And we thought things couldn't get worse," I say weakly. "Oh, Jamie, I'm so sorry."

"Bastards!" he says, skimming the article. "Feckin' bloodthirsty bastards. You're now only just a few points down in the polls and this is how they try to give their guy an edge! What really pisses the shite out of me is that someone in the Pot o'Gold yesterday afternoon probably nicked it while we were in the ladies', cleaning up Maeve. *This*," he rages, stabbing his finger into the paper, "is not news."

I'm too wounded for tears. "Oh, yeah, my love, I'm afraid it is."

Twenty-seven

 I call Gus Trumbo from the cab. "Is it over?"
I ask him.

He already knows what I'm talking about. "Sugar, we took a
bad hit—"

"*We?*"

"We. *I'm* not quittin' you. I signed on for the whole game.
All nine innings. You can't get rid of me. It's as bad as bein'
married."

"The *Post* claimed it as an exclusive. Has it hit the TV yet? If
NY1 has its hands on it for their hourly In the Papers segment,
no one in the city'll miss it. Wait—I need to put you on hold,
I'm getting another call."

I press the button and retrieve the new call. "Tess?"

"Oh, God, David." This is when I burst into tears. "I . . . I
don't know what to say other than I'm so, so sorry." I'm terrified
he's going to chew me out.

His voice sounds strained. "Welcome to the club," he says

ruefully. "I really, really hope, though bloodied, at least you can remain unbowed through this."

"Right now I want to crawl into a little hole and curl up and die. And of course it's the worst possible time for me to deal with a disaster. Jamie's mom ended up in the CCU last night. We're on the way to see her now . . . Yeah . . . I'm afraid I do have that effect on people . . . What? I can't hear you? You're breaking up . . . Oh . . . choked on a fishbone. But she may or may not have had a heart attack afterwards. We'll find out in a little while . . . What?"

I can't help smiling through my tears as I listen to David tell me, "Well, even though you wrote that I'm 'highly self-absorbed' and 'narcissistic'—August twelfth—which I guess isn't entirely unearned, at least everyone in the world knows I'm not gay now. And you did write *some* very nice things about me, even after I'd broken up with you. You're a good person, Tess. Fuck . . . I should have told you I loved you. Not because it hit the papers, but because . . . because I felt it all along, and I should have let you know. I should have let you know every day."

"Thanks, I suppose," I sniffle. "So . . . any advice for the eviscerated?"

"Same as you gave me a while back. Keep your chin up. Maintain your dignity. Stay on message. Counting today, we've got thirteen days until the election. That's an eternity in politics. A lot can happen between now and then. The voters have lots of time to forget or forgive."

"Tell that to Howard Dean. Or Gary Hart—well, he did something truly dumb, so don't count that one. And what about you, David? The *voters* might have been able to forgive and forget all that silliness about the is-he-or-isn't-he-gay shit, but the *press* wouldn't let it go. If they sink their teeth into this one, I'm sunk."

"Do you think a public appearance on my part will help at this point? We could all laugh it off and remind everyone that it's got nothing to do with the issues."

"I've got Gus on the other line. I'll ask him how he wants to play this. It's just happened so fast I can't think straight. My head feels like it's been invaded by a bunch of dwarves with pickaxes."

"Careful, if the wrong person hears you use that word, you'll be accused next of not being PC."

"Pickaxes?" I ask snarkily. "Dwarves, dwarves, fucking Disney dwarves! I've got to run; we're at the hospital. I'll try to call you later—or ask Gus to keep you in the loop." I flip the phone shut and turn to Jamie. "And you, my poor baby, caught in the crossfire." I try very hard not to cry. "Maybe you *should* go back home with your mother. As soon as she's well enough to leave the hospital, we'll get you a plane ticket, too."

Jamie steps out of the taxi and extends his hand to help me out of the car. "Are you daft, gorl?" He takes me in his arms. "Tessa Goldsmith Craig, I'm in this for the long haul." We head up the hospital steps. "Ya didn't write anything bad about me, did yiz?" he asks uncertainly.

"I said you were a dreadful slob," I confess meekly.

"Oh, that. Slob I can handle. It lends me a certain air of charm. I was afraid you might have written somewhere that I have a small wanker or something like that."

"But you don't. In fact," I say, blushing crimson, "I may have written somewhere that you don't suffer from the Irish Curse."

"Oh! I don't think the paper printed that comment."

"Just wait," I sigh. "It's only been one news cycle."

I am tremendously grateful that there are no television sets in the Cardiac Care Unit. This buys us some time with Maureen.

And we don't bother to tell her that Brigid didn't come back to the apartment last night . . . which of course means nothing . . . except that Brigid didn't come back to the apartment.

"Where's Brigid," Maureen asks us. Jamie and I exchange a glance. Do we lie? This could be a test of how in tune we are. Will we come up with the same answer on the spur of the moment?

"I don't know, Mum," Jamie says. "She's a grown woman."

"What's that supposed to mean?" Maureen demands.

"Mum, we've had a bit of a rough morning—"

"And I haven't? Hooked up to God knows how many tubes and wires over here. I feel like a human carburetor. Did ya bring me a puzzle, at least?"

There's no place to sit, so Jamie and I hover glumly near his mother's bedside. Dr. Gupta and Brigid appear within moments of each other, Brigid muttering a guilty "Sorry I'm late, Mum."

"Well, the good news is that you didn't suffer a heart attack, Mrs. Doyle," the doctor tells her. "But we would like to keep you here another day for observation, just as a precaution."

"Jamie, as soon as they release me from this filthy place, I want to go home. And you and Brigid are coming with me. I've had enough of this nonsense to last a lifetime."

The Doyle siblings exchange a glance. "Ya know, Mum, Goethe said, 'What does not kill me makes me stronger.' "

"Goethe said a lot of things, Jamie. But he was a German. Why should I listen to *him?*"

"Why not? He also said, 'Nothing is worth more than this day.' "

"You're talking nonsense. Have you been dipping into my morphine drip?"

"You're not on morphine, Ma."

"I'm taking the two of yiz home, and that's my last word on the subject. Chasing all the way across the Atlantic after some American woman, abandoning your family to manage the business without you. You're not an adolescent, Jamie."

"Well, you're right on that count, Ma. I'm over forty years old. Now, not only would I not consider retorning to Ireland with yiz, but regarding the bit about running off to the States to court an American woman—that's just about what Da did when he came a-wooin' you. Isn't it now? The way he tells it, Grandma had been wanting him to go back to Ireland but he'd just met you and didn't want to let a good thing slip through his fingers."

As Maureen blushes, Jamie removes an envelope from his coat pocket. "I figure now is as good a time as any to tell you this. Better, even. If your heart stops again, we've got the medics twenty feet away. You see what this is? It's a deed of sale. You're looking at the proud-as-shite new owner of the Pot o'Gold."

"Wh—this is madness, Jamie! What the hell did you use for money?"

"I sold my flat in Dublin. Feathered me new nest egg nicely." Maureen appears to be in shock. "I'm stayin' in New York. I might be middle-aged, but I'm finally going to own my own pub. I'm following me own dream now—which includes being with Tessa—and marrying her, if she's daft enough to have me."

Now this—my present state of being—is what "shock and awe" really means!

"Over my dead body!" swears Maureen.

"Too late, Ma!" Jamie says triumphantly.

And the evil spell is broken. And although my political career may be on a respirator, or so it certainly seems right now, there are little Disney bluebirds fluttering around my head, because any woman would be a fool not to be affected by Ja-

mie's sudden, and most romantic, declaration. If only I could
write it down in my diary.

"Thanks for that," Brigid says, giving her brother a shot in the
arm.

"For what?"

"Breakin' the ice with Ma. Maybe what I'm about to tell her
won't seem so bad now." She approaches the bed and gently
takes her mother's hands. "I was afraid I killed you last night
when I told you I met a man. Actually, I thought the real clin-
ker was when I said I was thinking of leaving the community
house. Well, I was up all night talking about it with Anto—"

"Who's *Anto*?"

"Forst of all, we didn't do anything—we just talked. And I
finally told him, after weeks of torning down so much as a cup
of coffee with the man, that I was planning to be a nun. And
you know very well who Anto is. *Captain O'Reilly*. I met him
at Holy Trinity. We kept running into each other there every
day. Torns out, we were both confused about a number of
things, and between the two of us we're straightening each
other out. I like him, Ma. And he likes me. So . . . I'm going to
end my candidacy. I'm goin' to write to Sister Genesius and
the Vocation Director, thanking them all for their faith in me,
but that I've realized I'm not a good fit for the community after all, and . . . I'm goin' to stay on in New York, and see what
happens."

Poor Maureen looks like she's at a funeral. "You—you're as
daft as yaw brother. But *you* don't have working papers. How
are ya going to stay here legally? I don't want no trouble with
the authorities. It's not the Doyle way."

"I've got sponsors. Father Mulligan at Holy Trinity offered
me a job as a receptionist when I told him I was thinking of

staying in the States. And now that Jamie's going to own the Pot o'Gold, he can hire me as a waitress."

"Oh, I can, can I? You've got it all thought out, haven't yiz?"

Brigid beams at her brother. "I have, actually."

Maureen is weeping. Too proud to ask for a tissue, she's trying to blink the drops back behind her tear ducts. I feel the urge to hug her. Ever so gingerly, so as not to disturb any of her tubes, I put my arms around her. "I'm not a good one for change," she confesses softly. "Never got used to miniskirts or rock music or Vatican II; I've even worn my hair the same way since I was twenty. Family and duty and responsibility are more important to me than anything in the world. Always have been. Father McCaffrey back home in Dublin is always telling me I need to let go. I don't know why I hold onto things so tight, but I do. It's just my way. I don't have any deep dark history of loss . . . there's just something in me that wants to see all my children as babies who need me, no matter how old they get. I was a nurse for a lotta years, ya know. In a children's hospital. And every one of them was like one of my babies. It's why I was no good at it when push came to shove; I cared too much. I couldn't bear it when we lost one of them. Well, maybe *that's* my history of loss, then, but I was like this long before I entered nursing. The reborn dolls I make are a part of that, too, I suppose. If everyone could stay a perfect little child . . . ach, ya probably think I'm crazy as a loon."

Well, maybe she's a bit of a head case, but who isn't in their way? We've each got our eccentricities. And one of us now has twenty laminated giant jigsaw puzzles hogging every bit of counter space in her duplex.

"Are you going to marry Jamie, then?"

I glance over at my beau. "Do you think he'll put his clothes in the hamper if I do?"

"Oh, you're asking for a lot, now. But if anyone can get my son to pick up after himself, you can, Tessa. Lord knows I never could. When you told him you loved him, within a day your flat looked like it had been Simonized."

"I will marry him. Especially if he still wants me after this morning."

Her expression darkens. "What's that supposed to mean?"

"You'll know soon enough anyway. Someone found my journal and brought it to the *Post*. They printed excerpts from it in the morning paper. Since the paper is also online, everyone in the world from my optometrist to Osama bin Laden now knows about my relationship with Congressman Weyburn. And with Jamie."

"Jamie do you know what you're getting into?" Maureen asks him.

"Tessa's entitled to her personal thoughts. It's not her fault that everyone is reading them. Ya know—I want to think positive on this for as long as I can. Nothing she did was against God's commandments, ya know. And would you want to vote for a candidate who *didn't* enjoy sex?"

Although the *Times* buries the diary story, relegating it to a page deep within the Metro section, the tabloids blaze it. The *Daily News* with its TESSA CONFESSA headlines lags a day behind the *Post* by virtue of the latter's exclusive; and the *Post* never does reveal how my journal got into their hands.

The letters to their editor, published the following day, castigate the paper. People have written everything from "Shame on you for trying to smear Ms. Craig!" to "I always thought Ms. Craig was a babe, but now I'm certain of it" to "Mind your own business; don't you newspapers have anything substantive to write about?" But those are a drop in the bucket compared to the flood of correspondence mailed to my campaign headquarters. Brigid, Venus, Imogen, Jamie, and I open hundreds of letters from supporters. "Yeah, I admit I read the articles," one note stated, "but I still think that printing excerpts from your journal was totally sleazy. I'm a betting woman and I promise you it'll go as a strike against Mr. Dobson and cost him dearly on Election Day."

Another letter said, "I'm sorry this had to happen to you. I wasn't sure I liked you because, I mean, after all, who are you? I didn't know what qualified you to run for Congress any more than Bob Dobson. But when the paper published your diary, I found myself feeling violated on your behalf. Reading something so personal showed me that you're not a *politician*; you're just like me: a woman full of hopes and fears and dreams. I admire you very much now."

And then there was the person who wrote "You rock, girl! David Weyburn is a hunk!"

Of course, there was a fistful of sobering notes, such as the one from a man named Buck who wrote, "I'm glad the newspaper showed you to be a slut so that everyone else knows now. You're going straight to hell where you belong."

Jamie took that letter from my hand and ripped it into tiny pieces. "Don't give it another thought, me darling. Hell must be his euphemism for Congress."

Twenty-eight

 November 6—Election Day

It still feels strange to write in the same book that was stolen. Every time I open it I wonder whose hands sullied its pages, how much of it they read, whether portions were scanned into some creep's computer—where they still remain—or photocopied and stashed away in files marked "privileged information."

It's 5 A.M. The polls open in an hour. Jamie's in the shower, and Brigid is drinking coffee beside me as we get ready to hit the campaign trail for the very last day, handing out literature to voters at subway stops and street corners.

Both the New York Times *and the* Daily News *endorsed me last week. The* Post, *naturally, threw their support—lukewarm though it was—to Bob Dobson. The only thing they had to say about him was that he could never be accused of being a "Washington insider," whereas I had years of Beltway experience under my belt.*

According to local pollsters, I've now got a four-point lead—which means it's anybody's ball game—but you can never predict anything. Even weather is a factor. For instance, if it rains, the little old ladies tend to stay home, especially when they figure their candidate will win anyway.

It's pouring its ass off this morning.

And my favorite local weatherman—the hunk who looks like a Ken doll—predicts all-day inclemency.

Unions are good for getting the last-minute word out and mobilizing units to take voters to the polls. However, the formidable teachers union, though pleased with many of my views on education reform, bristled at my call to remove the pedagogical deadwood from the classrooms. While they couldn't bring themselves to endorse my opponent, they didn't exactly throw a piñata party for me either. At least the cops and firefighters are behind me—and I seem to keep EMS very busy—so they're in my corner, but unless those folks are off-duty today, they're not in a position to do a door-to-door canvas to get out the vote for me.

Time to stay focused and think positive. Tomorrow at this time, my future will be sealed.

It's a whirlwind (and very wet) day. A long, day, too. Jamie and Maureen spend it readying the Pot o'Gold. It's where we'll all gather tonight with my campaign staff and volunteers to watch the returns come in over the TV. The polls don't close until 9 P.M. so it could be a late night. I get a flutter in my chest and butterflies in my stomach when I enter the voting booth and pull the lever for myself. Whenever I vote, I feel a tinge of empowerment—that personal connection to one of the things that made a bunch of radical royalist refuseniks into American citizens. As it wasn't in the founding fathers' minds, thousands of crusading suffragettes fought like hell to correct the oversight. Funny . . . of an American's two key civic duties one (voting) is as great a pleasure as the other (jury duty) is a pain in the ass.

And this time, of course . . . *Wow*. The feeling, the event . . . it's all so momentous, so huge. Even half a year ago I never could have imagined any of this. My life has taken so many big curves lately, I've just been trying to keep up without losing traction.

Our first stop of the day is the subway station at Seventy-ninth Street and Broadway, a block from Zabar's and H&H Bagels, where I wish we had free samples to hand to the hungry masses headed to work. "Good morning! Don't forget to vote today," Imogen reminds them, as she hands them a flyer stating my key position points. It's business as usual in New York for people to ignore such electioneering, but my crew has a better than average record of "takers" (those who accept the literature) and a low percentage of "dumpers" (those who take the paper but immediately toss it into the nearest receptacle). Common sense isn't always common on the campaign trail, but Craig volunteers know to offer my flyers with a smile to everyone who looks over eighteen and has a free hand—in other words, they don't foist the handout on a struggling mom juggling a baby and a bag of groceries, or the elderly man with a cane in one hand and a health care aide on the other.

"Step up and meet your next Congresswoman," Jamie announces mid-morning in front of the giant bookstore near Lincoln Center. "Tessa Craig: a candidate with no skeletons in her closet!"

"Oh, that's real cute, Jamie," I sigh.

"I'm just makin' lemonade, mo cushla! See, they're laughing."

"Oh, my God, you're *Jamie!*" a young woman exclaims. "You know she was really on the fence about you in the beginning, but then again, I can't say I blame her, since she'd just been dumped so bad. But I was really rooting for you two to get it together."

"Thanks so much." Jamie grins. "Now don't be forgetting to vote for her today."

And so it goes throughout the day. In the pounding rain my team fans out to snag the parents picking up their kids midafternoon at area schools, and to hit the senior and community centers from Chelsea at one end of the district to the edge of Harlem at the other.

Of course we end up crisscrossing paths several times with Bob Dobson's people, who are handing out plastic bags with the Pet-o-Philia logo, encouraging people to use them as rainhats. Once upon a time, dorky plastic rainhats that unfolded like a roadmap—the kind everyone's grandmother used to wear—bearing the candidate's name, were among the typical premiums handed out to voters. But gone are the days of the rainhats and refrigerator magnets, the emery boards and pink rubber erasers. Suddenly I feel a bit nostalgic for old-school politics.

We don't stop until the polls close, and then, soggy and exhausted, we trudge into the Pot o'Gold, where television cameras record my entrance. The place is awash with red-white-and-blue buntings, punctuated by crepe paper garlands of bright kelly green, and silly leprechaun cutouts strung up over the bar. You can tell I didn't engage a pricy party planner for the occasion.

And there's Suki Glassman, all rouged and lip glossed, chirping into her mic, speaking evidently to the anchor desk. "You know, Bill, some people might think this is kind of a dingy spot for a victory celebration, but Tessa Craig is the hometown honey of this Upper West Side watering hole. In fact, she is the honey of the pub's new owner, a handsome transplanted Irishman named Jamie Doyle. Oh, wait, here's the candidate now!"

Gus Trumbo yanks me out of my yellow slicker so I don't resemble the Gorton's Fisherman on camera.

Suki shoves the mic into my face. "Tessa, how did you feel going into the last moments of the campaign?"

"I feel very good, very confident," I beam. "It's been a long road, but I'm looking forward to extending it several miles to the south after tonight."

"Do you expect the current holder of the Congressional seat, David Weyburn to arrive here later?"

I should have been prepared for this question, but I wasn't. I glance at Gus who gives me a subtle nod in the affirmative.

"David has been very supportive of my candidacy, so I expect we'll see him sometime tonight. He's always liked the fish and chips here," I quip.

"I read that he even craved it after his heart surgery. Tell me, Tessa, how did you feel about your private diary being published in the daily papers?"

Is she kidding with this one? I look her straight in the eye and ask, "Did your mother ever snoop and find yours?" The young reporter's face registers a sudden flashback of horror and embarrassment. No words are needed to describe her reply. "Exactly," I say, and press into the crowd.

"Tess-a, Tess-a, Tess-a," they chant, stomping as though they're at a barn dance.

And suddenly I think we *are* at one, when a band, which must be tucked into a corner, because I can't even see them in the crush, strikes up a traditional Irish melody. Leave it to Jamie to find some authentic musicians. More transplants, I imagine. These guys are as good as any group I heard in Dublin.

"Hot stuff coming through, and I don't mean the cook!" shouts Maureen, barreling her way though the crowd, bearing aloft a corned beef. I've never before seen her jovial side. "And we've got homemade soda bread and cabbage for the Catholics and rye bread and mustard for the Jews!" she jokes. "Brigid, clear the tables; we've got hungry mouths to feed! Drinks are on my son, everyone," she bellows. "Jamie Doyle, the new owner of the Pot o'Gold!"

Three rousing hip-hip-hurrahs for Jamie are sounded, and suddenly I feel a hand on my waist. "David!"

He gives me a gentle kiss on the cheek. "Mazel tov, Tess. I knew you could do it." He points toward the TV set mounted above the bar. The noise in the small pub is so loud that the sound is all but drowned out. "Early returns coming in. Look." I glance at the crawl. Twenty-five percent of the precincts reporting and I'm up by three points. I want to shout, send up a *whoop-whoop*, but it feels a bit undignified for the candidate herself to do so. And it's still way too premature to celebrate. The race really got down to the wire in the last few days of the campaign. "You're going to be brilliant down there," David assures me. "You've got the personality and the ability to bring people together and that's what this country needs right now."

"What are you going to be doing come January?"

"I've been invited to be a poli-sci lecturer at Columbia."

I laugh. "You and Al Gore! You're not going to grow a beard and gain a hundred pounds though, are you?"

David pats his stomach. "I might on Maureen Doyle's cooking. Actually, Habitat for Humanity wants to talk to me, I've fielded a couple of calls from one of the Progressive think tanks . . . I've got a few options on the table. Maybe I'll just sail around the world . . . I've always wanted to duplicate all of Nelson's routes."

"Well, that'll take some time." I realize that I'm going to miss him. Very much. "Well, get yourself one of those international cell phones because I may need to call you from time to time for some good advice."

"Will do. But I'm betting you won't need it."

"Hey, pipe down, everyone!" Imogen yells. "Turn up the TV."

". . . And with ninety percent of the precincts reporting, we are projecting Tessa Craig as the winner of David Weyburn's Upper West Side congressional seat, carrying fifty-six percent of the vote."

A shout rises from the crowd, followed by "Tess-a, Tess-a, Tess-a!"

". . . So it looks like Congressman Weyburn's former head speechwriter—and former girlfriend, as we learned a couple of weeks ago—will be following in his much respected footsteps. Weyburn himself was the target of some scandal earlier this year, as you may recall, when rumors—erroneous ones, as it turned out—began circulating with respect to his sexual orientation. It was those rumors that tanked his re-election campaign and opened the door for Ms. Craig. Now, exit polls conducted throughout the day today showed that many of the voters were turned off by what they perceived to be dirty tricks employed by the Dobson campaign in the final days leading up to the election. In particular, the *New York Post*'s publication of portions of Ms. Craig's personal diary was cited as giving people more than they'd bargained for in terms of each candidate's character."

But no one in the Pot o' Gold can hear those last remarks. The anchorman has been drowned out with the sound of cheering and popping corks, as bottles of champagne are passed through the crowd. Off-camera, I slug down a gulp and hoist the bottle aloft in a victory salute.

By the time Gus tells me I should make my acceptance speech, all precincts have reported and I have won the election with 58.9 percent of the vote. On the television, Bob Dobson, from his headquarters at one of the fancy midtown hotels, is giving his concession speech. "Well, the little lady had a lot of fight and bite in her and I wish her well," he says.

"Carpetbagger!" Venus shouts at the screen. "Go back to your dog house!"

This may be the first acceptance speech in political history to be made from a barstool. Actually, I forgo the stool and stand before a phalanx of microphones, flanked by Gus Trumbo, Jamie and his family, Venus and Imogen, and the local politicians who'd endorsed me. David remains discreetly out of the picture until the crowd calls for him to step into view as well.

"Thank you, New York!" I say, as the crowd cheers. "And thank you to every person who heard my message and voted for me today. We're going to take that message to Washington and hold them accountable for their promises to *truly* make America stronger and safer in *every* way. We won't accept their merely giving lip service to programs they won't properly fund and things like color-coded charts instead of true solutions. We're going to compel them to put their money—our money, in fact— where their mouth is. I can't tell you how much I look forward to serving you. And just as I've done throughout the campaign, I'll keep the lines of communication open. Anytime you've got a question or a concern, e-mail me and I'll get right to work on it.

"I have a number of people to personally thank tonight . . ." and I name them all as the rest of my acceptance speech goes by in a blur of jubilation. The next thing I know, Jamie is right by my side, saying, "Wait, wait! I've got something I want to add!" and after "Welcome all of yiz to my new home away from home," he adds, "Tonight we're here to honor Tessa Craig and to celebrate her grand and glorious victory, and I certainly rejoice in it—even if it's gonna mean, I suppose, that I won't get to see her as often come January, though from now on I'll be here every night till closing time anyways. So, Tess, I'm wanting to give yiz a reason to come back to your district and spend as much time as ya can here. We have a bit of a saying back in Ireland—that a man won't marry his sweetheart until his mother dies. Now me mum over there had a bit of a mishap with a fishbone this week—don't worry, we double-checked all the filets tonight—and the paramedics told us she'd bought a ticket to the Pearly Gates. Lucky for us, she never got her boarding pass, so she's still with us today. But the corse is lifted, and I am free to marry the beautiful princess who put me heart in a half-nelson the night I met her. Tess, remember that evening in Blackpools when I jotted something down on a paper napkin?"

Jaime takes a folded cocktail napkin from his inside jacket pocket. "Mo cushla, would ya read what it says?"

He hands me the napkin. I glance at it and my voice begins to tremble. " 'August ninth. I am going to marry Tessa Goldsmith Craig.' I remember you stuffed this in the pocket of your jeans."

He smiles: sheepishly, expectant, and tugs on his earlobe. "I don't recall hearing yer answer just now."

"It's yes, Jamie." I slip my arms around his neck and kiss him. "It's yes."

And the crowd cheers once more. Imogen hunts for a tissue as Venus wipes her eyes with the back of her hand and blows me a kiss. I hear Brigid send up a holler, and out of the corner of my eye, I catch Maureen smiling. Well, her eyes are, anyway.

And I can't help smiling too, because the camera crews are already packing it in for the night. "Tsk-tsk. After all that, they missed the money shot."

"Then let's do a second take, just to see if they're payin' attention to us." Our lips meet in a passionate kiss and when I close my eyes, the lights behind them flash red, white, blue, and green.

And the music swells just like in the movies, a joyful Irish tune, and Anto O'Reilly shyly extends his hand to Brigid and suddenly everyone starts dancing. Now *this*, I'm thinking, is a political *party*!

"I love ya, Tess," Jamie murmurs into my mouth. "And if I don't remember to say it to yiz every day for the rest of our lives, you can . . ."

"I can what?" I whisper, teasing his lower lip with the tip of my tongue.

"You can make me clean the apartment. Top to bottom, dishes to laundry. I'll do yiz one better. If I don't tell you I love ya every day from now on, I'll even forsake all *Star Trek* episodes till death us to part."

Now *that's* big. "Well, then! You've got yourself a deal, partner."

"Sealed with a kiss?" he asks impishly.

"Sealed with a dozen."

A+

AUTHOR
INSIGHTS,
EXTRAS, &
MORE...

FROM
**LESLIE
CARROLL**
AND
AVON A

Sunday in New York
Wedding of the Week

Tessa Craig and Jamie Doyle

You would think a congresswoman-elect from Manhattan would elect to have her wedding at one of New York's poshest hotels, or perhaps get away from it all with a destination wedding in Cancun or Cabo San Lucas. But Tessa Goldsmith Craig, who takes her seat next month on Capitol Hill, representing the Upper West Side, celebrated her nuptials on December 23 in a local bar.

Of course, it wasn't just any bar. For years the Pot o'Gold on Amsterdam Avenue was a rather dingy neighborhood fixture, a lone holdout against the gentrification that swept through the area over the past twenty years. Its clientele preferred their no-frills menu, their limited beverage selection—no cosmos or apple martinis here please!—and no one seemed to mind the sawdust on the floor, or the faded wallpaper. It was all part of the charm.

Ms. Craig, a longtime local resident, used to frequent the Pot o'Gold long before she met Jamie Doyle. Following the breakup of a romance that could have spelled the end of her job as a political speechwriter, her girlfriends had recommended she take a vacation to Ireland, and it was in Blackpools, the Dublin pub owned by Doyle's family, where she met the man who would follow her all the way back to New York to woo her.

Jamie Doyle bought the Pot o'Gold in late October and proposed to his colleen on election night with the news of her victory flashing on the television screen above their heads. But after Tess said yes, the venue underwent a radical transformation. Now known as *Jamie Doyle's*, the bar will offer traditional Irish music nearly every night and a menu based on Blackpools's celebrated fare. Gone is the peeling wallpaper and the sawdust has been swept away. The floors are polished oak; the booths are upholstered in leather and separated by stained glass partitions. A brass foot-rail enhances the highly polished curving antique bar. The space was even reconfigured to include a snug, the classic cozy hideaway where a woman (or lovers, nowadays) might enjoy imbibing in relative anonymity. Doyle's only concession to American kitsch would seem to be the occasional *Star Trek* marathons he plans on hosting on weekday nights.

It's the perfect place for Mr. Doyle and Ms. Craig to hold a wedding, hosting a hundred of their nearest and dearest. Who needs a choice between grilled sea bass or Cornish hen, when you've got steamed corned beef or fish and chips? Oh, sure, the champagne flowed, but so did the whiskey and the Guinness. Guests were encouraged to wear whatever they wanted to, so there was a mixture of styles, from black tie to corduroys and from beaded evening gowns to flirty cocktail dresses—as usual, the women were more turned out than the men. In keeping with his relaxed outlook on life, the groom, ever the genial host, wore a purple tee shirt under his black dinner jacket, while the bride wore an ivory satin bias-cut gown that would not have looked out of place on a screen siren of the 1930s.

Arriving at the pub in a horse-drawn hack, Tessa Craig, who

had been married previously, exchanged I do's with Jamie Doyle as the snow gently fell outside the windows of the now-eponymous pub, muffling the intrusive sounds of a busy city. Inside, a heavily decorated Christmas tree sparkled with handmade ornaments and twinkled with colored lights, while an electric menorah blazed, despite the fact that Chanukah ended nearly two weeks earlier. But it was part and parcel of the bride and groom's own religious cocktail. Ms. Craig, who has been using that surname professionally for several years, was raised as a Reform Jew; Mr. Doyle had a strict Roman Catholic upbringing.

Rabbi Rhona Lehman from Stephen Wise Free Synagogue and Father Mulligan of the Church of the Holy Trinity married the couple, while the guests were encouraged to join the band in singing their favorite songs, a repertoire that ran the gamut from "Ave Maria" to Alanis Morissette. During the ceremony, the couple stood under a chuppah made of pine boughs and held aloft by four women: Ms. Craig's cousin, Imogen Beckstein, her former college roommate, the still-exotic dancer Venus deMarley, and the groom's mother, Maureen, and his youngest sister Brigid.

Brigid Doyle herself has apparently been sprinkled with a handful of romantic stardust. Although she confessed to having been conflicted about her path for a while, she's now considering a major lifestyle change, abandoning her plans of becoming a nun back in Dublin to put down roots in New York City, with the hope that someday she'll be taking a very different set of vows. She told *Sunday Styles* she'd met a police officer here, adding, "I can't tell you for sure because it's never happened to me before, but I think I'm in love." She's also thinking of going back to school, with an eye toward a new career in social work. "I really want to help people. And there are so many ways to do it; I've done a boatload of reflectin' and the long and the short of it is, I really don't think I'm cut out for a convent."

With no young children in the family, Tessa and Jamie decided to conscript Maeve, the bride's Irish setter puppy, into performing the duties of the ring bearer. But with so many treats on the buffet table, the pooch became distracted and it was a matter of several minutes before she could be persuaded to stick to business.

Reminding the couple that an enduring marriage, like a good sauce for boiled tongue, incorporates both sweet and tart, Rabbi Lehman shared an anecdote containing the secret of a long marriage—a recipe of sorts where a wise wife made a great deal of lemonade out of the sourer moments in her marriage.

"Tessa's an avid knitter, and she's pretty handy with a crochet hook as well, so she should particularly appreciate this story: There was once a man and woman who had been married for more than sixty years. They had shared everything. They had talked about everything. They had kept no secrets from each other, except that the old woman had a shoebox in the top of her closet that she had cautioned her husband never to open or to ask her about. For all the years of their marriage, he had never thought about the box, but one day, the old woman became very ill and the doctor said she would not recover. In trying to sort out their affairs before the end came for his wife, the old man took down the shoe box and brought it to his wife's bedside. She agreed that it was time for him to learn what was in the box. When he opened it, he found two crocheted doilies and a stack of money totaling $25,000. The old man asked his wife about the contents. 'When we were married,' she began, 'my grandmother told me that the secret of a happy marriage was to never argue. She told me that if I ever got angry with you I should just keep quiet and crochet a doily.' The old man was so moved, he had to fight back tears. Only two fragile, lovingly handmade doilies were in the box. Imagine—his wife had been angry with him only two times in six decades of living and loving! He almost burst into tears. But he had to know something. 'Where did all that money come from?' he asked his wife. She gave him the most winning smile he'd seen in years. 'Oh, that's the money I made from selling the doilies.'"

Apparently, the bride and groom have more in common culturally than a predilection for corned beef. As the guests shared a knowing laugh, the groom's father Eamon jumped to his feet and exclaimed, "Rabbi, you stole my wedding toast!"

The elder of the groom's two sisters, Mary Margaret O'Connell, the mother of twin girls, offered a toast of her own. "Now Tess, this is all in fun of course, but as a longtime married woman—to an Irishman—I wanted to share with yiz this little prayer. Trust me, it'll help ya through some of the tough days when they come.

"Dear Lord: I pray for Wisdom to understand my man; Love to forgive him; and Patience for his moods; because Lord if I pray for Strength, I'll beat him to death. Amen."

The bride roared with laughter. But so did the groom. "Oh aye, you're a troublemaker Mary Mags," he told his sister.

Midway through the reception, the door to Jamie Doyle's burst open and a blast of icy wind preceded the appearance of jolly St. Nick ("I'm on the groom's side")—in the person of NYPD Capt. Anthony O'Reilly, with the prosthetic aid of a pillow. Opening his enormous sack of goodies, he proceeded to dispense a plethora of wrapped gifts addressed to each of the wedding guests. According to those who opened their presents on the spot, each one of them seemed to have been personally selected with its recipient in mind. No generic bubble makers or bags of Jordan almonds for this group.

"I love giving presents even more than I enjoy receiving them," Ms. Craig told us. "And I've been on the receiving end of such wonderful things over the past few months. I've already gotten plenty!"

During that time, Tessa told us, she found herself embarking on a journey of self-discovery and self-actualization. "I kind of imagined myself as a passenger on a train with all my personal and professional baggage around me—everything that had been familiar and comfortable for years was on the rack above my head, nestled beneath my feet—you get the picture. And then suddenly, when I thought everything had been chugging along just fine, even though there'd been some delays at a station here and there," she chuckled, "the train suddenly switched to a different track. And it hit me that this serendipitous change in travel plans meant that maybe there was another destination I should consider."

The groom approached his forty-year-old bride and gave her a quick snog. It's clear that despite the surface differences between the two of them—the new pub owner and the future public servant—they are totally smitten with each other. "She's just beginning to hit her stride, don'tcha think?" Mr. Doyle asked this reporter. "Tess was born to be a leader . . . as well as the love of me life," he grinned. "It's just taken her a wee bit of time to find herself."

Acknowledgments

Thanks again to Sharon O'Connell, who, when she was juggling so many of her own plates, generously dispensed copious advice and information on the Irish lifestyle. Former New York City Councilwoman Eva Moskowitz and her helpful staff provided a clearer road map through the mire that is the NYC Dept. of Education, giving me a starting point from which I reimagined a better system. Nicole and David Gruenstein steered me between Scylla and Charybdis on issues of Jewish arcana. den farrier's suggestions early on were both provocative and golden. Sr. Pat Boucher explained the process of becoming a nun; Ross A. Klein provided information regarding cruise ship dumping (any errors are my own). Gail Matos's e-mails offered daily moral support and *Star Trek* trivia. M.Z. Ribalow asked the hard questions, and answered a bunch of mine. And of course, thanks always to my agent Irene Goodman and my editor Lucia Macro, who continue to inspire and encourage me to push the envelope.

Ron Rinaldi

Native New Yorker **LESLIE CARROLL** is also a professional actress, dramatist, and journalist. In addition to her contemporary fiction, she writes historical fiction under the pen name Amanda Elyot. Visit Leslie on the web at www.tlt.com/authors/lesliecarroll.htm.